The Collected Thraxas Volume Eight

Thraxas Book Twelve

Thraxas Meets His Enemies

CW01496237

Martin Scott

Thraxas Meets His Enemies

Thraxas book twelve.

'Sources at the Palace indicate that a very large sum of money in the form of gold bullion has disappeared from the Palace vaults. This was earmarked for the purchase of food and is a terrible loss to a city already on the brink of starvation. The whole affair smacks of corruption at the highest levels. Our revered War Leader Lisutaris, Mistress of the Sky, is of course beyond suspicion but the sad truth is she's surrounded by a coterie of very dubious characters including assassins, degenerate sorcerers, half-Orcish ruffians and several shady figures from the lower depths of Turanian society. Our readers will be amazed to learn that among these figures is Thraxas, about whom the Chronicle has had reason to warn the city before. As the food intended for our starving population disappears to the Simnian, Samsarinan and Niojan encampments, many curious glances will be cast towards the Mistress of the Sky, wondering why her most trusted companions all seem to be characters of the very lowest repute...'

For more about Thraxas visit
www.thraxas.com
www.martinmillar.com

Cover Model: Madeline Rae Mason

Thraxas Meets His Enemies
Copyright © Martin Millar 2022

This edition published 2022 by Martin Millar

ISBN 979-8421592259

Introduction to Thraxas Book Twelve

Once again it's taken me longer than I intended to produce the next Thraxas book. The world has been in the grip of a global health crisis and I didn't find that very good for the creative process. With Thraxas and with other writing, I had some periods of creativity and other times when the world's problems seemed to send me into a despondent state where I couldn't get on with anything. I probably should have coped better and I regret the delay. However it's ready now and there would have been no point putting out a new Thraxas book before I was completely happy with it.

Thraxas is finally back in Turai. There are enemies to be faced, investigating to be done and beer to be found. Or not, as the terrible beer shortage shows no sign of ending. This has been afflicting Thraxas for some time now. Perhaps in the next book I should just let Thraxas sit in the Avenging Axe drinking beer all day to the exclusion of anything else, a sort of golden age for him.

Martin Millar

Thraxas Meets his Enemies

Chapter One

I walk over the smouldering foundations of Turai's ruined west wall. Makri catches up with me. She carries a sword in each hand. I have a sword in hand too though I'm also carrying a shield. It's cumbersome but as I'm soon going to find myself confronted by the elite core of the Orcish occupying army plus an assortment of their strongest sorcerers I'd rather protect myself. Both Makri and I wear spell protection charms. They're good though probably not good enough to protect us from the power of an Orcish sorcerer like Deeziz the Unseen. I wouldn't be walking in her direction if our War Leader Lisutaris wasn't right behind me. Lisutaris, Mistress of the Sky, Head of the Sorcerers Guild, is the most powerful sorcerer in the West. Behind her is her team of attack sorcerers, chosen for their ability to fight. We're here to take our city back. Lisutaris brought the wall down but we've already suffered casualties. Sareepa Lightning Strikes the Mountain and Coranius the Grinder both perished as the wall fell. They were two of our strongest sorcerers. I didn't expect them to die before we even entered the city.

As for non-magical troops, there are many of them following us through; Simnian units, Samsarinans, Niojans, Elvish archers, all led by a Turanian phalanx and the Sorcerers Auxiliary Regiment whose job it is to keep the sorcerers alive while they work their spells. Among their ranks is my friend and companion Gurd, one of the strongest warriors ever to pick up an axe. It's taken us a long time to return to our city since the Orcs evicted us and we're not planning on retreating. I just wish I had a better idea of what we're about to face. There's so much dust and smoke from the fire that destroyed the wall's foundations it's impossible to see more than a few feet in front of my face. We march through the gloom. I noisily kick my way through the debris; beside me Makri walks as silently as a cat. I wasn't expecting to be first man into the city but

Lisutaris chose to lead the assault herself and I'm her Security Chief so here I am. I don't mind. Since Turai fell I've thought of little else apart from retaking the city. Sometimes I've thought about beer. But mostly retaking the city.

The smoke thins. I can feel grass beneath my feet. We've emerged into the broad park south of the Palace. I halt and look around. Lisutaris is close behind and next to her are her strongest remaining sorcerers. Around them are the heavily armoured assault troops. More and more of them force their way through the gap in the wall. Lisutaris is dressed in a leather jerkin and breeches with only a short rainbow cape denoting her rank. It's an unusual sight. Even when she led the army to victory in the Mountain Battle she wore the standard flowing cloak of the senior sorcerer. The sorcerers around her are similarly attired, with tough leather breastplates they'd normally scorn to wear. Everyone knows that defeating the Orcs is going to be a very tough battle. The only exception is the brightly clad Tirini Snake Smiter who would not wear a common soldier's breastplate even if her life depended on it, which actually it might. So far there's been no opposition though I was expecting to meet hordes of screaming Orcs the moment I came through the walls.

'Dragon!' yells a soldier.

Here in the broad expanse of the park we're vulnerable to dragon attack. Shields are raised as the troops prepare to withstand the ravages of dragon fire. Lisutaris remains calm. She turns to Gorsoman, a Simnian, and Harmon Half-Elf, a Turanian, both powerful sorcerers.

'Deal with this as planned.'

Harmon and Gorsoman advance quickly. Picked soldiers from the Sorcerers Auxiliary Regiment accompany them, some protecting them with their shields while others raise bows and crossbows to fire at the approaching dragon. Gorsoman and Harmon raise their arms. Purple sparks appear round their fingertips as they prepare to launch their spells. It's a tactic that's been practised and it's efficiently done, though I'm surprised that Lisutaris isn't dealing with the dragon herself. She has more power than either Gorsoman or Harmon Half Elf; probably more power than both combined. I've seen her bring down dragons with spells so ancient and powerful that the earth rocked beneath our feet. Despite this, she leaves it to her companions. The dragon roars, but

2

doesn't press its attack. Instead it retreats under fire from Gorsoman and Harmon. Lisutaris speaks to the young sorcerer Anumaris Thunderbolt. I'm close enough to overhear.

'Have you located him?'

Anumaris studies the palm of her hand. Something's written there in a language I've never seen; the words change as she reads. 'Not precisely but he's somewhere north, towards the Palace.'

Lisutaris calls to General Acarius, commander of the Sorcerers Auxiliary Regiment. 'We're heading towards the Palace. Protect me.'

The grey-haired general salutes smartly. I notice a flicker of doubt in his expression. I understand why. I'd assumed that after breaking into this park we'd head for the city streets east of here. That's the quickest way into cover and safety from the dragons. Heading north through the open parkland around the Palace invites danger. While camped outside the city walls our sorcerers provided the army with a continual shield against dragon attacks but that's not so easy for them to do while we're on the move. We've already been weakened by the loss of Sareepa and Coranius. If dragons manage to penetrate our defences while we're still in the open there won't be much of the army left by the time we encounter their troops.

Lisutaris strides forward. I barge my way in front of her, as does Makri, her official bodyguard. I'd rather Lisutaris wasn't leading the army. It's a vulnerable position for our War Leader. It wasn't part of the original plan. She changed it at the last moment. Again, I'm not sure why. Walking north towards the Palace I'm continually scanning our surroundings for signs of defending troops. So far, no Orcish units have attacked. Even those Orcs on the remaining section of the wall seem to be keeping out of sight. It makes for a strange few moments, unlike any other occasion when I've been involved in taking a city. Usually fighting is incredibly fierce as you go through or over the walls. Either the defenders break and flee or they throw you back out of the city. The lack of action doesn't last for long.

'More dragons!'

Suddenly we're in the thick of it, besieged by the remaining Orcish dragons, some of them carrying sorcerers on their backs. The air above crackles with energy as our sorcerers attempt to erect their dragon shield. Outside the city this required assistance from every person with the remotest trace of sorcerous power, even me. Here there are less people to add their strength. Huge dragons pound against the magical barrier, sending sparks soaring through the sky. The maintenance of the shield is directed by Hendrith Seawave, a powerful Elvish sorcerer. From the way he's screaming at the sorcerers around him I'd guess he already knows we're in trouble.

We'd be in less trouble if Lisutaris were to join in with maintaining the shield but again she declines to use her power. 'Keep going,' she cries, and we keep advancing towards the Palace. This is looking somewhat the worse for wear though not as bad as might have been expected after so many months under Orcish control. Apparently Prince Amrag didn't let his conquering force despoil the building too much. I ignore the noise above and concentrate on protecting Lisutaris. Makri does the same. The ranks of the Sorcerers Auxiliary Regiment guard our flanks. I caught a glimpse of my friend Gurd earlier though we didn't have a chance to speak. He's a large, ageing barbarian, and just knowing he's close boosts my confidence. Makri too; If I have to take on the entire Orcish army it's good to have two such warriors at my side.

Hendrith Seawave is calling out orders as we advance, directing the sorcerers. 'Glixius — we need more power forward left!'

Glixius? Glixius Dragon killer? That's a name I haven't heard for a while. Glixius is a powerful sorcerer. He's also a criminal. He was outcast from society because of his illegal activities. The Sorcerers Guild allowed him back because they needed all available practitioners to fight the Orcs. I didn't realise he'd joined up with the assault force. I glance round and recognise his large frame, square jaw and thick grey hair. Like the other sorcerers he's put on light leather armour but he's still wearing quite a fancy rainbow cloak. I always figured the Dragon Killer part of his name was just made up for effect. Perhaps he'll get the opportunity to prove me wrong. I'm further surprised to recognise the man following him with a spear in his hand. Casax, leader of the Twelve Seas branch of the Brotherhood, one of the city's most powerful gangs. It's not uncommon for a sorcerer to have physical protection during battle — helps prevent an enemy sneakily sticking a knife in their back while they're busy with their spells — but I wouldn't have picked Casax for the task. I didn't even know he'd joined up with the army. It makes me think a little better of

4

him. I'd have expected all of our leading criminals to have scuttled off and hidden, rather than help with the war effort.

For the moment our sorcerers are managing to keep the dragons at bay even if the shield above shows dangerous signs of buckling and warping. We march on. On our right are several small buildings, summer houses in the Royal Park. As we approach, a band of light Orcish troops emerges. General Acarius despatches some of our own light troops to engage them. I look at Lisutaris.

'Keep going towards the Palace,' she orders.

I don't like it. We're in danger of being both overwhelmed from above and outflanked at the same time. Lisutaris is leading us to disaster. I'm finally back in Turai and the idiocy of our leaders is going to get me killed. It's not a surprise. Turai has always been badly led. An honest hard-working man like myself has never had the chance to shine. Makri is glowering over at the engagement to our right. I know she'd rather be there, fighting the Orcs. She hates Orcs. She used to be an Orcish gladiator slave and now she likes to kill them. Nonetheless she remains in formation, protecting our Commander.

I don't know how many of our troops are now in the city. Prior to breeching the walls there were Turanians, Samsarinans, Niojans, Simnians and others from the North and Furthest West, along with a strong contingent of Elves, all ready for the assault. I hope they've all followed us in but in the confusion I can't tell. For all I know they could have been driven back, leaving me, Makri, Lisutaris and a few others to march on to our doom. I curse everything and keep my shield raised. The dragons are pounding us from above, rocks and arrows are raining down from the Orcish troops on our right and Lisutaris is still strolling towards the Palace, apparently without a care in the world. The sun is blazing down, it's hot as Orcish hell and I'm sweating inside my armour. Damn them all.

Chapter Two

Everything is about to go disastrously wrong. By now we should have been in cover, engaged in street fighting, methodically dislodging the Orcs from their positions. Instead we're wandering through a park, barely in formation, with no cover, under attack from all directions. Anumaris Thunderbolt is currently holding her hand in front of Lisutaris's face and Lisutaris seems fascinated by the sight. Apparently our esteemed War Leader has lost her senses. An arrow falls onto my shoulder, fortunately having lost its momentum due to the sorcerous shield overhead. It won't be long before the shield buckles. The dragons are still pounding away at it. I've had enough of this.

'Commander, where are we going?'

Lisutaris ignores me. I raise my voice against the din. 'Commander, we're going to be overrun! We need to head into the buildings and regroup!'

Lisutaris looks at me. 'Keep advancing towards the Palace, Captain Thraxas.'

We're two hundred yards or so from the Palace. The walls and towers are packed full of hostile Orcs and there are more dragons flying overhead.

'We're assaulting the Palace with this small force? That's a terrible plan.'

Our Commander smiles. Incongruous in the circumstances, I'd say. Maybe the war has finally driven her mad. I did have a commander down in Juval who lost his senses after a brutal spell of fighting and leapt into a river in full armour, never to be seen again.

'Just get us close to the Palace, Thraxas. I'll end it there.'

Anumaris shoves her hand in front of Lisutaris again. I catch a glimpse of figures and numbers moving over her palm. Some sort of sorcery I've never seen before. 'Prince Amrag straight ahead,' she says.

'Amrag? We're going straight for him? Is that the plan?'

'Pick up the pace, Captain Thraxas. Ensign Makri, protect me.'

'Yes, Commander,' says Makri, marching along confidently in front of Lisutaris. As Lisutaris's official bodyguard she's resolute in her duties. Either she's unconcerned by the dragons, rocks and arrows, or she's pretending to be. I've never seen Makri show fear. Of course she's part Orc with pointed ears so she probably lacks sensitivity. She's dressed in her light Orcish armour which is decent enough but not the sort of protection you'd want at the front of the line. The soldiers from the Auxiliary Regiment have bronze breastplates and helmets. They carry shields and long spears. It's good battlefield protection but it's heavy and they'll soon tire in this heat. If Prince Amrag is really in the Palace he's not going to let us stroll up unopposed. Any moment now the gates are going to open and heavily armoured Orcs will pour out. We're doomed. There are screams to our left as part of our sorcerous shield begins to cave in under the weight of two huge war dragons. I can see the pale blue light that marks the shield being forced towards the ground. The troops beneath that section begin to retreat towards our centre. Suddenly there's an extremely bright yellow flash and a loud bang that resonates even over the sounds of the dragons' fury. The shield rises in the air, sending both war dragons spinning away. An Orcish sorcerer falls from one of the great beasts and slams into the ground.

'Good work, Glixius!' yells Hendrith Seawave.

Glixius raises a fist in acknowledgement. His sorcery has saved our left flank. Apparently he's not useless in combat. Good to know, I suppose. There's nothing else good happening. Lisutaris is leading us into the heart of the enemy. It strikes me that if Anumaris Thunderbolt is tracking Prince Amrag, the Orcish leader, then it's very likely Deeziz the Unseen is also tracking Lisutaris. Deeziz, leader of the Orcish sorcerers, is an extremely powerful Orcish woman who took us completely by surprise with the strength of her magic. Human and Elvish sorcerers, particularly those of Turai, were always held to be the strongest around. For years they protected us. Deeziz changed that. Under her leadership the Orcish sorcerers grew in power. When Deeziz successfully infiltrated Turai, I actually heard her mock Lisutaris for wasting her time at balls and parties while Deeziz studied for years on a mountaintop, perfecting new skills. As the result of this was the fall of our city, it would have been hard to argue with her.

'Thraxas! What's happening?'

Gurd appears at my side. I'm surprised to see him. 'Shouldn't you be with your unit?'

'What unit? We didn't get a chance to form up. Before half the men were through the walls our War Leader just took off and we had to follow as best we could. It's chaos on the flanks.'

'It's chaos here too.'

'The Palace is too well defended. Why are we marching straight towards it?'

'Because Lisutaris has lost her mind.' Lisutaris is only a few steps behind me. I don't care if she overhears. Gurd grips his axe and curses. 'I always knew I'd die fighting the Orcs but I didn't think our Commander would throw my life away.'

I've always known I'd die fighting the Orcs too, but I thought it would be as a result of my own carelessness, probably involving over-indulgence of beer. I didn't think the most powerful sorcerer in the West would hand me over on a plate to the enemy. We're a hundred yards from the Palace. The Orcish archers on the walls start firing. Orcs on our left and right are closing in. I've no idea what's going on behind us but I expect we're surrounded. I glance round. I can tell from Anumaris's expression that she's frightened. She's young; she'd only just completed her studies before we were run out of Turai. She's done well in battle but she realises the trouble we're in. The sight disheartens me further. Another huge dragon crashes into the shielding above us and Tirini Snake Smiter struggles to fling it off. Perspiration streams down her face, ruining her carefully applied make-up.

We advance under severe pressure. Unexpectedly the dragons draw back. The relief lasts only a few seconds before a huge wave of rocks, arrows and crossbow bolts slams into the sorcerous shield. The sky is so thick with missiles it's difficult to see where we're going. Hendrith Seawave screams at his sorcerers to keep our protection in place. Many of them are flagging. They've had a tough task keeping the dragons out. Sheltering us from the relentless barrage is exhausting them further. Making this worse, our strongest sorcerer isn't helping. Lisutaris declines to add her enormous power to the defensive efforts of her companions. I don't understand what's happening. I know I'm about to die. I'm sober and I'm hungry; it's no way to go. I curse at everything and raise my sword in fury. I'm not going down meekly. 'I'll kill you all, damned Orcs!'

'Admirable sentiments, Captain Thraxas,' declares Lisutaris, choosing this minute to move alongside me. 'Trumpeter, sound the halt.' A young military trumpeter who's been hurrying along beyond our Commander raises her bugle to her lips and blows, giving the signal to halt. We come to a confused stop, only fifty yards from the Palace, the gleaming white and gold edifice in the north of the city, home to our King, now presumed dead. It's surrounded by innumerable Orcs who probably can't believe their good fortune: our War Leader has walked right into their midst. Unnervingly, a much louder blaring of trumpets sounds from within the Palace. It's a shock. The Orcs don't normally use trumpets. A gate opens in the Palace walls. The Orcs on the parapets fall silent. The dragons withdraw further, spiralling upwards. The archers and crossbow wielders cease firing. Several figures walk out of the Palace, approaching us.

'Prince Amrag and Deeziz the Unseen,' says Makri, whose Elvish blood has given her eyesight as sharp as theirs.

I turn to Lisutaris. 'Were you expecting this?'

'Not at all. Apparently the Prince has a taste for the dramatic.' For some reason Lisutaris doesn't sound worried.

'Send an arrow into his throat!'

'No use. Deeziz has put a strong shield around them. No weapon would penetrate. Time to talk.'

'Talk? To them? Are you insane?'

'Ensign Makri, step forward with me. You too, Captain Thraxas. Everyone else stay back.'

I used to wonder what it would be like to be an important figure in the city. A man worthy of attention and respect. I've been constantly denied the opportunity to shine by the wealthy aristocrats of Turai who've always conspired against me, refusing to let a man from the lower classes advance, no matter his talents. The way I've fought for this miserable city I should be a general at least and probably a Senator as well. Somehow, as I walk out in front of several thousand Orcs under the bemused eyes of our own soldiers, it doesn't feel that great to be a prominent citizen. I'd be much happier drinking beer in my favourite tavern.

Prince Amrag approaches. Deeziz is beside him. Behind them are six Orcs. Advisers, generals or bodyguards, I've no way of telling. It's not a large entourage. Amrag doesn't have a reputation for ostentation. Mostly his reputation is for being an extremely able commander, undefeated until last month when Lisutaris won a convincing victory against him, sending him and his army

9

scurrying back to the safety of the occupied city of Turai. That can't have been good for his reputation though it hasn't weakened his authority. He still leads the combined forces of the Orcish nations, without any rival.

Prince Amrag is said to have some human blood. As does Makri. They're half-brother and sister. The only people in world who know that are Makri, Amrag, Lisutaris, and me. Makri has some Elvish mixed in as well, which Amrag doesn't. It's a complicated family history and quite how it all led to Makri being brought up in a slave gladiator pit and Amrag going on to be ruler of the Orcish nation of Kose remains mysterious. Makri has never been forthcoming about it. The Orcish leader is dressed in armour that's practical and not too fancy. On his head there's a plain gold circlet. He's taller than his companions. His features are a little less craggy though his skin is the same dark red. I can sense the discomfort behind me as our troops find themselves in such close proximity to Orcs. Everyone in the West grows up to hate and fear them. Generally we've good reason too. It's less than twenty years since the last invasion from the East.

Prince Amrag comes to a halt less than ten yards from us. I can tell he recognises Makri as his eyes rest on her for a second. When he speaks, he addresses only Lisutaris. 'I might congratulate you on breaking into my city, Lisutaris, Mistress of the Sky. Though you seem to have taken a wrong turning to bring you here.'

I get the impression that Prince Amrag might be expecting a lengthy conversation. I'm not certain why. Perhaps it will make him look good in front of his followers if he calmly chats to the enemy leader before eliminating her and her army. Perhaps he's genuinely interested in what exactly made Lisutaris lose all reason and approach the heavily defended Palace without any sort of preparation. Perhaps he wanted to see his half-sister again. As it turns out, Lisutaris isn't interested in conversation. She produces a vial of blood from beneath her tunic. The blood she took from Makri, acting on instructions from the spell book of Julia the Bad. She crushes the vial. Then she speaks a short sentence in a language I've never heard before, a secret language so awful that just the sound of it makes my blood freeze. There follows the strangest, most terrifying sight. The air around us turns purple as Amrag, Deeziz and their companions are thrown back as if shot from the mightiest catapult. Even before they hit the Palace their

10

bodies are coming apart. They slam against the wall in a bundle of flesh and blood, creating a gigantic red stain and a tangle of heads, torsos and limbs that slides to the ground.

Simultaneously Makri cries out and falls to the ground, clutching her abdomen. I stand over her and raise my shield. The Orcs on the Palace walls begin to wail and those on our flanks edge backwards nervously. Lisutaris regards the destruction she's caused. 'Bugler, sound the attack.'

The bugler blows her bugle. The troops around us charge. The Orcs fall back in panic, completely demoralised by the shocking death of their leader. There's no one to step up and take Amrag's place. In the confusion I help Makri to her feet. She's looking unhappy.

'My womb hurts,' she says. That's not something I've ever heard before, I admit. Makri rubs her abdomen. 'I knew that spell would have a bad affect on me.'

'It certainly had a bad affect on Amrag. I suppose Lisutaris knew what she was doing. Are you all right?'

Makri nods. 'I want to join in the fighting.' By now the advance troops have followed Lisutaris to the Palace where she's busy bringing down a wall to let them in. The Orcish defenders are disappearing. The rest of our army is catching up with us, advancing unhindered as the Orcs flee. Makri is limping and we can't keep up with the soldiers streaming past. I ask her if she wants to find a safe place to rest but she shakes her head.

'I need to join in the battle. I have to fight.'

We trudge on. Makri's still in discomfort though she's trying not to show it. I look up at the sky. The dragons have disappeared. The Orcs are disappearing. We're in the middle of a city being retaken yet we're strolling along without any apparent danger. It's an odd feeling. 'At this rate I'll be back in the Avenging Axe this evening, drinking beer.'

'If it's still standing,' says Makri, which is a reasonable point. Destruction around the Palace is not severe but we don't know what the Orcs have done to the rest of the city.

'If the Avenging Axe has been destroyed I'll make the Orcs pay for it.'

'There aren't any Orcs!' Makri sounds frustrated. 'I wanted to join in the battle.'

11

We enter the South Wing of the Palace, picking our way through the debris. There we meet Lisutaris, walking towards us. 'Commander! What are you doing wandering around on your own? It's dangerous.'

'My Bodyguard and my Security Chief didn't follow me,' says Lisutaris, wryly.

'Sorry, Commander. Makri was affected by your spell, we couldn't keep up.'

'My womb hurts.'

'She keeps saying her womb hurts. Is that possible?'

'Of course it's possible,' says Lisutaris. 'Why wouldn't it be?'

'I've just never heard anyone say it before.'

Lisutaris rolls her eyes. 'I'd be surprised if you knew what a womb actually does, Thraxas.' She reaches out to Makri. 'I'm sorry you were hurt, Makri. Your family blood was vital for the spell, it wouldn't have worked without it. Obviously it reserved a little of its potency for you.'

Makri takes a deep breath. 'I'm feeling better now.'

'Good. The Orcs are in full flight. Destroying their leaders has destroyed their morale. Our sorcerers are helping our troops chase them out the Palace and then out the city.' Lisutaris puts her hand to her brow. 'I'm out of sorcery. I need to rest.'

At that moment six heavily armed Orcs drop through a hole in the ceiling. I grab our Commander, shove her into a corner and stand in front of her, sword at the ready. The six Orcs race towards us, or rather five of them do because Makri has already killed one of them by throwing a knife into his throat, the sort of thing only she can do in a tight spot. I don't want to move away from Lisutaris but I'm forced to advance because I can't let Makri take on five Orcish warriors by herself, no matter how skilled a fighter she is. There's rubble everywhere from the collapsed wall and the damaged ceiling. Broken furniture is strewn around, making for a difficult fighting environment. I trip over a rock as I'm engaging the nearest Orc. It nearly lets him in but I catch the edge of his axe on my shield and run him through with one well placed stroke. I step back sharply as another Orc crashes to the ground at my feet, victim to Makri's swordplay. Makri uses a sword in each hand, a technique she learned as a gladiator. She's barely withdrawn one sword from her victim before she's used the other to pierce the throat of another and suddenly there are only two opponents left.

As they're both facing Makri I take the opportunity to stab one in the back while Makri deals multiple blows to our last remaining enemy. He falls down dead with blood spurting from his wounds. Makri has an expression of grim satisfaction. Prior to this she hasn't felt she's been given enough opportunities to kill Orcs.

Lisutaris rises to her feet. She looks down at the six corpses. 'You're good at this. I appreciate it. Let's go.'

'Can you walk, Commander? We could just stay here.'

'I'll be fine as long as I don't have to do anything strenuous. I need to find Hendrith Seawave and take control.'

As we walk into the next room Anumaris Thunderbolt appears, supporting Tirini, who's bleeding from wounds in her left arm and left leg. 'Commander! I was worried about you!' Anumaris is flustered, and she has a rag tied around her forehead, covering a wound.

'I'm fine, Anumaris. Tirini, you're bleeding. Sit down while I attend to you.'

Tirini stands up straight. 'I'm quite all right, Lisu. Just a few scratches.'

It's incongruous to hear anyone using a familiar name for Commander Lisutaris. No one but her old friend Tirini would ever think of it. Lisutaris manages to smile. 'You're not all right. Sit down.'

'Tirini saved me from a platoon of Orcs,' Anumaris tells us. 'Just blasted them all away.'

'It was nothing.' Tirini Snake Smiter, interested only in parties, fashion, scandal and romance, is not going to admit to any interest in war. That would be a rather common thing to do. Even so, she won't be unhappy if people learn of her exploits. Same as any sorcerer, really. Lisutaris lays her hands on Tirini's wounds. Our War Leader is not a specialised healer but has enough common sorcerous skills to stop the bleeding.

'You'll be fine, Tirini but you need to rest, you can't go into action again.' She looks around a little uncertainly. Six members of the Sorcerers Auxiliary regiment enter the room. They halt and salute smartly. 'Corporal Laniax, accompany Tirini Snake Smiter and Anumaris Thunderbolt to the throne room. Protect them until I return.'

'Yes, Commander.'

13

Lisutaris turns to Makri and me. 'We have a city to clear. Follow me.' We walk through the rest of the Palace. A long time ago I was employed as a senior investigator by Palace Security but I've never seen these exclusive royal rooms. Damage is slight, with rich furniture and trappings almost unharmed. I'm encouraged. I don't care about the royal furniture but I am worried about beer. I've been beer-deprived for far too long. If the Orcs haven't caused too much destruction in the rest of the city there might be a few breweries still operational. Heartened by the thought of an end to the terrible beer shortage I follow Lisutaris. Makri seems to have recovered, the satisfaction of fighting having raised her spirits and cured any lingering effects of Lisutaris's terrible spell.

Chapter Three

We don't get to engage in any more fighting. The Orcs are in full retreat and most of them have fled through the north gate. Lisutaris authorises pursuit by our cavalry to cut down as many of them as possible before they disappear into the Wastelands. Other troops are assigned the task of combing through the city, checking for any remaining enemies. After ensuring that her senior officers all have their orders, Lisutaris leads us to the throne room. There Tirini, having recovered some of her power, has treated both her own wounds and those of Anumaris and both now seem quite healthy. Tirini rises to her feet, embraces Lisutaris and kisses her lightly on both cheeks, the sort of greeting you might see aristocratic ladies perform at fashionable events but has previously never been seen in wartime. Tirini is apparently already over the war and intends to return to her favourite pursuits.

'So glad I could help, dearest Lisu. But now I must leave your army and return home. One dreads to think what the Orcs may have done to it. If my dresses have been damaged in any way I shall be quite upset.'

Lisutaris almost smiles, though stops herself. 'Tirini, you really should wait until you're formally discharged...'

'Discharged? I never joined the Sorcerers Regiment.'

'Didn't you?'

'No. I never thought it was quite suitable. I simply accompanied you through these considerable hardships out of friendship and my overwhelming sense of duty. But now my dresses await. And my shoes. One is terribly concerned about them. Goodbye.' And with that Tirini leaves, her part in the war effort apparently over.

'She disintegrated that entire Orcish platoon,' says Anumaris. 'It was something to see.'

Lisutaris sends the soldiers from the Sorcerers Auxiliary Regiment from the room then sits down, not on the throne but on one of the couches used by royal attendants. She looks fatigued. The spell she used to defeat Amrag might have taken more out of her than she wants to admit. It certainly was a mighty spell. Both Prince Amrag and Deeziz the Unseen were protected by layers of powerful sorcery but Lisutaris's attack reduced them to bloody pulp. I walked past the bodies and they were unrecognisable as anything.

'I've sent a message to Cicerius telling him it's safe for him to enter the city.'

'Do you really need him?'

'Of course,' replies Lisutaris. 'With Consul Kalius dead and the entire Royal Family also presumed dead, Deputy Consul Cicerius is the senior remaining Turanian politician. We'll have to establish some sort of government while we set the city in order.'

Makri isn't convinced by this. 'Can't you just stay in charge? People will follow you. You're the War Leader who took the city back.'

Lisutaris shakes her head. 'I never had any ambition to be War Leader. It just became necessary. I've no desire to be in charge of Turai. I'll stay around until we have things in order but after that I'm going home to sit on my balcony and smoke thazis.' Lisutaris is smoking a slender thazis stick as we speak. It's still technically illegal in Turai but that's never concerned her.

'Not that I'll be able to concentrate on repairing my gardens,' continues Lisutaris, sounding dissatisfied. 'Not with the state of the Sorcerers Guild in Turai. We've lost so many good sorcerers recently it's seriously weakened us. I have to do something about that.'

Turai is a small city-state, much less powerful than our neighbours, but the talents of our sorcerers have always protected us. Our Sorcerers Guild was more than a match for any of them. Recent losses have combined to undo that.

'We'll have to recruit the most advanced students from the Sorcerers College, even though they're not really ready.'

'Can you recruit sorcerers from abroad?'

'Possibly. We've done that in the past. Unfortunately we don't have much to offer them at the moment. The city is in a bad way.' Lisutaris glances around the throne room. 'Though you wouldn't know it to look at this place.' The throne room is extremely luxurious with its golden throne, gold and purple hangings, fine ancient tapestries and glittering chandeliers. Lisutaris makes a face, signifying frustration. 'When Cicerius arrives we're going to be busy. There are armies from Simnia, Samsarina, Nioj, the Elvish islands and others. They all need to be housed or camped somewhere. They need to be fed. Turanian citizens are going to be heading back here as soon as they can which is another problem. I don't know how we're going to feed them all. Security is difficult. I'm not having hostile Niojans looting the place but we don't have great numbers of Turanian soldiers apart from the Auxiliary Regiment. We'll probably need to ask the Elves for help. As for our infrastructure — water supplies, sewerage, roads, aqueducts — it's all in a bad state. I'm sending out military engineers to make assessments. It's all a very large task. That's why we need Cicerius. He's far more used to dealing with these sort of problems than I am.'

Lisutaris lights another thazis stick. For a woman who's just retaken a city after a long campaign she's not looking so bad though she has a bruise on her cheek from flying debris and her hair is as matted and dirty as everyone else's after coming through the chaos at the walls.

'Well, Commander, I can see it's a big task. Lot of work ahead. I wish you the best of luck. Me, I should be going. I have to get down to the Avenging Axe to see if my home still exists and then make a start on checking the city's beer supplies.'

Lisutaris glares at me. 'Amusing, Captain Thraxas.' She doesn't sound amused. 'You won't be leaving the Palace any time soon.'

'But I have to–'

'You're still my Head of Security. You'll remain with me while I organise things. As will Ensign Makri.'

'Yes, Commander,' says Makri. Ever since Lisutaris appointed Makri as her bodyguard she's had this annoying tendency of making a great show of doing her duty. Bit rich coming from a woman with pointy ears, Orcish blood and the manners of a wasteland savage, if you ask me, but there you have it. I'm not happy with these developments. 'I've been keeping myself going for months with the thought of getting back to the Avenging Axe. Can't I even check it's still standing?'

'No, you can't. I'm sure Gurd will send you a message letting you know how things are in Twelve Seas. Right now we have a meeting to attend. All the military leaders are due here in forty minutes.' Lisutaris looks down at her leather tunic which is covered in dust, and then at the palms of her hands, also filthy. 'There's still running water in the bathing area next to the Queen's dressing rooms. Makri, come with me. We should get clean before

17

the meeting. Thraxas, find another bathing room and make yourself look respectable.'

'I refuse to wash just because I have to meet Simnian generals.'

'Captain Thraxas, are you going to complain about everything I tell you to do? I hope not, for your own sake. Go and wash, and if you come across a royal wine cellar anywhere, don't drink anything. I need you clean and sober.'

'This is the worst retaking of a city in history. Clean and tidy? I should be rolling around drunk in the gutter, as is traditional in the circumstances.'

Noticing a dangerous glint in Lisutaris's eyes, I say no more, and depart to find a bathing room, of which there are many in the Palace. No point in making her angry, I suppose, even if I have reason to be annoyed. When a man has marched countless miles over hostile territory, battling Orcs every step of the way before finally breaking down the walls and retaking his city — I was, of course, first man into Turai — he should get some reward. A few ales, a hearty meal, maybe a medal or two. So far, none of those things is looking likely. I direct a few hostile thoughts towards Lisutaris. The woman may be as sharp as an Elf's ear when it comes to winning a war but she's not great at man management.

I find a bathing room nearby, in good condition apart from the dead Orc on the floor with a huge gash in his chest. I drag his body to one side and clean myself as best I can. It's impressive that the Palace still has clean running water, I suppose. Excellent plumbing, built to last. While I'm a lot cleaner when I finish, my clothes aren't and I still make for a shabby figure as I arrive at the meeting. I'm not the only one. The generals, officers and senior sorcerers in attendance have only just come off duty and there are few clean uniforms on view. There are some ambassadors, older men, smarter in appearance.

Outside, soldiers will be celebrating our victory but the mood here is restrained, sombre even. Discussions are long-winded, wide-ranging and extremely tiresome. I'm glad there are comfortable armchairs in the conference room. It's all I can do to stay awake. There's talk of which troops are to stay in the city and which are to remain camped outside. Can the fleet that's been shadowing us off the coast provide food for the combined armies, and who's going to pay for it? Are we convinced the Orcs are fleeing home and how far should our cavalry pursue them? What

18

sort of defensive formations do we need inside and outside Turai now that we've retaken it? The only relief is the arrival of a trolley of wine, rescued from a cellar by an enterprising general's assistant. While he's filling goblets for everyone I discretely snatch a whole bottle for myself and retreat to my chair. Makri notices. She frowns at me. Once again, she's on her best behaviour out of loyalty to Lisutaris. There was a time when these military officers and senior sorcerers were troubled by the presence of a woman with Orcish blood at Lisutaris's side. They appear to be over it now. Even the Elves seem reconciled to her. Makri speaks fluent Common Elvish and some of their commanders can even be heard greeting her politely these days.

Lisutaris deals with the complex problems competently enough though much of this involves delaying decisions until Cicerius arrives. The Deputy Consul is expected tomorrow. Cicerius is now the senior politician in Turai though he doesn't have nearly the respect from our allies that Lisutaris commands. Lisutaris is renowned not only as the strongest sorcerer in the West but a fine military tactician too. Her Guild is completely loyal to her, both Turanians and those from other nations. Maybe we don't need Cicerius, I muse, as the discussions drag on. Lisutaris is still War Leader till hostilities are officially declared to be over so she outranks everyone else. Let her take care of everything. Meanwhile allow the doughty warriors like myself to return to our homes and start hunting for beer. I'm waiting for a message from Gurd regarding the state of the Avenging Axe. Nothing will have prevented the old barbarian from making straight for his beloved tavern to see if it's still standing. Tanrose has probably joined him by now. Tanrose, esteemed cook from the tavern and love of Gurd's life, is currently expecting a child and won't want to be separated from Gurd for long. She'll have had an anxious wait outside the city and will be relieved he survived. I'm pleased Gurd finally worked up the courage to ask Tanrose to marry him. I spent a long time worrying a rival tavern might snatch her away by offering her better pay for her services in the kitchen. That would have been a disaster. I rely on her food to keep me going, I'm a man who requires a lot of food and Tanrose is the most talented tavern cook in Twelve Seas.

By now, with wine inside me and the stress of the day starting to drain from my body, I'm staring at my feet, no longer paying attention to anything. I'm about to doze off when the sound of chairs being pushed back wakes me. I look up to see the generals filing out of the room. As soon as they're gone Lisutaris sits down heavily. She looks weary. Her assistant, Captain Julius, arrives.

'There's a large bedroom not far from this room, Commander, suitable for your use. There are smaller rooms near it, suitable for Ensign Makri and Captain Thraxas, as you requested.'

'Thank you, Captain Julius.'

'Tirini Snake Smiter has sent you a message. It's verging on the hysterical. Apparently there's been considerable damage in Truth is Beauty Lane.'

Lisutaris nods. 'I feared as much.'

Truth is Beauty Lane is in a wealthy part of Thamlin, where all the best sorcerers live.

'Tirini reports great structural damage and an almost total looting of her wardrobe. The message she sent was damp, possibly stained with tears.'

'I wonder if my thazis plants have gone?'

Lisutaris owns a glasshouse — an actual small house made of glass, an unheard of extravagance — for the cultivation of her own special brands of thazis which she prepares herself and smokes through a water pipe. For a moment she looks troubled, but then shrugs. 'I'll sort it out when I have time. Send a message to Tirini telling her not to worry, there are always new clothes and shoes to be had. Has Captain Hanama reported?'

'She's waiting outside.'

I'm not keen to encounter Captain Hanama, or Hanama the Assassin as she should be known, a ruthless member of the Assassins Guild, recruited by Lisutaris as Head of her Intelligence Service in a rare lapse of judgement. Captain Hanama is as cold as the Ice Queen's grave; not a person whose company I enjoy. I'm pleased when Lisutaris dismisses Makri and me before Hanama makes her report. Hanama was nowhere to be seen during the assault on the city. I wonder what she was up to? Something nefarious, no doubt, sneaking around on private business for Lisutaris, who is capable of fairly nefarious behaviour herself when she deems it necessary. I follow Captain Julius along to the small room that's to serve as my bedroom while I'm in the Palace. As I look around the chamber with its comfortable furnishings, thick rug, two Elvish paintings on the wall and a small Samsarinan decorative sculpture in the corner I feel uneasy. All though the city there will be soldiers and returning citizens looking for somewhere to spend the night; none of them will find a place as comfortable as this. Most of them will be camped in tents, inside and outside the walls. Here I am, in a plush little room at the Palace. I wonder what will become of this place now the King and his family are all dead? The King was well into his dotage and I wouldn't say either of his sons were a credit to the city. I remember Princess Du-Akai a little more kindly. She was a client of mine, a few years back. Will there ever be another King? Is Turai about to move permanently into a different form of government? I finish off my wine and fall asleep on the comfortable bed, trying not to reflect that until today, it was probably home to an Orc in the retinue of the now deceased Prince Amrag.

Chapter Four

I waken early. The light is streaming in through the window. The glass here is far higher quality than anything you'd find in most of the city. I'm wondering what the day will bring when Makri arrives in my room.

'Can you never learn to knock on a door?'

'You've been complaining about that for three years.'

'You ought to have learned some civilised manners by now. Especially if you're actually going to the University.'

Makri smiles, but then her face falls. 'Do you think they'll really let me do that?' Makri has an inexplicable appetite for education and learning. Since arriving in Turai she's expressed an overwhelming ambition to attend the Imperial University. That seemed impossible. The University mostly caters to sons of the upper classes and doesn't admit women. It doesn't admit anyone with Orcish blood either, meaning Makri was disqualified on two counts. Undaunted by this, she attended the community college in Twelve Seas, coming top of every class. That earned her a qualification that would be sufficient to guarantee entrance to the University for anyone else. Unfortunately the problems of her being female and part-Orc appeared insurmountable. The situation would have been hopeless had it not happened that Deputy Consul Cicerius promised he'd use his influence to let her attend as a result of some very valuable service she did for the city.

'I think it will happen,' I tell her. 'Cicerius promised and he's the only politician in Turai you can actually trust. He won't go back on his word. Even if the professors rebel.'

'Will they rebel?'

'Yes, probably. But you've faced worse. Don't worry, if they give you a hard time I'll sort them out.'

I used to mock Makri's aspirations. I don't know how or when it came about that I started encouraging her; it just happened. I can see difficulties ahead. Even if Cicerius supports her ambitions, being part-Orcish in a city that's just been despoiled by Orcs might lead to more than her usual difficulties.

'I don't even know if the university building is still standing. It might be ruined. Will they rebuild it? What if all the professors are dead? Some of them were too old to flee the city. What if the Orcs burned all the books and manuscripts? What if they burned the library too? There might never be a university in Turai again.'

'Makri, what is this? Ever since you arrived in this city you've expressed nothing except ridiculous optimism about going to the University. Why get pessimistic now? They can get new professors and new books. It will open again.'

Makri looks overwhelmingly gloomy. 'I keep thinking things might go wrong.'

'Once Thraxas chases Orcs out of a city, they stay chased out. Nothing will go wrong. Unless we all starve to death. That might happen.'

Food is going to be a problem. No crops were harvested this year. The grain warehouses are empty. None of the livestock in the farms around the city will have survived the invasion. We're in for a very hard time.

'What about Turai's allies? Will they help?'

'Difficult to say. In my experience allies generally help when there's something in it for them.'

'I remember Lisutaris talking about that with Coranius,' says Makri. 'Something about Simnia and Samsarina both wanting better access to our harbour for trading. And Nioj not wanting them to have it because they want it for themselves.'

'They'll all be trying to increase their influence, that's for sure.'

'Coranius died in the attack,' says Makri.

I don't reply. There's an uncomfortable silence.

'He was a very powerful sorcerer,' continues Makri. 'Turai will miss him.'

Again, I don't reply. Makri becomes frustrated. 'Are you going to say anything about Sareepa?'

'What am I meant to say?'

'I don't know. Something. You were having a relationship with her. It's the only relationship I've ever known you to have. She died outside the walls, fighting beside Coranius. You must have something to say about it.'

For a moment I feel angry. I swallow it back and shake my head. 'I don't have anything to say about it.'

We're rescued from a further uncomfortable silence by one of Lisutaris's young messengers who knocks on my door and informs us that Lisutaris wants to see us right away.

'Are you going to keep that Orcish armour on?' I ask Makri, as we leave my room.

'It's all I've got. This and the chainmail bikini. I don't know what happened to the rest of my things. Got lost somewhere in the confusion of taking the city.'

I'm dressed in the old tunic I wore under my armour. It's threadbare and faded. I'm not sure where my other belongings are either. Somewhere in a wagon outside the city walls, I think. We walk through unfamiliar corridors, heading back to the rooms set aside for our War Leader.

'You notice how cool it is in here? Even though it's hot as Orcish Hell outside? The Palace has cool air pumped through it. Not just by sorcery, there's some sort of machine does it.'

Makri is interested to learn this. She's enthusiastic about all sorts of engineering. I've heard her enthuse about Turai's underground sewerage system which is, according to her, a marvel of construction.

'Summer in Turai is always bad and this one is going to be worse. I tell you, the city badly needs beer and if Lisutaris has any sense she'll release me from security duties and let me go around ensuring there's a good supply.'

'Like a beer commissioner?' Makri laughs. 'It would be your ideal job.'

'It would. But Lisutaris won't see it that way. She's always been short-sighted when it comes to beer.'

Our Commander is waiting for us in a room that's been rapidly adapted for use as a command centre. She's discarded her leather breeches and tunic, replacing them with a robe and sorcerer's cloak. Neither of them are as sumptuous as she'd normally wear but she is looking more like her old self, with an elegant silver necklace and her hair styled in a manner resembling that of aristocratic Turanian ladies before the war. Lisutaris does actually come from a wealthy, aristocratic family. That's unusual for a sorcerer. Most of them come from respectable backgrounds but not from the highest echelons of society. The aristocracy generally look down on the profession of sorcery, or any profession really. Makri's hair, once a huge, unruly mane, is tied back neatly in a long ponytail as it has been since Lisutaris recruited her for military service. My own hair is tied back in a ponytail too. I noticed a few more grey streaks in the mirror; soon I'll be as grey-haired as Gurd. As we arrive, Harmon Half Elf and Hendrith Seawave are leaving. Lisutaris has wasted no time in getting to work. 'I've spread out all the Turanian troops we have through the city to prevent looting. I'm trying to confine the foreign troops to duty at the walls, and outside.'

'Wise move, Commander. We can't let a bunch of foul Simnians and Niojans loose in Turai.'

'We can't. But be politer about it in public. They helped us retake the city. Cicerius has arrived, we're going to meet him and then we have another task to attend to. Makri, do you have anything else to wear apart from that Orcish armour?'

'No. But it's light armour, I can manage with it.'

'I'm not worried about your comfort, I'm worried about you resembling an Orcish invader. Look in that small room, there's a selection of leather tunics and leggings discarded by my sorcerers, pick some that fit you.'

Makri departs into the adjoining room. I inform Lisutaris I've been hearing troubling rumours. 'The army is complaining about the lack of beer. Probably be best if you let me sort it out.'

'They'll survive. As will you. Don't look so downhearted, there's still Elvish wine stored in the Palace, the Orcs wouldn't touch it.'

'It's not the same. Don't blame me if the troops revolt.'

Makri re-appears, clad in a leather jerkin and leggings.

'I suppose that's better,' I say. 'If it wasn't for the pointy ears you'd look almost human.'

'You know you're the only person to actually gain weight during the war?' says Makri. 'How did you manage it?'

It's a scandalous and untrue assertion. The way weight's been rolling off me I'm a shadow of my former substantial self. I'm about to reply when Lisutaris informs us sharply she had enough of us bickering like children on the way to Turai and would rather not listen to any more of it now we're here.

'Follow me,' she says, and walks out into the corridor. Even though I knew the Palace was a luxurious dwelling I'm still surprised by the opulence of some of the rooms and hallways we pass through. There are carpets here that would cost more than an entire house in many parts of the city, and works of art on the walls from some of the finest painters in the West, spanning hundreds of years of history. Our Royal Family always did like to look after themselves well. While Prince Amrag hadn't allowed his troops to

25

despoil the Palace there are exceptions. Elvish statues lie broken and Elvish paintings have been defaced. Some gilded furniture has had the gold stripped from the edges. Mostly it's not too bad. Some Turanian politicians would not be impressed by the opulence on display while the population are suffering. Senator Lodius for instance, leader of the Populares Party, opponents of Cicerius and the Traditionals.

Lisutaris finally halts outside a door and turns to us. 'We're meeting Deputy Consul Cicerius. Cicerius and I will be talking to other politicians later today to sort out some form of government but there's something we need to do first. Thraxas, don't annoy him by demanding he makes you beer commissioner or anything ridiculous like that.' Lisutaris reaches for the golden door handle, then pauses. 'Makri, don't immediately demand he sends you to the University. That can wait.'

We enter a small stateroom. Sitting on a gilded chair is Cicerius. He looks much the same as I remember him. Older, but still the same thin, stubborn, honest, unfriendly soul, respected but never loved by the citizens. He's wearing a plain white toga, presumably not having a spare supply of the gold-rimmed garments that properly denote his rank. That must rankle. Cicerius has his share of vanity. He rises to his feet, greets Lisutaris politely, then glares at us.

'Thraxas. Now a Captain, so I understand. And Makri. Ensign Makri.' It's obvious we're not the two people he was most looking forward to meeting. The door opens and Hansius appears, Cicerius's chief assistant. He too greets Lisutaris very respectfully but frowns when he sees Makri and me. 'I understood we were only accompanying Lisutaris, Mistress of the Sky.'

'We are,' says Cicerius.

'Captain Thraxas and Ensign Makri will be coming with us.' Lisutaris's tone invites no arguments. That doesn't prevent Cicerius from arguing. 'It's for the most trusted eyes only.'

'That's why they're coming. Thraxas and Makri have accompanied me every step of the way. I left Turai with them and returned with them, Deputy Consul.'

'Acting Consul,' Cicerius corrects her. 'Following the death of Kalius I'm automatically promoted until a new Consul is selected. Traditionally I should now be addressed as Consul.'

Lisutaris manages to avoid rolling her eyes. 'Very well, Consul. Without Captain Thraxas and Ensign Makri I wouldn't have survived the sack of Turai, let alone managed to lead the army back here. I trust them completely.'

Cicerius is surprised at the strength of Lisutaris's speech. I'm surprised too. I'm not used to being described in such glowing terms. I deserve it of course, but it doesn't happen often. The Consul shrugs, acquiescing to Lisutaris's demands. Wherever they're going, Makri and I are going too. Hansius leads our small party along more corridors, taking various turns till I've lost all sense of where we are. I hadn't realised how labyrinthine the Palace was. In a room decorated in Samsarinan turquoise, there's a sorcerer waiting for us. Dominius Iron Strike, a Palace sorcerer I know by sight but have never spoken to. He's youngish for a sorcerer, his short beard showing no signs of grey and his long black hair tied neatly back. He's wearing rather a splendid rainbow cloak. With him is another man, older, greying hair, wearing the garb of a senior member of the Merchant's Guild. Lisutaris introduces him as Lemusius. I recognise the name. He's one of Turai's richest men. I've no idea how he could have returned to the city so early. He certainly wasn't fighting with the army.

By now I'm mystified as to our destination and wondering if we're just going to keep wandering around the Palace picking up people as we go. Things become clearer in the next room when Dominius Iron Strike utters an obscure word of power and a hidden door slides open in the wall revealing concrete steps leading down to a secret part of the Palace. I'm curious. I have no idea what we're about to find. We come to a metal door which Lemusius opens with a key. Dominius is carrying an illuminated staff to light our way, though I notice that Lisutaris has caused another light to float above her head, the sort of everyday sorcery she can do without even thinking about it. We come to another metal door, strongly encased in a thick metal frame, suggestive of a bank vault. Lemusius the merchant produces the largest, fanciest-looking key I've ever seen, a key with so many teeth and prongs it seems absurd it could ever be necessary for anything. He inserts it in the lock. As he does so, Dominius intones rather a long sentence in one of the private languages used only by sorcerers. Both actions are apparently necessary to open the door. It opens smoothly. We step inside. Lisutaris causes the light above her head

27

to grow in strength and it's immediately reflected back at us by rows of gold bullion on shelves and gold coins spilling out of chests and sacks on the floor. Lisutaris nods her head in satisfaction. 'The Orcs never located it, Consul. This should be enough to help the city through the crisis.'

'This is very good news.' Cicerius manages a rare smile. 'Turai will have many expenses while we recover from the war. Simply existing through the next few months will be difficult. No one must know of this reserve.'

I get the strong feeling that Cicerius is mainly addressing Makri and me. I can see problems. 'So what's the plan, Commander. Are you just leaving this gold here?'

'It seems the best place for it.'

'I don't like it. It's not secure enough.'

'Not secure enough? It survived an Orcish occupation.'

'They had no reason to look for it. How many people know about this?'

'No one knows of it.' Cicerius is adamant.

'The people in this room do. Lemusius, you were the King's senior financial advisor, I believe? How many of your associates know about this?'

'None of them.'

'Someone will know. Your predecessor will have mentioned it to someone. Or your wife will have. Or the clerk at work who looks after your diary and knows more about your business than you realise.'

Lemusius looks offended. 'Preposterous.'

'What about your close associates, Commander? Did you mention this to Anumaris? Tirini?'

Lisutaris compresses her lips for a second. 'It may have been mentioned on a rare occasion.'

A rare occasion when they were all smoking thazis, no doubt. 'As for you, Consul Cicerius, and your assistant Hansius, are you going to tell me you're the only politicians in the whole of Turai who know about it?'

'We are!' says Cicerius, sharply. Unfortunately for him, Hansius is another rather honest man and is moved to remind him that the last chancellor in the Senate, Senator Trappius, certainly was aware of the gold. 'Trappius was involved from the start, when the King ordered a proportion of the new product of our gold mines be hidden in the Palace. More of his staff may have known.'

'Trappius and his staff are presumed dead during the war.'

'To sum up,' I interrupt. 'We don't know how many people know about this. As Lisutaris's Head of Security, I don't like it. This is an isolated section of the Palace and we didn't pass any guards on our way here. It's not safe to leave this gold unattended.'

'Captain Thraxas,' says Lisutaris. 'You saw the security protecting the vault. Opening it requires a unique key, which remains safe in the senior financier's hands. It must be used simultaneously with a spell which is known only to a few members of the Sorcerers Guild. Even I could not open that door on my own.'

'I'm not so sure about that, Commander. I've seen you do a lot of things. Anyway, spells can be learned and keys can be copied. This isn't safe. Either surround the sector with guards or take the bullion to the centre of the Palace where it can be guarded continuously.'

'That would simply draw attention to it,' protests Cicerius.

'I can't spare the Turanian troops,' says Lisutaris. 'They're all needed in the city.' She pauses. 'I appreciate your concerns but I do think the gold is best left here. I can assign two men to guard the corridor. I'll have another member of my Guild place a watchful spell over the area to warn us of any unauthorised approach.'

Cicerius asks Lemusius how much is in the vault.

'Around two million gurans. The Palace never provided us with an exact figure.'

'I'll ask Dearineth the Precise Measurer to count it,' says Lisutaris. 'Calculating the exact amount will only take her a few moments.'

I don't bother pointing out that inviting Dearineth to count the gold bullion will mean another person knows about it. I don't like this. Nothing in Turai is secure at the moment, not even the Palace. Lisutaris and Cicerius seemed satisfied so there's no point arguing. I'm thinking about the Avenging Axe. I haven't heard from Gurd. I really need to find out what happened to the tavern. I have to see for myself what my old neighbourhood looks like after all these months of Orcish occupation.

Chapter Five

It's a long, difficult walk from the Palace in the north of the city all the way down to Twelve Seas. The main streets are crowded with soldiers, refugees, baggage carts and beggars. The sun is beating down. It's hot as Orcish hell and there's devastation everywhere. We skirt past Thamlin so I don't see how much damage has been done to the homes of our wealthiest residents, but south of there in Jade Temple Fields the city's in a bad state. The temple with its famous jade columns that gave the area its name has been severely damaged. Several of the columns are broken and most of the roof has caved in. The Orcs have always been very hostile to the western True Church. It wouldn't surprise me if many of our shrines and temples have been destroyed. Houses, shops, taverns and markets have all suffered. Jade Temple Fields was home to the city's civil servants, Palace workers, merchants — the middle classes of Turai. It's all going to need a lot of rebuilding. No one really knows how many Turanians managed to save their lives by fleeing as the Orcs swept through Turai but from the way refugees are already returning many of them have survived. Some wealthier inhabitants who'd made their way to the small city states further along the coast are returning too, in merchant vessels hired for the purpose.

'Lisutaris and Cicerius are bringing people back quickly,' says Makri, who does appreciate a well-organised operation.

'They are. That's good, I suppose. Except their houses are in ruins and I don't see how we're going to feed everyone. I've been underfed for months.'

We walk past the remains of the Wandering Bard, a tavern I've spent many enjoyable evenings in but now lies in ruins. Next door to the tavern was one of the city's finest bakeries. That's been destroyed too. It's a depressing sight. We carry on southwards. Makri is sad to see the destruction though her main concern is the library. Turai's Imperial Library housed a famous collection of books and manuscripts. A wonder of the world, according to Makri. I wouldn't go that far but there's no denying it was a great resource for the city. Makri's convinced it will have been looted, burned and destroyed. She may be right. When Lisutaris gave us time off to visit our home Makri wanted to go straight there, but as it wasn't on our way to Twelve Seas, I dissuaded her.

'If every manuscript has been burned you won't be able to do anything to help. It will only depress you.'

Makri's already uncomfortable at being separated from Lisutaris. She takes her duties as bodyguard very seriously. I tell her not to worry. 'Lisutaris is the strongest sorcerer in the West. Strongest in the world since she defeated Deeziz. She'll be fine. No one is going to attack the Palace.' Reports from our scouts indicate that the combined Orcish armies have left the field completely, retreating over the Wastelands then going their separate ways into their own nations. With the death of Prince Amrag their alliance has disintegrated. Our victory is complete.

We're forced off the main road, Moon and Stars Boulevard, by the weight of carriages struggling their way past the innumerable potholes and the debris that lies everywhere. We continue through the streets of Pashish. Pashish, a poorer part of Turai, is in a bad state. Orcish soldiers would have been billeted here and they haven't looked after the place well. Few dwellings have escaped damage. Some is minor, broken windows and doors, but other houses have collapsed and there are huge scars in the road from dragon fire. The aqueduct running through Pashish that's supplied water here for two hundred years now lies broken and dry.

'Can sorcerers repair aqueducts?' asks Makri.

'I've never seen them involved in building work. I think it's beneath them. They might be able to help in a crisis.' We pick our way over the debris. 'This aqueduct was in poor repair even before the Orcs got here. I remember the local council applied for help to repair it and the Senate told them there was no money. Strange, when you think about it, with millions of Gurans in gold hidden under the Palace.'

'Not placed there for helping poor people.' Makri has become as cynical as everyone else about our politicians. She's only been in Turai for a few years but it didn't take long to discover they're not in the business of helping the needy. We're now on the borders of Twelve Seas, our home. It looks the same as Pashish, badly damaged though not entirely ruined. We make our way towards Quintessence Street which is not far from the harbour. I remember the last time I was here. Makri and Lisutaris were sick with the Winter Malady. I dragged them out of the Avenging Axe when the

Orcs attacked and we escaped through the sewers. Makri is remembering the same events.

'I was the stake in a card game. If you lost I had to marry Horm the Dead. Did that really happen?'

'It did. Fortunately my superior card skills saved the day.' In reality, an unexpected interruption from Deeziz the Unseen brought the game to an end. Close to Quintessence Street there's a great deal of damage. There was heavy fighting here with dragons overhead. The harbour in Twelve Seas was attacked as people tried to flee. Buildings have collapsed and everywhere there are scorch marks and twisted lumps of stone and metal. I have vivid memories of citizens running along the beach while I desperately tried to push Makri and Lisutaris into a tiny fishing boat. We sailed in that boat for weeks till we finally washed up in Samsarina. We've been through a lot since then. I've been dreaming of settling back into the Avenging Axe with a tankard of ale and a plate full of Tanrose's excellent stew. When we enter Quintessence Street it's obvious that's not going to happen for a while. The shops and houses are devastated. Former residents are already setting up tents. Some of them are military surplus, others no more than sheets of canvas stretched over broken walls.

Makri and I come to an abrupt halt, speechless at the sight that greets us next. The Avenging Axe is a burned-out shell. Our home has been destroyed. Gurd is picking through the ruins. I approach my friend. He actually manages to grin. 'I'll build it again' says the old Barbarian.

'You will.'

Makri is despondent. Her room in the Avenging Axe contained her own collection of books and scrolls. It was a small collection by the standards of wealthier students but precious to her. 'I thought I'd hunt in my room to see what was left.' She sighs heavily. 'But there's nothing left.' The upper stories of the tavern have collapsed into rubble. The people passing by look dazed. There are returning citizens, soldiers on duty to prevent looting, and one or two food vendors trying to sell what scraps they have. All over there's an air of utter gloom. It's worse than I expected and I realise I was foolish to ever dream of things getting back to normal.

Chapter Six

I step on something and it splinters beneath my feet. A thin wooden sign — 'Thraxas, Sorcerous Investigator.' I shake my head. It's hard to believe I was ever a Senior Investigator at the Imperial Palace. A man with a respected position. That didn't last long. When they threw me out I ended up in Twelve Seas, a cheap private detective in a cheap part of town. I never had much sorcerous power despite what it said on the sign. A few easy spells, learned during my brief attendance at sorcerers college, were all I could ever manage. These days I could hardly use any of them.

Gurd is still wearing his brown military tunic. Like most Turanian soldiers he's not yet been discharged from the army. That won't happen for a while yet. Those military citizens currently trying to put their lives back together will have to do it at the same time as guard duty on the walls and regular shifts with street patrols. He leads us round the remains of the tavern to the yard at the back where Tanrose is standing over a small campfire, stirring a pot. Behind her is a small army tent. Gurd must have given her his own. That's against army rules but I doubt he's the only soldier who'll be secretly donating army equipment to their loved ones to help them survive. The moment Tanrose sees me she rushes to my side and embraces me.

'Thraxas! We were worried about you.'

I appreciate Tanrose's concern though her embrace makes me uncomfortable. I haven't been embraced much in recent years. In the last few weeks I was, by Sareepa, a Matteshan sorcerer who for some reason always had a soft spot for me. Her warmth and touch were a comfort on the long march back to Turai. I don't want to think about her death at the city walls.

Tanrose asks me where I'm billeted and when I tell her I'm at the Palace it actually raises a laugh. 'You managed to land on your feet.'

Gurd is amused. 'I hope you're not too comfortable.' He's putting on a show of good humour for Tanrose. His partner is pregnant and they've nowhere to live. It's a bad situation.

'Gurd, I'll do something to help. Lisutaris and Cicerius and some other politicians are all meeting to work out how to get the city

33

back on its feet. Whatever re-construction crews they can raise, I'll get one down here.'

'I think they'll be fixing the walls and the aqueducts, Thraxas. And the roads. Maybe the villas in Thamlin.'

'I'll get someone down here to help.'

We're interrupted by a high pitched, familiar voice. 'Thraxas! Makri! I've come to get you!'

I turn round to see a young Elf with spiky blonde hair hopping off an army wagon. Sendroo-ir-Vallis, commonly known as Droo, temporarily seconded to the Sorcerers Auxiliary Regiment and formerly part of my Security Unit. Perhaps she still is. I don't even know if I still have a unit. She marches up to me. Sendroo is a teenage Elf several inches shorter than me and about a quarter as wide. Her diminutive size doesn't prevent her from glaring up at me in an unfriendly manner. 'I'm so angry with you! You wouldn't let me join in the attack!'

That's true. Makri and I were at Lisutaris's side as she brought down the city wall. The other members of my unit, Anumaris and Rinderan, both sorcerers, were there too. Droo wanted to come but I forbade it, banishing her to the back of the lines. The assault force was no place for a small teenage Elf whose main concerns in life before the war were drinking wine and writing poetry.

'I had to sneak in behind some big infantrymen!'

'I'm glad you survived, Droo.'

Droo grins. 'I shot an orc with my bow!' Her bow is still slung over her shoulder, quite jaunty against her worn and faded green Elvish tunic. Her hair is as unruly, blonde and spiky as ever. 'You shouldn't have sent me away! But that's not why I'm here! Our Commander sent me to get you.'

'Lisutaris?'

'Yes. I was sent to the Palace to be a messenger again and as soon as I walked into the grounds Lisutaris appeared and told me to go and find you and Makri and bring you back. Something urgent, I think. Look, I've got an army wagon with two horses and two soldiers to shout at anyone who gets in the way.'

I turn to Gurd. 'You see? I always said this city couldn't manage without me. I've only left Lisutaris's side for half an hour and already she needs me back. Probably they'll end up making me a General. I don't suppose any beer survived the wreckage?'

Gurd shakes his head. 'Cellar was completely destroyed. No beer, and I don't know when anyone will be brewing again.'

'This day keeps getting worse.'

Makri and I depart, knowing we can't ignore an urgent summons from our Commander. The military wagon has right of way and other vehicles move aside but progress is still slow. Everywhere you look there are soldiers, citizens and workmen, trudging through the debris-strewn streets, straining under the blazing sun. It's uncomfortable and chaotic. At several junctions along the way we see signs at street corners asking all citizens with any sort of organisational or construction skills to report to the Palace where they'll be assigned to reconstruction work. You have to hand it to Cicerius. He's an efficient organiser and he's managed to get things moving faster than I'd have expected. Droo produces a small carafe of wine from her canvas bag and hands it to me. 'I couldn't find any beer.'

Droo has a talent for sniffing out alcohol. 'Not even the Simnians?'

'They might have some but Lisutaris is keeping them out of the city. Am I still in your Security Unit?'

'I don't know if I still have a unit. A lot of things haven't been sorted out yet.'

'Some of the Elves will be sailing home soon in the good weather,' Droo tells us. 'But I want to stay here a while.' She beams. 'I'm still having an adventure!'

I drink some wine and offer it to Makri, who shakes her head. 'We're not supposed to drink on duty.'

'We're not on duty, we have leave to visit Twelve Seas.'

'Our Commander called us back so we're on duty again.'

'Makri, just drink some damned wine.'

'No.'

Ensign Droo has no interest in army rules and takes the carafe and pours wine down her throat. 'Elvish soldiers are always allowed to drink wine.'

'That's completely untrue,' says Makri.

Droo laughs. 'I'm sure I read it somewhere.'

I notice an unusual brooch on Droo's tunic. Three small pearls on a silver frame. Not expensive, but quite a nice piece.

'Where did you get that?'

'I found it outside the Palace, trodden into the ground. We have pearl fisheries on Avula, it reminded me of them.'

We have a long wait outside the Palace. Wagons, soldiers, officials, civil servants, a few senior sorcerers, all here on business, either heading for the requisitioned rooms at the Palace or the administrative buildings around it. We disembark and walk through the grounds, past the great fountain of St Quatinius, a marvel of engineering that used to shoot three great plumes of water high in the air. It's no longer working, and the shrubs and flowers in the surrounding gardens are parched and dry under the blazing sun. Inside the Palace things are a little quieter though we still pass plenty of officers and officials scurrying along the corridors. As ever, Makri's slightly Orcish features attract attention. Tying her hair back does tend to expose her pointed ears. Even though she's discarded her Orcish armour she still looks barbaric to anyone unfamiliar with her, with her man's tunic and leggings and a sword at each hip. Several Niojan scribes step back in alarm as we pass. That's not the only reaction she gets. Makri's part Elvish as well, with large dark eyes and fine cheekbones. Young men have fallen for her plenty of times. Young Elves too, which tends to confuse them.

When we reach Lisutaris's conference room the guards tell us to wait. I look back along the marbled corridor. I wonder again what will become of the Palace now we no longer have a Royal Family. I'm not sad about their passing. It's a long time since I felt any affection for them. That's not uncommon among the population. The door opens. Lisutaris emerges. Before it closes, I catch a glimpse of a familiar figure inside.

'Lodius?'

'Senator Lodius has joined our Ruling Council.'

'A triumvirate with you and Cicerius?'

'In effect, yes. Cicerius isn't happy about it but I didn't see any other option if we're all to work together.'

Senator Lodius is the leader of the Populares Party, implacable opponents of Cicerius's Traditionals. Lodius's calls for the improvement in the lives of Turai's lower classes has gathered him a lot of support over the years. That support extends through much of Turanian society and it would be difficult to exclude him from efforts to re-construct the city, particularly as he managed to serve honourably in the war. He didn't do anything spectacular but he did raise a military unit at his own expense and marched it back to Turai so there's no criticising him on that front.

'Follow me,' says Lisutaris, and walks swiftly along the corridor.

'Can I come?' asks Droo.

Lisutaris halts and considers for a moment. 'Yes, Ensign Sendroo. You're still part of Captain Thraxas's Security Unit. As such, you will comply with our security rules. Tell anyone of this business and I'll personally explode your head.' Lisutaris doesn't sound like she's joking. We follow her along the corridor, wondering what might have happened.

When I notice that the Head of the Sorcerers Guild is leading us down the familiar route to the underground vault containing Turai's secret gold reserves, I begin to develop a shrewd idea of what might have happened. Lisutaris and Cicerius might have confidence in the impregnability of a fancy lock supported by sorcery but they haven't spent their lives dealing with Turai's criminals.

'So how much is missing?'

Lisutaris glares at me but declines to answer. We descend several more floors and travel along more corridors. Two uniformed guards smartly salute our Commander. We turn the final corner and approach the door of the vault. The door has been pushed shut but obviously it's not properly locked because Lisutaris makes it swing open with a simple spell. She snaps her fingers, illuminating the interior. It's completely empty. Someone has made off with the entire contents.

'Why are we looking at an empty vault?' enquires Droo, innocently.

'Because there should be two million gurans worth of gold here,' I explain. 'And someone's stolen it.'

Lisutaris shakes her head. 'This is a disaster. Without it we can't buy food. The city will starve.' She turns to me. 'Captain Thraxas. You need to find out who's responsible and recover the gold. You and your security unit are to engage in nothing else. Just find the gold.' She pauses. 'And don't say anything annoying like "I warned you this would happen."'

'Did Thraxas warn you this would have happen?' Droo gazes round the empty vault. 'Probably you should have listened to him.'

'Yes, perhaps we should.'

'Because Thraxas does seem good at solving crimes so he probably knew what he was talking about.'

'Thanks you for your opinion, Ensign,' growls Lisutaris, menacingly enough to make even Droo realise she shouldn't say any more. Makri strides into the empty vault. 'How could anyone move so much gold without being caught? There was more than a wagonload in here.'

'I presume someone had access to a magic pocket,' says Lisutaris.

It's a reasonable suggestion. You can pack anything into a magic pocket and carry it away easily. It won't weigh anything or take up any space. Even so, it wouldn't be a quick task, you'd still have to load the gold into the pocket. There aren't too many magic pockets around either, they're regulated by the authorities. Our late King was always nervous that someone might use one to produce a sword out of nowhere and end his reign earlier than anticipated. I ask Makri, Lisutaris and Droo to step out of the vault. 'I need to examine it for traces of sorcery.'

'I've already done that.' Lisutaris sounds impatient. 'There are no traces.'

'For you, maybe, but you're used to bringing down dragons, not investigating crime.'

'I'm the Head of the Sorcerer's Guild!' exclaims Lisutaris, angrily. Her aura of calm is quickly slipping away. I'm not surprised.

'Just let me look.' I examine all the walls and the floor and the ceiling. I have a highly developed skill for detecting sorcery at the scene of a crime, but I can't detect anything. Nor can I see any sign of any other means of entry to the vault. I go back outside to talk to Lisutaris. 'What happened to the man with the key?'

'Lemusius? We haven't heard from him.'

'Isn't that strange?'

'No, he had no reason to contact the Palace.'

'I don't like that you haven't heard from him. I'll have to talk to him anyway. What did your vault sorcerer say?'

'Dominius Iron Strike was informed by a guard that the door to the vault appeared to be ajar so he went to check and found the vault empty.'

'Did the guards have any idea how the door came to be open?'

'They claim to have seen nothing.'

'What about the sorcerer you'd told to keep watch on this place?'

Lisutaris shifts uncomfortably. 'Dearineth placed a spell to alert her to any unusual movements in this location. She observed none.'

I'm tempted to inform Lisutaris that her security arrangements were about as much use as a one-legged gladiator but I refrain. True, she should have listened to me in the first place but I can let her know that at some future date. 'I'd have thought there'd be some sort of sorcerous mark on the gold so government sorcerers could trace it.'

'There was. A sorcerous tracer mark we should be able to locate. But we can't. I've looked.'

'If the gold was still in a magic pocket would that mean you couldn't find it?'

Lisutaris is uncertain. 'It's difficult to say. I'd have thought I'd be able to locate it even inside a magic pocket but that's not certain.'

'Could another sorcerer have removed the mark?'

Lisutaris hesitates. 'The tracer mark was placed on the gold by Old Hasius the Brilliant. It would be very difficult for another sorcerer to undo his work.'

'Difficult but not impossible?'

Lisutaris shrugs her shoulders. 'Nothing is completely impossible in sorcery.'

We can't ask Old Hasius himself, he was killed in the sack of Turai. Another grave loss for the Sorcerers Guild; Hasius was the most senior sorcerer working for the government.

'I'll need to talk to Dearineth, Dominius Iron Strike, and every guard who's been on duty here. I'll also need to talk to Lemusius. If you can find some spell for tracing unrecorded magic pockets that would help. We don't want the gold to leave the city if possible. Is there any chance that someone had a supply of Red Elvish Cloth?'

Red Elvish Cloth creates a barrier that's impenetrable to even the most powerful investigating sorcerers. Only the authorities have access to it and there's very little in Turai.

'I wouldn't think so,' says Lisutaris. 'There are several private rooms in the Palace lined with it and one at the Abode of Justice, but that's all. It was completely outlawed for anyone else.'

'Have someone check these rooms to see if any of the cloth is missing. Are Rinderan and Anumaris still part of my security unit?'

Since we retook the city, I don't even know where the two young sorcerers have got to.

'Anumaris could be. I assigned her to sorcerous protection of the walls but you can have her back. Rinderan's not available, he's assisting the ambassador from the Southern Hills and I promised Queen Direeva I'd look after him.'

'I'd like Makri too, if you can spare her as bodyguard.'

'That's fine. I'm not in danger here and I have Tirini.'

I'm expecting Makri to protest about this but she remains silent. Maybe she likes the idea of helping me in an investigation. She has some talent for it. Not as much as she thinks she has. 'I'll need a wagon to get us round the city and some sort of official authorisation.'

Lisutaris reaches inside her robe and pulls out a small bronze badge. There's nothing on it. She speaks. 'Captain Thraxas, Senior Palace Investigator.' Immediately her words are inscribed on the badge. That's a piece of sorcery I've never seen before and quite an impressive one. I take the badge. 'It's going to be a temporary position,' I tell Lisutaris. 'When I've sorted out this mess I'm going back to Twelve Seas to help rebuilt the Avenging Axe.'

'Was it badly damaged?'

'Destroyed. Tanrose is living in a tent in the yard. I promised Gurd I'll help. Whatever re-construction crews are available I'd like some sent down to Twelve Seas.'

Lisutaris knows Gurd is a good citizen as well as a warrior who's served the city well. Despite that, and despite the fact that Makri and I live in the Avenging Axe and are now homeless, she can't promise assistance any time soon. 'I'll keep Twelve Seas in mind but all the reconstruction teams are working on the walls and the aqueducts. We can't manage without them. Then there are the main roads and sewers, all in a bad state. We don't have that many workers and if we want to hire more from our neighbours that's going to cost money we don't have.'

We walk back along the corridor and up the stairs. 'I haven't even seen my own house,' says Lisutaris. 'I haven't had a moment to visit Thamlin.' For a moment the Head of the Sorcerers Guild appears seriously depressed. 'I knew it wasn't going to be easy getting the city back in order but it's worse than I expected.'

'What's the status of Glixius Dragon Killer these days?'

'Glixius? He's in good standing after the war. Why?'

'I saw him just before we attacked the Palace.'

'He was with the assault force. He's a strong sorcerer.'

'He was with Casax, the leader of the Twelve Seas chapter of the Brotherhood. Seeing them together made me suspicious.'

'Is that a lead?'

'It's somewhere to start. Casax is aware of most crime in Turai. In normal times anyway. He might be able to tell me something. I'll talk to him after I've seen Lemusius.'

Chapter Seven

The stables outside the Palace have been requisitioned by the new authorities. We head there to pick up our wagon. 'Droo, I don't need you to come with me. Find Anumaris and tell her she's back in my unit. Tell her to make a list of everyone who might have known about the secret vault. And I mean everyone. If the King's chef's kitchenmaid learned that there was gold hidden under the Palace, I want to know about it.'

Droo nods, but she's looking doubtful. 'Can we find that out?'

'I taught you all how to investigate on the march. Anumaris is well organised when it comes to making lists. Do the best you can and do it quickly. If you find any beer along the way, that'll help too. Bribe people if necessary, we have a government budget to spend.'

Droo grins. Scouring the city for beer and bribing people if necessary is right up her street. She departs to track down the young sorcerer Anumaris. Droo, while sober, is an enthusiastic and efficient helper. I climb into the wagon, a small cart with one black horse. Not a great vehicle but it does come with an official looking sign on the side — *Palace Vehicle, priority access* — so that will be helpful for manoeuvring our way through the crowded streets. Overhead the sun is beating down. Whoever founded this city didn't give much thought to the weather conditions which are often terrible. Makri climbs in after me. So far today she's been unusually quiet. She remains so as we head northeast towards the house of the rich merchant Lemusius.

'I didn't think I'd be investigating so soon after reaching Turai. It wasn't what I had in mind.'

'Did what you have in mind involve beer?' asks Makri.

'Yes. Barrels of it. I pictured myself rolling around in beer while eating an endless supply of Tanrose's pies. I should have known that wasn't realistic.' I shake my head. 'Maybe it's not so bad to be investigating again in Turai. I'm getting back to normal.'

'You're far from normal,' says Makri. There's an odd tone in her voice.

'What do you mean?'

'When Tanrose embraced you, you shrank back.'

'Shrank back? What are you talking about?'

'You shrank from her embrace. Only slightly, but you did.'
'No, I didn't.'
'Yes, you did. I saw you.'
'Why would I do that? Tanrose has kept me going for years with her pies and stews. She's the only person in Turai I don't mind embracing.'

Makri won't let it go. 'You weren't comfortable when she put her arms round you.'

I'm starting to feel irritated. 'I was not uncomfortable.'
'Yes, you were.'
'No, I wasn't.'
'We could keep on like this,' says Makri. 'It doesn't change what I saw.'

Now I'm annoyed. What's Makri doing observing me anyway? She should mind her own business. 'Why are you going on about it?'

'Since Sareepa was killed and you haven't said a word about it. So I'm postulating you've internalised your grief and it's made you uncomfortable with human contact. It might remind you of Sareepa. You don't know how to deal with the way it ended.'

Makri's the only person I know who'd use the word *postulating*. It's a further irritation though only minor in comparison to the general outrage I'm feeling about her sticking her nose into my private affairs. 'Is that what this is about? Some nonsense about me not coping with something? Dammit Makri, ever since you went to Community College and met Samanatius the Philosopher you've had nothing but fancy theories. Internalising my grief? What does that mean?'

Makri responds calmly. 'It means you can't express your feelings so they'll start eating you up inside. It's very unhealthy.'

The sun is beating down. Two workmen and two soldiers are blocking the road, arguing about something or other. I suddenly feel angry at everything. 'Has Turai come to this now? A man can't go about his business without half-Orcish women lecturing him about his feelings?'

'I'm one quarter Orcish and it has no bearing on the matter. Nor, before you insult them, do my pointed ears. I'm trying to help you.'

Fearing I'm about to explode, I take a deep breath and concentrate on manoeuvring the wagon past the arguing workmen

43

and soldiers. 'This is ridiculous even by your standards. Never mention it again.'

Makri shrugs. 'Fine. Eat yourself up. I don't care.'

'You're just in a bad mood because you haven't seen your damned library yet.'

'Me worrying about the library doesn't have any bearing on your inability to talk about Sareepa.'

We ride on in angry silence. I should be celebrating with a barrel of beer. Instead I'm investigating a crime in the relentless heat in a ruined city with an annoying woman who's in a bad mood. It's a poor homecoming for a war hero. By now we're close to Lemusius's home, an impressively large mansion on the fringes of Thamlin. Lemusius was rich enough to live in the smartest part of the city, even if wealthy merchants are never quite accepted by the top layer of Turai's society. The aristocratic class don't entirely approve of anyone who's sullied their hands by participating in trade or industry. Normally there'd be servants peering out of windows as we approach but there's no sign of anyone here. The rich people of Turai might be short of servants for a while. Many of those who survived will still be required for army duties.

There's a fancy bronze bell on the ornate front door but as I go to ring it I notice the door is slightly ajar. I'm immediately on the alert. No one leaves their front door open in Turai. I glance at Makri. Simultaneously we draw the army-issue knives we're wearing at our belts. I push the door open. Inside it's gloomy but there's enough light coming in from the windows to show us the scene. Coats and a coat rack are strewn over the hallway floor. It could be war damage but I sense it's more recent. We step into the first main room we come to. Inside, Lemusius is lying dead on the carpet, face down with a wound in his back. Next to him is an overturned chair.

Makri and I search the house quickly, remaining close together. The place is empty. There's little damage. In one room we find a few small Orcish figurines and a mat that's required for certain Orcish prayers.

'Looks like an Orcish officer was billeted here and Lemusius hadn't cleared it all out yet.'

We return to examine the body. It's cold. I'd say Lemusius has been dead for around twelve hours. There's no sign of his fancy key but I've no way of knowing where it might be kept. It could still be secure in a hidden safe or it might have been stolen. I can't sense any sorcery. I study the wound in his back.

'Looks like a knife wound. It's the only wound on his body so I'd guess he was taken by surprise and killed quickly. Probably never saw his assailant. An investigating sorcerer might be able to learn more from the body.'

'Are there any investigating sorcerers left?'

I shrug. It's a reasonable question. The Abode of Justice did employ several sorcerers with experience in investigating crime. Specialists who could conjure up pictures of the past, or trace items over long distances. 'I don't know if there are any specialists left. Anumaris has some experience, I'll ask her to examine the house too, she might be able to pick up something.'

Makri looks down at Lemusius's body, then shakes her head. 'Welcome back to Turai. Didn't take long for people to start killing each other.' We depart, leaving the body on the floor. Makri takes the reins in the wagon while I write a note for Lisutaris. Turai has always had an efficient Messengers Guild and they're already re-opening their outposts. We find one on the main street. I hand over my message and the clerk seals it with wax and promises a swift delivery to the Palace. Makri wants to take the reins again.

'Where now?'

'Twelve Seas.'

'The Avenging Axe?'

'No, the Mermaid.'

'The Mermaid? Home of the Brotherhood? Do you think they have something to do with this?'

'It's possible. I don't like it that I saw Casax and Glixius close to the Palace.'

'Is Casax the leader of the whole Brotherhood?'

'No, just the Twelve Seas chapter, but he's one of their most important bosses. There's a lot of crime around the harbour, the Twelve Seas chapter has always been powerful.'

Once again I'm reminded of the card game at the Avenging Axe on the day the city fell. Casax was one of the participants. There were other wealthy gamblers there too, all making a rare visit to the rough part of town because it was one of the few places where gambling was still to be found, the rest of the city being plagued by the winter malady at the time. 'Even if Casax wasn't involved,

45

the theft of the gold bullion is a major crime and he generally gets to hear about things.'

'He's not the sort of man who'd volunteer information.'

'He's not, but he's not as smart as he thinks he is. None of these criminals are. I might learn something. Who knows, he might think it's his patriotic duty to help Turai.'

Makri laughs at the thought. That's probably justified. Although Casax did fight in the war and he didn't have to do that. He's well-connected enough to have simply hidden till it blew over but he chose to march back with the army. Maybe he does harbour some loyalty to the city. When we reach Moon and Stars Boulevard we should turn south. Makri however drives straight over the road and into the streets beyond.

'I want to look at the Imperial Library. I need to see what state it's in.'

'We don't have time, we're investigating.'

'I just want to look.'

'Do you really need to look at it now?'

'Yes.'

'Fine. We'll just tell Lisutaris the gold is lost and Turai is going to starve because you couldn't wait to check on a bunch of old scrolls.'

'It won't take long.'

I shake my head wearily. We might as well get it over with. Makri won't be happy till she's seen the Library, and while she's unhappy there's always the chance she'll start talking about feelings and emotions. I'm keen to avoid that. Not far from the main road, a little north of the Palace, stands the headquarters of the Honourable Merchants Association. It's suffered heavy damage. Several wealthy-looking individuals are gathered around the shattered columns at the entrance, talking with a group of workmen they've hired to repair the damage. Just past the building the road is completely blocked by the remains of a collapsed building belonging to the Honourable Guild of Goldsmiths. A few men are standing forlornly beside the wreckage. Honourable goldsmiths, presumably. I don't recognise any of them. We dismount and walk past into a small private park. Here the fences have all been broken and the trees have been hacked down. There's a dried up pond and the flower beds have been trampled beyond repair.

Makri halts, scowling. 'I used to come here and read.' We walk on. 'The Merchants didn't like me coming here,' mutters Makri, almost to herself. 'But they got used to it. It was a nice park.'

Across the park is the Imperial Library, a large building, three stories, previously white but now darkened by the effects of smoke and flames. At first glance it doesn't seem to have suffered too much structural damage. Some green tiles from the roof have been sheared off and lie on the ground and many of the windows are broken, but the walls seems secure.

'Makri!'

A woman hurries towards us. She's wearing a blue robe, similar to the other employees in the library I've seen on the few occasions Makri dragged me there. There's a bandage round her head. Clean and well-applied, I notice.

'It's so good to see you, Makri!'

Honestly, not many Turanians say that to the part-Orcish ex-gladiator.

'I was worried about you with all the fighting.'

Makri smiles at her. 'I'm fine. But you're wounded.'

'It's nothing. My brother's in Turai's First Phalanx and I was following along behind. I rushed into the city a bit too quickly to see the library and an arrow grazed my head. It's just a little cut, I'm fine.'

Another scroll and book fanatic, rushing past flying arrows to see her damned library. No wonder she gets on well with Makri.

'Thraxas, this is Aridinis. She's the deputy librarian. Aridinis, this is Captain Thraxas. We work together for Lisutaris.'

Aridinis is somewhere around thirty-five and I can tell her background just by looking at her. Moderately wealthy family, father a civil servant, older brothers and sisters respectably married, leaving her to make a career for herself, either through choice or because there was no family money left for another wedding. One of that strange breed of Turanian women, few in number, who go into the arts and sciences, ending up at the Imperial Library or the Imperial Record House, happy to be around scholarly works. Still respectable, but not particularly well-regarded by the rest of the city. Well-regarded by Makri, however.

'How are the books?' ask Makri, anxiously.

'Not too bad. I was so scared the Orcs would destroy everything but they seem to have left most of the collection alone. There was a fire round the other side of the building so there's a lot of smoke damage and water damage too. We still have about eighty percent of the collection and we might be able to recover more.'

I don't know what Aridinis means by *eighty percent*. I've never heard the words before.

'Do you want to come and see for yourself? All the librarians will be pleased to see you again.'

'Are there many of them here?'

'Quit a few have made it back.'

I tell Makri we really should be heading down to Twelve Seas.

'I have to look inside. I'll only be a few minutes.' And with that, Makri hurries off with Aridinis, leaving me on my own in the ruined park with the sun beating down and not a drop of beer to be had anywhere. I consider leaving Makri here and just continuing on my own, but decide to wait for a few minutes. It's not like I'm about to solve this crime any time soon. I can see the possibility of never solving it. Removing that gold from the underground vault without leaving a trace behind, under the very noses of the Palace guards, Lisutaris and her fellow sorcerers, required a level of skill and organisation that points to something that may be beyond my powers to solve. What if the gold was stolen by Nioj or Simnia, in an effort to damage us? If the combined sorcery, state intelligence and manpower of one of our rivals was behind it then it's probably too late to do anything about it. The city will starve and I'll never taste beer again.

I look over towards the goldsmiths gathered around their destroyed headquarters, all of them still forlorn. I'm sympathetic, though it's not like they ever hired me to work for them. These honourable associations don't care for the services of a lone investigator in Twelve Seas, preferring instead to rely on the services of one of the reputable investigating agencies in the smarter parts of the city. More fool them. Makri arrives back, interrupting my thoughts. She's smiling. 'It's really not as bad as I thought it might be. Most of the collection survived and there's hardly any damage to the Elvish history section.' Her face falls. 'The advanced celestial mechanics section did suffer some losses.'

We return to the wagon. This time I take the reins and steer us back to the main road.

'It's still bad though.' Makri frowns. 'Everyone there is relieved they've saved eighty percent of the collection but twenty percent is still a substantial loss. There are valuable books and scrolls that will be very difficult to replace.'

'What does *percent* mean?'

'It's a way of measuring things,' explains Makri. 'You divide everything into a hundred parts. So the whole collection of books would be a hundred percent and if you lose one-fifth of them that means twenty percent. The librarian started using the system after Samanatius suggested it.'

'What's wrong with the normal system of parts in three hundred?'

'Nothing. But the new system is easier. It's progress.'

'I don't like progress. It's never good.'

Our journey through the city is as slow as before. Debris and traffic everywhere. Workmen blocking every route. Soldiers marching this way and that. Refugees streaming along, carrying their meagre possessions in canvas bags. Children screaming, mothers becoming angry, ruined shops, nothing but splinters of wood where the markets used to be. Not a functioning tavern to be seen. Those that escaped destruction haven't bothered to open, no beer being available. It's a poor state of affairs.

'If Lisutaris cared for the city she'd be doing something about the beer shortage.'

'She has other things on her mind.'

'Nothing as important. I don't see how we can carry on without it. It's typical of this useless city. Men fight and shed blood to defend it and how are we repaid? With no beer. It can't go on like this. Lisutaris and that fraud Cicerius have never cared for the common man. I hope Senator Lodius is giving them a hard time about their lack of care for all the decent citizens who're suffering while they roll around in luxury at the Palace.'

'You detest Senator Lodius.'

I do detest him. Nonetheless I refuse to concede. 'Lodius himself may be a rabble-rouser but that doesn't mean his policies are bad. He'd distribute the wealth in Turai more fairly. It's time these rich people in Thamlin stopped exploiting the poor.'

I've had some involvement with Lodius in the past and know him for the power-hungry politician he is. Even so, his party, the Populares, do make a series of reasonable points. The wealth in Turai is badly in need of redistribution and the Traditionals, on behalf of the King, have never been keen to redistribute any of it. 'At least Lodius pretends to care about people.'

'That's not the most convincing argument I've ever heard,' says Makri. 'But you're right. Since I've been in Turai I've been surrounded by poverty. Now it turns out there was millions in gold hidden in the Palace.' She pauses. 'Do you think Lodius knows about that?'

'I doubt it. Cicerius will keep it from him. Lisutaris too, I expect. She'll support Cicerius over Lodius.'

'We don't know that.'

Makri is loyal to Lisutaris and doesn't like to admit she has any faults, but a wealthy sorcerer like Lisutaris, Mistress of the Sky, will support the Traditional Party over Lodius and his Populares. I shake my head. Any discussion of politics in Turai rapidly reminds me that I loathe all our politicians. None of them care that the common man is suffering from the worst beer shortage in recorded history. I despise them all.

Chapter Eight

We pull slowly into Twelve Seas. More rubble everywhere, and the closer we get to the harbour the worse it is. I vividly remember the dragons flying overhead as people fled. We make our way to the end of Quintessence Street then turn into Tranquility Lane. It's a miserable little alleyway. Before the city fell it was always full of dwa addicts and hopeless beggars. They haven't yet returned. It won't take them long, particularly as the Mermaid tavern at the end of the alley is still standing. It seems to have suffered little structural damage.

'The Mermaid, home of the Brotherhood, criminal centre of Twelve Seas, untouched by the war. Meanwhile our honest tavern's in ruins.'

Makri leaps from the wagon, much more nimbly than I do. I check my sword is loose in its scabbard. You never know what might happen in the Mermaid. 'I wonder if they have any beer?'

'This place is run by criminals,' says Makri, disapprovingly.

'Beer is beer.'

They don't have any beer. I can tell as soon as we enter. I'd smell it if it was here. There's a barman lounging behind the bar but no sign of any ale. A few customers at the tables have glasses in front of them, probably cheap wine. It's a pitiful sight for a tavern in Twelve Seas. I notice a number of Brotherhood members have already made their way here. It won't take long till they're all back, stealing from the docks, running illegal gambling and selling dwa. I don't know where they'll find their supply but they'll find it; they always do. I head straight for the staircase at the back. Three men rise from a table and stand in my way.

'That's a private area.'

'I'm here to see Casax.'

'He's busy.'

These are petty thugs, not trained fighters. Makri and I could bat them out the way if necessary though I'd prefer not to have to fight. It doesn't come to that because a loud voice comes bellowing down the stairs. 'Is that Thraxas? Here already?'

It's Casax, Brotherhood boss. He laughs, mockingly. 'The big investigator is here to interrogate us. Just like old times. Couldn't wait to visit, Thraxas. Did you miss us?'

Now everyone laughs, even Karlox, the huge man at Casax's side. Karlox is a large, violent and not particularly bright individual who works for Casax as an enforcer. He dwarves his boss, which is not to say Casax is small. He's a brawny figure with a shaved head and a fancy gold earring in each ear. He has some scarring on his jaw though he's still a better looking man than most of the miscreants in the Mermaid. I notice the dagger on his hip, or rather the scabbard, a rather elegant Elvish item that he must have picked up during the war.

'And he's brought his girlfriend. Always good to see you, Makri. You here to accept my job offer? We always need dancers.'

His men laugh some more. Makri shifts uncomfortably, not liking this, but manages not to rise to the bait. Casax tells his men to let us pass. 'It won't feel like home till Thraxas has dragged his fat frame over to investigate us.'

I'm overweight. I'm fine with it. I don't like Casax mocking it. I walk up the stairs with Makri at my side. The Mermaid is undamaged though I notice some changes. There used to be pictures on the staircase walls and Elvish tapestries in Casax's office. Good works, far to good for a shabby tavern in this part of town. Now they've all gone. 'I see you've lost a few things.'

This makes Casax scowl. 'Damned Orcs, stripped the place bare. At least they left it standing. I'm sorry about what happened to the Avenging Axe. Gurd's a good man, he didn't deserve that.' Casax sounds sincere about this and he probably is. 'You remember our last night there, playing cards when the Orcs attacked the city? I can barely remember how I made it out alive.' He takes a seat and lounges back, inviting us to sit on the seats facing him at his desk. 'And now we've taken the city back. We're war heroes.'

I wouldn't describe Casax as a war hero. He did march and fight with the army so perhaps it's fair enough.

'Of course, it was tough for us regular soldiers,' continues the Brotherhood boss. 'Doing all the heavy work. We weren't all walking alongside Lisutaris with sorcerers to protect us.'

I glare at him. I'd forgotten how easily he could irritate me. 'You've got it the wrong way round, Casax. We were protecting Lisutaris. I was first man through the walls and Makri was right there with me. But maybe we could save the war stories for another time. I have some questions.'

'About what?'

This is awkward, as I knew it would be. I can't come right out and tell Casax what I'm investigating. The theft of the Palace gold, and even its existence, is a state secret. 'When we entered the city, I saw you approaching the Palace. What were you doing with Glixius?'

'Fighting the Orcs or course. What did you think we were doing?'

'When did you and Glixius become friends?'

'We're not friends. He was the sorcerer assigned to my unit as we came through the walls. You mind telling me what this is about?'

'Did you and Glixius enter the Palace?'

'No, we went round it and carried on fighting. You're already boring me, fat man. Get to the point.'

I don't mind that I've riled Casax a little. I'd like to ask him more about his activities around the Palace after we marched into Turai but again I'm wary of giving anything away about the missing gold. 'I've just been looking at a body.'

'In the Palace?'

'No, on the edges of Thamlin. A man called Lemusius. He was murdered last night. You know him?'

'I've heard of him. Some sort of Palace financier, wasn't he?'

'Something like that.'

'Why would you think I had anything to do with it?'

'Because you're a notorious criminal and you might be involved in anything.'

Casax smiles, quite broadly. 'I'm not denying that. But Palace financiers in Thamlin are a bit out of my way. Even if the Brotherhood were involved, which I'm not saying we were, there's closer people to Thamlin than us. The Kushni chapter, for instance.'

I nod my head. 'Is Barilox back in town?' Barilox is the boss of the Kushni Brotherhood and one of the most influential criminals in Turai.

'Not yet. On his way.' Casax leans forwards. 'Thraxas, I'd have thrown you out already except I have the feeling this has something to do with Lisutaris and the Palace. You're still in her Security Unit so it must be something that concerns her. I'm not necessarily opposed to helping with that. Lisutaris was a fine War Leader. I put in enough effort helping her take this city back, I don't want to see it go all to hell now. But I'm not going to sit here answering questions from an investigator who won't tell me what it's about.'

'I can't do that, Casax. But yes, it is an important matter and it does involve our War Leader. Something happened at the Palace and it involved Lemusius and now he's dead. It feels like something that needed organisation and resources.' I pause, and look him in the eye. 'Organisation and resources like the Brotherhood have.'

Casax shrugs. 'We're not the only ones. The Guilds, the Honourable Merchants' Association, the army, the church, the sorcerers, they've all got resources.'

'None of them are actually dedicated to crime.'

Casax laughs. 'They're all capable of it when necessary. You'd be surprised what they've been involved with in the past.'

'No, I wouldn't be. I know what this city is like. I'll get round to investigating them if necessary. But I didn't see any of them hanging round the Palace. Unlike you and Glixius.'

'You're way off target with that, investigator. We were fighting the Orcs and I don't like you suggesting otherwise.' There's a pause while Casax wonders if he's fed up talking to me yet. 'Are you going to tell me what's missing from the Palace?'

'No.'

'Then I'm not going to be able to help. If this murder happened up in Thamlin, have you considered asking the Society of Friends? It's closer to their territory than ours.'

The Society of Friends is the main criminal organisation in the north of the city. They're bitter rivals of the Brotherhood. I've come across them though not often as they generally stay out of the south of the city, that being Brotherhood territory.

'It's possible they're involved,' I admit.

'Do you have any contacts there?'

'No.'

'You're not really a well-connected man, Thraxas. Must be a problem for you, in your line of work.'

'I get by.'

'Barely. You've been scraping a living for as long as I've known you.' Casax looks around at the bare walls, dissatisfied. 'I miss my tapestries. Going to take a while to replace them. Damned Orcs.' He looks at Makri, who's been silent the whole time. 'You're part Orc. Might make things difficult for you in this city after what

54

we've been through. Though you didn't do so badly for us in the war, so I hear. Bodyguard to our War Leader. Still planning on going to the University? Plenty of people won't like that. If they try and stop you, let me know. Maybe I'll be able to help.'

Makri doesn't know how to take this. She remains silent. Casax turns his attention back to me. 'Before the war the Society of Friends was re-organising. They'd had some trouble because their leader Artinus fell out with the Civil Guards who gave them protection. Darisax took over. He's a clever man, used to have a lock on all the pearl trade down the coast before moving into Turai. Any crime that's been going on around the Palace or Thamlin, he might know something about it. Of course, you wouldn't be able to talk to him. He's not going to bother with a small-time investigator from Twelve Seas.'

I ignore the insult. 'I'm working for Lisutaris at the Palace.'

Casax nods. 'That might help. You could ask for an introduction from our new government. Cicerius and his friends. These aristocrats all have connections with the Society.'

'That seems unlikely.'

'The Society of Friends have been paying off their contacts at the Palace for years. You'll find someone at the Palace who can introduce you to them.'

It's time to go. I stand up. 'Is there any chance of this tavern selling beer any time soon?'

Casax looks genuinely regretful. 'Not soon. We've nothing to sell and not much prospect of the brewers bringing in barley or hops. There were no harvests this year, no one has anything.'

'Dammit Casax, the Brotherhood must be able find beer.'

'Are you suggesting we steal it?'

'No,' says Makri, immediately.

'If necessary,' I say, glaring at Makri.

'Don't encourage people to steal beer!'

'Why not? It would be the first useful thing the Brotherhood ever did for the city.'

Casax holds up his hand. 'Thraxas, if I had any beer I'd give you some just to shut you up. But there's none to be had.'

Casax has something else to say before we go. 'You're an informer short.'

'Am I?'

'You're old friend Kerk. He was killed when the Orcs invaded.'

55

Kerk. I'd almost forgotten about him. A dwa user, so addicted he'd risk his life selling me information to raise money for more of the drug. I shrug my shoulders. 'He was never much of an informer anyway.'

Chapter Nine

We ride the wagon back towards the Palace. Makri's looking at me with disapproval. 'Encouraging the Brotherhood to steal beer for you is bad, even by your standards.'

'I have no standards when it comes to beer. The Brotherhood are going to be involved in crime anyway, might as well make themselves useful.'

'Are you really not bothered by Kerk's death?'

I consider this. 'I suppose I am. He did give me useful information, once or twice. But there's no point in feeling much about dwa addicts. They're never going to recover. If the Orcs hadn't killed him the drugs would.'

The streets are becoming busier and more chaotic by the hour. The navy has been transporting displaced citizens back to Turai. Already several large vessels have discharged their human cargo at the docks. Whether this is the best idea, I'm not certain. Citizens are coming home to ruins and the possibility of starvation. It's a facet of human nature I've noticed before. Everyone wants to go home. Turanian citizens, sheltering in neighbouring territories, aren't going to wait any longer than necessary to return.

'It's really bad,' I mutter to Makri, as we wait among a huge snarl of wagons on the main road.

'It will take a while for the workers to clear the roads.'

'I was still talking about the beer shortage. I can't believe the Orcs destroyed the breweries.'

'That's not really the problem, is it?' says Makri. 'You heard Casax. There's no barley to brew with. The breweries can probably be repaired easily enough but it's no use if there are no supplies.'

My face is screwed up. I'm deep in thought. 'It only needs barley, hops and water. The city still has plenty of water coming in, even if the aqueducts have been damaged. How hard can it be to get hold of hops and barley? Someone must have some. Now I think about it, Rinderan's family own a brewery down in the Southern Hills. He's an expert on the subject. Just give him the right equipment and he'd get things moving. I wonder if Lisutaris has any spells for making it quicker? She might have, she's always helping her thazis plants along with some sort of magic.'

57

'People need food and shelter. I can't see Lisutaris taking time off to make alcohol.'

'She'd do it if she needed thazis.' I urge the horses on. 'There's no reason we can't solve this problem, working together. Beer could be produced with a little effort from the authorities.'

Makri scowls. 'I refuse to talk about beer any longer. Do you even remember why we went to the Mermaid?'

'Of course. We're investigating the theft of gold bullion from the Palace.'

'Did you learn anything?'

I pause, quickly reviewing my conversation with Casax. 'Not really.'

'Did you even pay attention to what he said?'

We're still caught up in an immovable snarl of wagons and pedestrians. I turn to look at Makri. 'Yes, I was paying attention.'

'So what did you learn?'

I'm starting to feel annoyed. 'Are you questioning my investigating?'

'Yes.'

'I'm number one chariot at investigating. Did you just roll your eyes?'

'Probably.'

'Casax didn't tell us anything useful.'

'He might have,' says Makri. 'Pearls, for instance.'

I've no idea what Makri is talking about. 'Pearls?'

'Casax mentioned a new Society of Friends boss called Darisax. He said he was once involved in the pearl trade.'

'So what?'

'So Droo found an unusual pearl broach trampled into the ground outside the Palace.'

I'd forgotten about that. I nudge the wagon forward. 'It's a tenuous link.'

'I know,' says Makri. 'But it's the sort of thing you'd have picked up on if you weren't obsessed with beer.'

Makri is looking pleased with herself. It's annoying. A gap in the traffic appears and we move forward. The sun is beating down. It's hot as Orcish Hell. I'm pouring with sweat. Makri doesn't suffer from the heat as much as I do but even so her forehead is covered in perspiration, slightly matting her huge main of hair. Even tied back it still takes up a lot of space.

'It's going to be difficult for me to talk to the Society of Friends. I've never had any contacts there.'

'Not even when you were a Senior Investigator at the Palace?'

'That was a long time ago. Anyone who was a member of the Society back then will be dead or in prison by now.'

'Casax said that some of the politicians at the Palace have links to them. Was that true?'

'Probably. I'll ask Lisutaris.' We move forward at a slow pace. 'The Society of Friends might have some beer stashed away.'

'If you mention beer again I'm going to get out and walk.'

It takes a long time to reach the Palace. Droo and Anumaris are waiting for me in the small room I've been allocated as an office.

'Droo! Any progress in the beer situation?'

The young Elf shakes her head sadly. 'No, The Simnian and Samsarinan quartermasters claim they've completely run out and the Niojans wouldn't even let me in their camp. There are some ships coming into the harbour from the Southern Hills tonight but I think they're just bringing refugees.'

'Typical. You'd think a few of these people might have stepped aside to let them carry a few barrels. Selfish, all of them.' If Droo can't find me a flagon of ale, no one can. I'm gloomy as I turn to Anumaris. She's a young Storm-Class sorcerer, a relatively new member of the Sorcerers Guild. Since we re-took the city she's tidied herself up and is wearing a clean black cloak over her tunic, with the sorcerers' rainbow motif on the collar and a single bronze star on her chest. I ask her what the star means.

'Lisutaris gave them out to every sorcerer who took part in the attack.'

I purse my lips. They've already got medals. No one's given me a medal yet.

'I've been making a list of people who knew about the gold.' Anumaris produces a sheet of paper from beneath her cloak. I examine the names on the list, written in her neat handwriting. Cicerius and his assistant Hansius. Lisutaris. Lemusius. Dominius Iron Strike. Former Chancellor Senator Trappius, now presumed dead. Dearineth the Precise Measurer. Tirini Snake Smiter. Ularax, former Head of Palace Security, also presumed dead.

I glare at Anumaris. 'What is this?'

'It's the list you asked for of people who knew about the gold.'

'No, it isn't. This is a list of people Cicerius and Lisutaris admit knew about the gold. Neither of them know how comprehensive it is. What about Lemusius's business associates? Cicerius's fellow Senators? The former Head of Security's family? Or his favourite whore, when it comes down to it? This list is a waste of time. I thought I'd taught you the rudiments of investigating but apparently I didn't.'

I hand the paper back to Anumaris, who's now looking rather abashed. 'Ask questions and make a proper list. Don't take Cicerius's word for who knew, he's not going to admit he got drunk one day and told his gardener about the gold.'

'I don't think that's likely.'

'You don't know how likely it is because you didn't investigate. I need you to do better.'

Anumaris nods her head though she doesn't look happy at being criticised. I ask her if she has any further thoughts on the case.

'It all seems impossible. A special lock and a secret spell needed for entry. A huge amount of gold to move while there were guards outside in the corridor. Dearineth had placed an observation spell on the vault.'

'Would you say Dearineth is reliable?'

'Very reliable,' says Anumaris. 'The observation spell she put on the vault should have warned her of any intruders.'

'There are lots of sorcerers around, some more powerful than Dearineth.'

'Not many could avoid a spell like that. Only someone like Lisutaris could manage it, and there isn't really anyone else like Lisutaris. Do you think the gold was removed by way of a magic pocket?'

'It seems most likely. Palace Security used to keep a record of everyone who owned one but that's no longer up to date. There were rich businessmen and politicians buying them in secret and the Palace didn't do anything to stop them.'

'Why not?' enquires Droo, who's naive in the ways of a city like Turai.

'Because our rulers were corrupt and probably got a share of the profits. As long as you're in Turai, remember that anyone you meet in our line of work is liable to be corrupt.'

The young Elf looks momentarily surprised. 'Then why were you all so keen to come back?'

'We're used to it. Anumaris, I have another thought about moving the gold. Could it have been moved through the magic space?'

'I don't think so. That would still need people to carry it.'

'Maybe not. After the city fell, Gurd, Tanrose and some others were all dragged through the magic space by Tirini Snake Smiter. She got them all far away from the city in an instant.'

'Really? Tirini did that? That would take a lot of power.'

'Anyone who took part in the final attack wearing pink shoes and her favourite jewellery does have a lot of power. Do you know anyone else who could do that?'

'I don't think so. Lisutaris, of course. Perhaps Coranius, but he's dead.'

'What about Glixius Dragon Killer?'

'I don't really know how powerful he is. He's never associated much with the Guild, being, eh…'

'A notorious criminal unwisely brought back into the fold. It's worth bearing in mind anyway. While you're asking questions, find out if anyone in the Sorcerers Guild is known to have transported people or things through the magic space. After you've examined the crime scene at Lemusius's house, that is. Makri will go with you to make sure your'e safe.'

Anumaris is offended by this. 'I'm sure I won't be in danger.'

'Sorcerers can get stabbed in the back while they're busy with their sorcery. Droo, go to the harbour in Twelve Seas and find out everything you can about the cargo on the ships that are arriving.'

'Do you mean find out if there's any beer?'

'That would be helpful. But find out everything else too. Ask around about any unusual cargo. On your way back, call in on Gurd and Tanrose and check on how they're coping.'

Chapter Ten

Samanatius's funeral comes as an unwelcome distraction. I'd thought that the elderly philosopher would have died during the sack of Turai but it turned out his students managed to get him out of the city, fleeing south towards Mattesh. There however, old age and a fever caught up with him. He was temporarily laid to rest in a small village in Mattesh and now his followers have brought his remains back to Turai for a proper burial.

Makri was upset when she learned of Samanatius's death. She greatly respected him and attended the philosophy lectures he gave free to anyone who wanted to listen. I never held philosophers in much regard though I do admit that Samanatius wasn't so bad. He might have spent his time lecturing about obscure subjects but he did fight honourably in the previous war, despite being too old even then. Furthermore he once rendered me significant help in a case. I'm moderately saddened to learn of his death but alarmed when Makri tells me I have to attend his funeral.

'They're burying him in the St Petrio's Park, next to the Palace grounds.'

'An actual proper funeral? For Samanatius? Are you sure?'

Since the city fell, many Turanians have died and burials have been perfunctory at best. While the army was fighting its way back to Turai there wasn't a lot of time for ceremony. Senators, Generals, common soldiers, camp attendants, mule drivers and cooks were all swiftly buried in hastily dug graves. A few words were said by a Pontifex, or their commanding officer if no religious figure could be found. I'm so used to this it's a surprise to hear that Samanatius will be sent off with ceremony. It's not one I'm keen to attend.

'I don't think I can spare the time.'

'You have to,' Makri informs me. 'Lisutaris will be there.'

'She will?'

'Yes. Plenty of people will be there. Samanatius was widely respected.'

I'm about to ask why but bite it back, knowing Makri will be offended.

'I have to accompany Lisutaris as her bodyguard and she'll want you there as her security chief.'

I sigh. 'Fine. I need to talk to her anyway.'

'An important person like Samanatius deserves a proper funeral.' Makri pauses. 'Sorry, maybe that was insensitive. Are you unhappy because you couldn't go to Sareepa's funeral?'

I feel an unpleasant tingle down the back of my neck. 'No, I'm fine.' The day after Sareepa died her body was taken away by two junior sorcerers from the Matteshan Sorcerers Guild, back to Mattesh for her own proper burial.

'Perhaps you can visit her grave one day,' says Makri, awkwardly. I can't think of any reply. The awkwardness continues as we walk in silence towards the stateroom Lisutaris has commandeered for her office. The Palace corridors have been cleared of debris. Already senior workmen can be seen examining broken statues, defaced murals and damaged tapestries with a view to repairing them. The Palace will be in excellent shape long before houses in Twelve Seas have been rebuilt.

Lisutaris is now looking as elegant as she did in the days before the war. She looks years younger than she did while leading the army to Turai. That might be aided by make up or even by sorcery; I can't tell. Female sorcerers in Turai have beauty secrets they don't divulge. Lisutaris was never counted among Turai's great beauties but she was always an attractive woman. I once heard Anumaris and Makri say she was becoming more attractive with age. I don't know if that's true. I'm mostly interested in food and beer these days. We have around ten minutes before we leave for the funeral so I take the opportunity to ask Lisutaris about the Society of Friends. She's surprised by the question. 'Why would I know anything about a criminal gang?'

'They're a criminal gang the Traditionals have used for their own benefit. Very helpful when it comes to election time and they need to disrupt their opponents. Helpful for all those little deals rich people don't want the public to know about too.'

Lisutaris professes to know nothing of this. I don't believe her. Before the war, Lisutaris didn't much involve herself in politics but her elevation to Head of the Sorcerers Guild must have made a difference. She'd have had regular contact with the city government, most of them allies of Cicerius and the Traditionals. 'No need to be shy about it, Commander. Just tell me who in the Palace has good relations with the Society of Friends so I can talk to them.'

Lisutaris scowls at me. 'I wouldn't know. Corrupt Senators never felt the need to confess their transgressions to me. What's this about, anyway? I've just come out of a meeting with the Simnian and Niojan military attachés and I've got a lot on my mind. Six ships full of grain will be arriving in Turai from the West in three days time. Turai needs that grain but we don't have money to pay for it.'

'Then you'd better help me recover the gold. It must have taken a lot of organisation to get it out the Palace. The Society of Friends are the obvious candidates in this part of the city.'

Lisutaris is sceptical. 'Isn't sorcery far more likely?'

'I'd think there must have been some physical help along the way. Though it's likely sorcery was involved. Powerful sorcery. The sort of thing only really strong practitioners like you and Tirini might be capable of.'

'I trust we're not suspects?'

'You both suffered a lot of financial pain when the city fell.'

'I'll let that pass as a joke, Thraxas. It's true that with Coranius and Sareepa gone, there aren't many top-rated sorcerers around. Not Turanians, anyway.'

I feel another pang at he mention of Sareepa but don't react to it.

'But there are others,' continues Lisutaris. 'From Simnia and Samsarina. Nioj, too. They all entered the city with the assault force.'

'I know, but you banished them all outside the walls soon after we'd cleared out the Orcs. When you showed me the gold in the vault there shouldn't have been any foreign sorcerers left around the Palace. Could any of them have stayed here hidden?'

'I don't think so,' replies Lisutaris. 'I'll check as soon as I can.'

'Do you have a spell for that?'

'Yes. I could still pick up their magical aura. But I don't have a spell for checking the identity of every single person who was in the Palace. Do you really think this gang could have been involved?'

Makri tells us it's time to go. We leave the stateroom, heading for the doors to the north of the Palace. From there it's a short walk to St Petrio's Park where some of Turai's most notable former inhabitants are buried. As we leave the Palace I'm still nagging at Lisutaris. 'I could really do with information on the Society of Friends.'

'I'm telling you, I can't help.'

'How about Cicerius? Will he be at this funeral?'

'Interrogating the Acting Consul on his links to the underworld wouldn't go well.'

'I could try to be tactful.'

'That's not one of your strong points, Thraxas. Given your past history I'd rather you didn't trouble him with this.'

'What past history? You mean the way I rescued you from Turai and helped you become War Leader?'

'Cicerius appreciates your military service. It hasn't erased his memories of the time you were carried drunk into the Palace, singing obscene drinking songs and insulting his record in government.'

'That was quite a minor incident.'

'It was widely reported afterwards. Then there were the terrible excesses of the Sorcerers Assemblage. He blames you for that.'

I'm outraged. 'He blames me? Are you serious?'

'The drunkenness, debauchery and corruption at the Assemblage in Turai have become legendary, Thraxas. You were responsible for a lot of that.'

'I was instructed by the government to do whatever it took to get you elected as Head of the Sorcerers Guild! Which I did. You were heavily involved in all that too.'

Lisutaris nods her head quite calmly. 'Yes, I was. But I couldn't take any of the blame afterwards, could I? Head of the Sorcerers Guild is a position of international importance. I could hardly acknowledge I was elected due to Turai providing enough gold, alcohol, drugs and whores to corrupt every voting sorcerer in the West. Wouldn't look good at all.'

'What about that upper-class woman, Tilupasis? She helped organise most of it.'

'You really couldn't expect her to admit to any involvement. It wouldn't look good for her either.'

'I take it no one minds it doesn't look good for me?'

'It didn't hurt your reputation, Thraxas. You didn't have one to begin with. And there was the matter of your behaviour during the card game at the Avenging Axe, just before the city fell.'

'The card game during which I protected the city from Horm the Dead with my amazing skills?'

'I think Cicerius more remembers the Bishop hammering on the door, demanding you be arrested for robbing his church.'

I shake my head. 'I shed blood for this city and this is the way I'm treated. Aristocrats get away with anything but an honest working man gets blamed for everything.'

Lisutaris smiles. 'I appreciate your work, Thraxas. I haven't forgotten that you were first man into the city.'

'I'm pleased to hear it. Can I get a bronze badge like your Sorcerers Regiment, showing I fought in the war?'

'We haven't got round to making them for other ranks yet.'

The gardens north of the Palace were devastated during the occupation. The flower beds are barren and the lawns are brown and trampled. We find ourselves in the midst of quite a crowd, all heading for the funeral. There are one or two senators in white togas but few people have formal clothes. Most just wear whatever they had on when we re-entered the city. I notice various military officers, including some from Simnia and Samsarina. Senator Lodius is walking in front of us with a crowd of his supporters. Again, I'm surprised. I'm sure most of these people never attended lectures by Samanatius or read any of his works. To our right, outside the gilded railings that mark the Palace grounds, a great throng of ordinary citizens can be seen heading for the park as well.

'Lisutaris, I need to talk to someone who knows something about the Society of Friends. I'm planning on questioning one of their bosses, Darisax, but he's not going to tell me anything for free.'

'Why not? You're an official investigator for the Palace. You represent the law.'

'He won't care about that. I need to know more about his business so I can put pressure on him. If you won't let me talk to Cicerius, I'll talk to Senator Lodius. He'll tell me which Palace figures have links to the Society of Friends.'

'I'd rather you didn't do that. I'm endeavouring to keep the peace between Lodius and Cicerius.'

'Dammit, Lisutaris.' I look her straight in the eye. 'I'm meant to be investigating. That means asking questions which I can't do if you keep forbidding me to talk to people. Either help me or get out of the way so I can help myself.'

'Captain Thraxas, you're still in the army and I'm still your Commander.'

66

'Do you want me to find the gold or not?'

'Obviously I want you to find the gold.'

'Then stop obstructing me and start helping.'

Lisutaris eyes me, very coldly. She's wondering whether it's worth cracking down on me for insubordination. 'Talk to Senator Statius's secretary Lieutenant Derigus. He came back to Turai with the Turanian Infantry and he's working in the emergency aqueduct repair unit.'

'Would you like to give me any more details?'

'Senator Statius was rumoured to have imported illegal thazis plants from the South. A particularly admired variety, difficult to get hold of. I did hear it said that his secretary made the arrangements.'

I'm raising my eyebrows. 'Statius imported illegal thazis plants? Via the Society of Friends? Was he the only one?'

'As far as I know, yes.'

I wouldn't say Lisutaris is a great liar. Even so, she manages this with a straight face though we both know that if any fancy new thazis plants were brought into the city, she'd have been first in line to acquire them.

When we arrive in St Petrio's Park the crowd parts for Lisutaris. I walk alongside her, a little uncomfortably, as does Makri. Neither of us are used to commanding much respect and I can tell some people are wondering who the large, poorly dressed individual is who's accompanying their War Leader. People always stare at Makri and here it's no different. Her role as bodyguard to Lisutaris did become well known among the troops but for the civilians in the crowd it's puzzling to see a woman with obviously Orcish blood walking alongside our War Leader. We pause at the front of the crowd. People are still arriving from all directions.

'Why are there so many people here? Don't tell me they all followed Samanatius's philosophy, I know they didn't.'

Lisutaris admits to being surprised. 'Perhaps it's the only chance people have had to come together. We haven't had much to celebrate so far, even if we won the war. Samanatius was widely respected.'

'He was the reason I came to Turai,' says Makri. 'He's the main reason other countries don't think Turanians are all stupid.'

If Samanatius was widely respected I notice that this didn't extend to the church. Given the importance of the event you might

67

have expected one of their senior officials to be present but the presiding official is a lowly local pontifex. He's standing next to a plain wooden coffin. Behind that is the newly dug grave.

'Turai's True Church isn't keen on philosophy,' whispers Makri. 'They're not going to send a Bishop for Samanatius.'

Standing next to the Pontifex is bearded, middle-aged man whom Makri informs me is Atlantius, second in line to Samanatius in his academy.

'I suppose he'll take over now.' Makri doesn't sound happy.

'Isn't he any good?'

'He's a reasonably good philosopher. But he's no Samanatius.'

Makri looks like she might have more to say about Atlantius but the crowd falls silent as the Pontifex steps forward to speak. At this point my attention starts to wander. It always does when Turai's religious officials are talking. As he praises Samanatius's contributions to the city my attention shifts, partly to the case I'm working on and partly to chariot racing. I wonder how long it will be before the races start up again? It probably depends on what state the Stadium Superbius is in. The Orcs occupied it so it could be in a bad way. Might take a long time to repair it. Chariot racing is a popular pastime in Turai but the authorities won't regard it as a priority. It strikes me how much I've missed gambling at the races. I want to be sitting in the Stadium with a flagon of ale in one hand, a full betting programme in the other, and a bowl of fried yams at my side. I drift off into a reverie about some of my favourite betting triumphs at the races. Occasions where I terrorised the bookmakers. Other occasions where cruel fate, bad luck and outright corruption denied me the success I should have had. There was the strange occasion when an Orcish chariot owned by Lord Rezaz the Butcher was allowed to compete, and the even stranger denouement where none of the favourites won due to a scandalous, corrupt and ultimately successful campaign by the Association of Gentlewomen to pick all the winners themselves. The memory of the money I lost that day makes me wince. On the other hand, you have to admire the audacity of the AG's successful scheme, even if they had an unfair advantage having recruited the services of Melus the Fair, stadium sorcerer. Makri was involved in that too, and Lisutaris. That reminds me that Lisutaris still has thousands of gurans belonging to me secreted in her own magic pocket, the proceeds from my successful gambling campaign during the great

68

sword-fighting contest in Samsarina. I hope she still has it; I wouldn't be amazed if much of it has disappeared in war expenses.

Lost in my gambling reverie, I don't hear any of the Pontifex's words. When I become aware of the funeral again, Samanatius's successor Atlantius is well into his eulogy and Makri is dabbing her eyes. All I really hear is the final farewell before four attendants step up to lower the philosopher's coffin into the ground. Lisutaris turns to us, informing us that she needs to return to the Palace right away. We walk back though the crowd. When we're close to the building the sorcerer suddenly picks up her pace.

'Why are we almost running into the Palace?'

'I just spotted Bishop Gzekius and Bishop Elakius. They've been agitating for a place on the Council and I don't want to deal with them right now.' The True Church in Turai is a powerful institution. It's not surprising they'd want to be involved in any new leadership.

'Fortunately Archbishop Xerius hasn't made it back to Turai yet. When he does I'm expecting trouble. It's hard enough making things work with Cicerius, Lodius and me. Xerius will only make it worse.'

The True Church and the Sorcerers Guild have always had an uneasy relationship. I can foresee difficulties when the Archbishop arrives back and starts demanding a say in things.

Makri is still dabbing her eyes. 'It was a much better eulogy than I was expecting.' A tear rolls down her cheek.

I'm uncomfortable in the presence of female tears. I can never say the right thing when it happens. Fortunately I need to speak to Derigus which gives me an excuse to depart swiftly. It takes me a while to locate the Emergency Aqueduct Repair Unit, located in the north wing. All sorts of administrative units have been quickly set up by Cicerius. The Abode of Justice buildings, just south of here, and the public works bodies nearby, were badly damaged in the war so perhaps the Palace will become our new seat of government. Or maybe Cicerius will find us a new King. I don't know what these people want.

Statius's secretary Derigus turns out to be more of a young soldierly type than I was expecting, possibly the younger son of an upper-class family who's chosen the army as a career, entering the ranks as a junior officer. He has a fresh battle-scar running down his neck. He's smartly dressed though his hair is a little longer and shaggier than you'd expect. I find him standing over a desk in a small office examining plans for the aqueduct that takes water through Thamlin. To my surprise, he recognises me.

'Captain Thraxas?'

'Derigus. Are you still in the army?'

He grins. 'Yes, still in the army. Lieutenant in the Second Turanian Infantry. I wasn't far behind you when we came through the walls.'

'Where did you get the wound?'

'Orcish battalion attacked our flank when we advancing towards the Palace. It's nothing, it's healing up. I saw our Commander's bodyguard in action. She was very impressive. Slew Orcs so fast you could hardly make out her moves. She's called Makri, isn't she?'

'That's right.'

'Does she really have Orcish blood?'

'She does.'

'Really? We though that was just a wild rumour.'

'We?'

'The junior officers in the regiment. She was the topic of some discussion on our way to Turai. Our Commander must really trust her.'

'Makri is very trustworthy. Especially when it comes to fighting Orcs.'

'Do you know her?'

I don't think Lieutenant Derigus realises how eager he's sounding here. I recognise the symptom. He's not the first well-bred young man to feel a surprising attraction to Makri. Usually that happens after they see her serving beer in her chainmail bikini at the Avenging Axe, but watching her dispatching enemies might have a similar effect in the right circumstances.

'I know her well.'

'What is she like?'

'She's a good companion and an excellent swordswoman. She's still working as Lisutaris's bodyguard so you might run into her. But I didn't come here to discuss Makri.'

Derigus looks embarrassed. 'Of course. Sorry. What can I help you with?'

He sounds open and friendly. Normally that would make me suspicious but if he took part in the final assault he can't be all bad. 'I want information on the Society of Friends.'

That makes him pause. His next words are more guarded. 'I'm not sure why you'd ask me that…'

'I've been told you handled the negotiations for the import of illegal thazis plants.'

Derigus shrugs. 'That's true, I did. But I couldn't reveal who I was working for.'

'You were working for your employer in Turai, Senator Statius. Don't worry, I'm not interested in him or his plants. I just need to know about the Society of Friends. Was that the only time you were in contact with them?'

'No, I knew Society of Friends people growing up in North Walls. I didn't join the Senatorial class till I was adopted as a twelve-year-old. When Senators needed to talk to the Society, I was a reasonable choice.'

'Do you know a boss called Darisax?'

'No, but I've met plenty of others.'

'What for?'

'Various reasons. Senators who needed emergency loans. Senators who wanted to sell valuable art works without paying the required taxes. Senators' wives who needed new jewellery for a ball at the Palace but whose income didn't quite stretch to acquiring it legally. A few Senators' sons who thought they'd like to try dwa.' He pauses. 'You understand I won't repeat any of this in front of witnesses? I'm willing to help with any enquiry for our Commander, but I'd never admit any of this in a courtroom.'

'That's fine. I'm not too interested in the dealings of our Senators. I already expect them to be corrupt. Tell me about the Society of Friends. Were you their main contact at the Palace?'

'Not by a long way. Stapiros was their chief contact. I was very small fry compared to him.'

'Who's Stapiros?'

'He's an accountant in the Palace treasury, or rather he was. He was killed outside the city walls.'

'Was he part of the assault force?'

'No, he was too old for that. He was working in the Paymaster's Unit. He was killed when the dragons almost got through our shield.'

While our army was outside Turai our sorcerers erected a huge sorcerous shield to protect us from dragon attack. It did protect us but there were times when it almost gave way under extreme pressure and some people died.

'Unfortunate for him. Did people know he was connected to the Society?'

'It wasn't really a secret.'

'Didn't that bother anyone?'

Derigus shrugs. 'It didn't seem to. If someone important like Consul Kalius needed something done by the Society — election expenses, vote buying, that sort of thing — Stapiros was the go-between.'

'Who's going to take his place as the Society's man in the palace?'

Lieutenant Derigus smiles. 'Not me, if that's what you're thinking. I did well in the war and I'm up for promotion. It's time to forget I ever knew people in North Walls.'

'That's probably wise. Tell me more about anyone at the Palace who's ever been involved with Turai's underworld.'

'That will take a while. It's not a short list.'

'I'm in no hurry. Someone could probably find me a glass of Elvish wine to be getting on with.'

Chapter Eleven

Makri takes the reins as we make the short journey to Thamlin. It's on our way north and Lisutaris asked me to check on her house and see if I can locate certain items for her. Work crews here are making good progress with their clear-up operation. In Truth is Beauty Lane, home to Turai's wealthiest and most powerful sorcerers, they're already repairing potholes and hauling away broken slabs of masonry from the fancy tiled pavements, pale green and pale yellow.

Lisutaris's villa appears to be in a bad state; broken windows, and doors hanging from hinges. Some of her clothes are strewn around the bushes in the front garden. Expensive items, no doubt. It's a depressing sight. A military guard waits outside the entrance. He lets us pass unhindered, recognising me as head of Lisutaris's Security Unit. We skirt the house, heading for the extensive gardens at the back. Immediately we're faced with a lot of damage.

'Wanton destruction,' mutters Makri, as we walk through a small grove of broken, blackened trees. Whoever was billeted in this mansion has ruined the gardens. Beyond the blackened trees is a large pond, now empty, with the bones of ducks and other birds lying on the banks. Just beyond are Lisutaris's greenhouses. They're in ruins. Inside I can't find any surviving thazis. Her extensive collection of the narcotic plants has been destroyed. As Makri looks on I hunt around among the roots for anything that doesn't look dead. I find a few tiny shoots, none of them healthy, and gather them into the bag I'm carrying. Maybe Lisutaris can do something with them. As we're leaving, I pause, and look back at the greenhouses.

'Everything's ruined but I suppose the land is still fertile. Crops would grow here. Like barley and hops. A sorcerer could hurry along the growth.'

'Lisutaris would blast you with a spell if you tried making beer in her precious greenhouses!'

I finger the spell protection charm round my neck, a good functional object but not one that could stand up to the full wrath of Lisutaris. 'She might not object.'

'She'd go crazy! Abandon the idea.'

'Once again, Makri, I'm disappointed in you. I come up with a sound, practical idea for making beer and you're sinking it like a trireme in a whirlpool. It shows a serious lack of imagination.'

'Look on it as a test of character. Surviving without beer for the good of Turai.'

'My character failed that test a long time ago.' The back door to Lisutaris's mansion, or rather the door to the splendid veranda that exits into the gardens, is hanging by one hinge. As I push it open it falls to the ground. Inside everything is in a bad state. I've been inside Lisutaris's mansion several times in the past, as has Makri. On one notable occasion I was trapped here with a group of sorcerers while a mob of maddened citizens tried to burn the place down, the result of a malevolent spell cast on the city by Horm the Dead, insane sorcerer and enemy of Turai. I last saw Horm at the card game in the Avenging Axe, just before the city fell. I don't know what became of him after that.

We pass though the lower floor quickly. Everything is ruined. Statues, furniture, tapestries, paintings, carpets, balconies, stained glass, everything. All broken and despoiled. Upstair Makri heads off to Lisutaris's library while I make for the large chamber with a balcony overlooking the gardens. This room, light, airy, filed with greenery, was the sorcerer's favourite location for sitting with her water pipe, sometimes alone, sometimes with her friend Tirini. The balcony room is as desolate as everything else. Plants are strewn on the floor, blackened and long-dead. Broken pottery shards are everywhere. Lisutaris's favourite water pipe has been smashed into small pieces. I hunt in the cupboards where Lisutaris kept her extensive collection of pipes from around the world. They're all broken. Wooden pipes, clay pipes, metal pipes. There were some with precious jewels but they've been stolen. I sigh. Lisutaris isn't going to take this well. I notice one small wooden pipe on the floor, still intact. I pick it up and tuck it into my bag along with the few pathetic remains of her plants. When I leave the room I meet a grim-faced Makri in the corridor. 'How was the library?'

'Destroyed. Not a book or a scroll left.' Makri is more appalled at this destruction than anything else. We walk down the stairs and leave the mansion in silence. It's time to talk to the Society of Friends. That's probably not going to improve our mood. Makri wears a sword on each hip. One a bright Elvish weapon, the other a foul black Orcish blade, the likes of which could not be found

74

anywhere else in the West. 'When we're talking to the Society of Friends, try not to kill anyone because you're in a bad mood about Lisutaris's books.'

Makri scowls. 'I'll do my best.'

We ride on in silence. The sun beats down. We're heading for North Walls, a poor area of the city and a Society of Friends stronghold. When Prince Amrag took the city his army entered this part of the city first and that caused a lot of damage. The destruction is even worse than in Twelve Seas. An annoying squawking noise erupts from the roof a warehouse. A flock of small black birds, stals, calling to each other on the rooftops. They squabble about something for a few moments before flopping back down in the heat.

'I never liked these birds. I was hoping the Orcs might have eaten them all.'

Makri doesn't reply. She's in a very poor mood. We enter Benevolence Lane, a miserable little road of ramshackle houses, pawn shops and a few scruffy looking taverns. Every building is damaged. Just as in Twelve Seas, returning citizens are living in makeshift tents while attempting to repair their homes. Water flows continually down the gutter either from a broken aqueduct or a fractured water pipe. A few children splash in the water while adults collect it in pans, needing it to stay alive. There are no government work crews here. The only proper reconstruction is taking place at the Hero of Turai, a tavern slightly larger than the buildings around it. Scaffolding has been set up and workmen are replacing slates on the roof while glaziers are busy repairing broken windows.

'You get your repairs done quickly if you're a criminal boss,' I mutter to Makri as we walk inside. It's busier than I'm expecting. The entire place falls silent. A tall man with long hair steps out from behind the bar.

'We're not open to the public yet,' he says, indicating that we should leave.

I show him my badge. 'I'm not the public. I'm an investigator from the Palace and I'm here to talk to Darisax.'

This doesn't endear me to the assembled members of the Society of Friends. Those standing near draw closer while those at the tables stand up. There are a lot of hands on sword pommels.

'Never heard of him,' says the barman, harshly. 'Leave.'

I notice his jerkin, a well-made leather garment with light metal plating sewn onto the front. An army garment, the sort of thing a member of the infantry would wear. Whether he's just come out of the army or if he stole it somewhere, I can't tell.

'I'm working for our War Leader. If I leave now I'll be coming back with an order to close you down and a squadron of troops to enforce it.'

'Who the hell do you think you are, fat man? And who's this Orcish bitch with you? Get her out of here, we don't serve Orcs.'

Makri's swords appear in her hands quicker than the eye can follow. I sigh. This is going to be more awkward than I anticipated. Makri should have ignored the insult but in her current mood that was probably too much to expect. As she draws her swords, the entire crowd, around fifteen men, all produce weapons. So do I. Good weapons; a bright Elvish sword, won by Makri in the great sword-fighting competition in Samsarina and given to me as a gift, and my army dagger with a good crossguard for parrying enemy thrusts. The Society of Friends men close in which will be unfortunate for them if they come too close to Makri. Just then a short, rather stout man pushes his way through the crowd. He's grey haired, middle aged, and the others defer to him, letting him advance. He stares at me, then at Makri, then back to me.

'You're an investigator from the Palace? Is this the way you normally investigate?'

'Not really, but I'll go along with it.'

A taller, bulkier individual has moved into position behind him. A bodyguard, I'd say, though not a standard physical enforcer, from the rainbow insignia on his shoulder. A sorcerer.

'We're not much worried by the Palace up here in North Walls. You can introduce yourself before we throw you out. Or bury you, maybe.'

'Captain Thraxas, Head of Security for Lisutaris, Mistress of the Sky, War Leader of the West.'

'Fancy title.'

'I take it you're Darisax, current leader of the North Walls Society of Friends?'

He doesn't answer my question. The sounds of sawing and hammering reverberate through the tavern from the workmen outside.

'I've heard the name Thraxas before. But he wasn't working at the Palace. He wasn't a Captain either. He was some cheap investigator in Twelve Seas. Drunken oaf, people said. I did also hear he claimed to have some sorcerous powers.' He turns his head to talk to the large sorcerer behind him. 'Mabzus, check him out.'

Mabzus is an unusual name, I'm not sure where it's from. He's dark complexioned, maybe from the Southern Hills or even further South.

'He's got no power, boss. He has a spell protection charm but it wouldn't keep me off.'

Makri strides forward. She raises her black sword. 'I'm in a really bad mood because all the books and scrolls have been burned and I thought I was going to the University but the University's been damaged so I might never get there and I don't like being called an Orc so now I'm in an even worse mood and if you try firing a spell at us I'll kill you before you can speak and then I'll kill everyone else here and then I'll go and kill your children too because I'm in a really, really bad mood and I've killed a lot better fighters than you and it might cheer me up to do it again.'

This, perhaps the most unexpected speech ever heard in the tavern, might in other circumstances raise a smile. No one is smiling. Makri's black Orcish sword is a troubling enough sight for anyone, a weapon with an evil aura that somehow seems to suck in light rather than reflect it. Her face is as grim as I've ever seen. The Society men are wondering how many of them she'd kill if they all attacked at once, and thinking that it might be too many for comfort. Several of the fainter-hearted criminals shuffle backwards.

Darisax remains calm. 'I'm guessing you're that Commander's bodyguard people were talking about. I never heard anything good about you.' He addresses his men, telling them to put their weapons away. 'Over here, Captain Thraxas.'

He leads us to a table in the far corner. Mabzus follows. 'Mabzus, make sure no one can hear us.' The sorcerer nods, then mutters a spell. A muffling spell isn't too difficult for an advanced sorcerer. Sitting down, Darisax is no more physically impressive than he was standing up but I've already seen his men respect him. You don't get to be a Society of Friends boss unless you're intelligent, competent, and a good leader.

'Tell me what this is about. Make it quick, I have things to attend to.'

'I know you have, Darisax. You've already got a consignment of dwa coming in from your friends in Attical. Should be docking any time now.' This is something of a guess on my part but not much of a guess. Derigus at the Palace was able to tell me a lot about the North Walls Society's contacts for importing dwa, and Droo already picked up rumours at the harbour that trade was about to continue.

Darisax narrows his eyes. 'No idea what you're talking about. If I did have any idea what you were talking about, I'd tell you it was a bad idea to interfere with my business. What are you looking for, a bribe?'

'I'm looking for information about a theft at the Palace. The Society of Friends has a lot of contacts there, so I hear.'

Darisax shrugs. 'I've never heard that myself.'

Some criminals might brag about their powerful friends. Darisax is too clever to do that.

'You were well acquainted with Stapiros.'

'Never heard of him.'

'You're a decent liar, Darisax, but not as good as me. Stapiros was the Society's man at the Palace. Killed outside the city walls. Who's lined up to replace him?'

'Someone at the Palace has too much imagination. Given you a lot of false information. I never knew any Stapiros and I don't know anything about any thefts from the Palace.'

Beside us, Makri shifts in her seat, making a metallic sound as one of scabbards bangs against her wooden chair. Darisax regards her sourly. 'Looks like your girlfriend is getting impatient. Maybe it's time for you to leave. If she starts threatening us again Mabzus will deal with her and that would be ugly.'

'Ugly for him, not for her. Your pet sorcerers don't worry me. The ones that end up with the Society of Friends are never any good. Tell me about that brooch you're wearing.'

My question takes him by surprise. He glances down at the small pearl broach on his collar. 'What about it?'

'A couple of pearls in a metal frame. Cheap piece of jewellery for an important man like you, isn't it?'

'I never like to be overdressed.'

'How's the pearl industry these days?'

'Bad. I got out a while ago.'

I nod. 'I heard the oyster beds along the coast weren't so good any more. But you still like to wear that broach. Reminds you of the days when you made your start in crime by stealing from legitimate pearl divers and strong-arming the others.'

'I'm getting fed up with your company, investigator.'

'Palace Investigator. With a lot of back-up to make your life difficult if necessary. You're not going to find your relationship with the new government so cosy. I found another broach like that, Darisax. Right outside the Palace. What were you doing there?'

'I haven't been near the Palace since we came back to the city.'

'Really? I'll soon find out if that's true. Lisutaris is in charge now and she's got plenty of sorcerers with her. Once they've examined the brooch they'll be able to tell me a lot about it. Might even get a clear picture of you dropping it there.'

Darisax abruptly rises to his feet. I've finally managed to annoy him.

'This talk is over. Mabzus, see them out.' The large sorcerer tries to shepherd us towards the door. I don't protest but I don't let him hurry us either. Outside the sun is beating down and workmen are struggling to load roof tiles on to a hoist.

'Did you learn anything?' asks Makri.

'Yes. You can be eloquent when you're angry. Nice speech in there.' We climb into the wagon. 'Darisax is hiding something, and it could have been him that dropped that broach near the Palace.'

We ride through North Walls. 'I had this idea that as soon as I was back in Turai I'd be off to the University.' Makri shakes her head. 'That was naive. Look at the state of this city. Everything's ruined.'

'Turai's been in a bad state before and we recovered. Last time the Orcs attacked most of the walls came down but we built them again. You were here when Horm the Dead unleashed his spell that drove half the population mad. The city was in flames but we recovered from that too. Turanians are stubborn. We have to be to live in a place like this.'

Makri manages to smile. 'I wonder what happened to Horm? I thought he'd be fighting for Prince Amrag.'

It was puzzling that Horm the Dead, one of the most powerful Orcish leaders, didn't appear to be part of Amrag's army. 'It's possible he fell out of favour after events at the Avenging Axe. He was working for himself. Then Deeziz appeared, working for Amrag. Probably didn't look good for Horm.'

'Did Horm really want to marry me or was that all part of some scheme?'

I shrug. Horm's motives were never easy to read. It's possible he was attracted enough to Makri to really want to marry her. We're held up by a team of workmen struggling to clear the remains of a collapsed wall from the road. I gaze around at the destruction. 'I thought I'd be heading straight back in the Avenging Axe, drinking beer. That was foolish as well.'

'At least you didn't ask the Society of Friends if they had any beer.'

'I'd have smelled it if they had. Do you really think it's a bad idea to try making my own?'

'Yes, it's a terrible idea.'

'I still think Rinderan could help things along with beer magic. What's the point of being a sorcerer from a brewing family if you can't do that?'

Chapter Twelve

Anumaris is waiting for me at the Palace with an expanded list of people who may have known of the existence of the gold bullion. 'I've added a few names and some them are interesting. Cicerius's assistant Hansius was more forthcoming when Cicerius wasn't around. He told me that before the war Cicerius was in the habit of discussing Turai's finances quite regularly with Senator Agresius, his party's treasurer.'

Agresius is a very senior member of the Traditionals and a close ally of Cicerius. He must be around fifty now but he took part in the recent campaign and he was already a hero from the last war.

'He's one of Turai's leading citizens,' says Anumaris. 'But it's rumoured that he was heavily in debt to the Society.'

'Really? Agresius was in debt to the Society of Friends?'

'According to Hansius, yes.'

'That's an interesting lead, Anumaris. Cicerius won't like it if we interrogate his close ally. We'll do it if we have to. Anyone else on your list?'

'I'm wondering about Captain Ularax. He was Head of Palace Security. He served with the army but was killed on the march back to Turai.'

Every conversation these days seems to involve some Turanian who's been recently killed. It's depressing.

'The thing is,' continues Anumaris. 'He was in the same unit as Casax, the Brotherhood boss. And Glixius Dragon killer was assigned to protect them on several occasions.'

This gets my interest. 'Did Captain Ularax know about the gold?'

'Yes. He was involved in security at the Palace for a long time and was sometimes tasked with carrying gold into the vault. He must have been trusted never to mention that to anyone outside but perhaps he said something to his unit on the way back to Turai?'

'Very possibly. A secret vault full of gold is a good story. He might have let something slip, either to Casax or Glixius. I'm still suspicious that they were so close to the Palace after we came through the walls.'

'There's more. Hansius told me that three soldiers — Senior Trooper Lubatox, Private Carox and Private Durun — sometimes helped to carry the gold into the vault. That seems like a security risk. Captain Ularax must have trusted them but we can't ask him why as he'd dead.'

'This secret vault is sounding less secret all the time. That's generally the way of things in Turai. We'll need to talk to the soldiers. Anyone else?'

Anumaris consults her list. 'There's Stapiros. He's a senior accountant at the Palace and he was actually responsible for keeping track of how much money was in the vault. Consul Kalius trusted him enough to deal with the figures.'

I'm raising my eyebrows. 'Stapiros? I've just been talking about him. He was the Society of Friends' main contact at the Palace.'

'That doesn't look good.'

'It doesn't. We can't question him because he was killed outside the city walls. There's no knowing who he might have talked to when he was travelling with the army.'

'Why would Consul Kalius trust him with confidential information if he was close to the Society of Friends?'

I shrug. 'Who knows what these people were up to? Kalius wasn't above using the Society when it suited him.'

'I tried to question our Commander about any sorcerer who might have known about the gold but she became annoyed and shouted at me.'

'Lisutaris doesn't like being questioned. Don't worry about it, I'll talk to her.'

Makri is wondering about the Society of Friends sorcerer we met in North Walls. 'Would he be powerful enough to steal from the Palace?'

'Mabzus? Good sorcerers tend not to end up working for criminal gangs but there are exceptions. I'll ask Lisutaris if she knows anything about him.' I arrange to meet Makri at our wagon outside then head off to see Lisutaris. When I get there she's looking harassed. I bring her up to date on my investigation.

'The so-called secret vault wasn't that much of a secret. Plenty of people knew about it. I knew that would be the case.'

'Are you any closer to finding the gold?'

'Possibly.'

'Possibly?' Lisutaris is disappointed at my lack of progress. 'We've only got a day or two to come up with the money for grain. Otherwise everything that's coming into the harbour will be sold to these Simnian merchants or agents from Nioj. They'll either sell it on at a profit to the armies outside, or sell it back to us in small parcels at an even bigger profit. Only the rich people in Turai will be able to afford it and Senator Lodius won't stand for that.'

'I'm surprised Lodius hasn't started trouble already.'

'He's trying to be responsible. Or pretending to be, I can't tell. If we don't manage to get hold of grain for the city he'll abandon that and then there will be trouble.'

'What sort of trouble?'

Lisutaris scowls. 'Anything from complaints to the other Senators to a full-on call to revolution to his followers. Cicerius fears the latter. Personally I don't think Lodius would want to oppose me, my sorcerers and the loyal army units, but that's not much comfort. After getting the city back the last thing I want is a civil war.' Lisutaris swears, a curse I don't think she'd have known before becoming part of the army, then produces a thazis stick from inside her cloak. She lights it with snap of her fingers and inhales deeply. 'I remembering why I never liked to be involved with politicians. Cicerius and Lodius hate each other and their supporters are just as bad. You'd think everyone might work together for the good of Turai but they're continually looking to use every little thing to their own advantage.'

I tell Lisutaris that I checked on her house. As I list the catalogue of destruction her expression changes to one of sadness. 'All the greenhouses destroyed? And all my artworks?'

'Almost everything. Makri checked your library, that was all gone too.'

I hand over the pathetic remnants of the still-living shoots I found in her greenhouses, along with two green leaves. 'That's all that was left alive. And I found this.' I give her the small clay pipe. 'It's all that was left in your balcony room.'

She takes the pipe and hold it in her hands. A tear forms in her eye. I'm immediately uncomfortable. The tear rolls down her cheek and she starts to cry. Quite softly, but she's definitely crying. I'm now very uncomfortable. I always am around women's tears. You'd think Lisutaris would know that by now. It's unreasonable behaviour on her part, especially as I had to watch Makri dabbing her own eyes only a few hours ago.

'Well, I probably should leave you to it, Commander.' I take a step backwards. Tears roll down the sorcerer's face as she stares at the last remnants of her balcony room, where she passed away the hours with her water pipes, her views of her gardens and her friend Tirini. At that moment, Tirini enters the room, resplendent in a silver dress with matching accessories.

'Lisu!' she exclaims, seeing our Commander's tears. 'What's the matter?' She produces a yellow silk handkerchief, hands it to Lisutaris, then glares at me angrily. 'What did you do to her?'

'I didn't do anything!'

'Then why is she crying?' Tirini puts her arm round her friend and talks to her soothingly. 'Don't let him upset you.'

I'm about to protest my innocence when Captain Julius walks into the room. Lisutaris's young assistant raises his arm to salute but halts in confusion at the sight of Lisutaris in tears, with Tirini trying unsuccessfully to comfort her. Captain Julius immediately rounds on me. 'What did you do?'

'I didn't do anything!'

'You must have done something! Our Commander doesn't cry for no reason.' Julius hurries to Lisutaris's side. 'Did Captain Thraxas insult you?'

Neither Tirini's silk handkerchief nor Julius's solicitations seem to have much effect on Lisutaris, Mistress of the Sky, mightiest sorcerer in the West. The sight of the pathetic remnants of her gardens appear to have pushed her over some sort of edge. There's a brisk knock on the door.

'Come in,' wails Lisutaris, hopelessly. To my great annoyance, Captain Hanama marches in. Hanama is a small woman, very pale, almost childlike in appearance, but she's remarkably skilled in her work. I know she assassinated at least one person on the march and possibly more. As soon as she enters she comes to an abrupt halt, surprised at the sight that greets her.

'What is going on?'

'Thraxas insulted Lisutaris,' cries Tirini. 'He's gone mad for lack of beer.'

Hanama glares at me. 'Really, Captain Thraxas. You spent most of the march insensibly drunk. Surely you can stay sober for a few days without insulting our Commander?'

'Oh for God's sake!' I look over at Lisutaris, hoping for some support against these ridiculous accusations. None is forthcoming. Lisutaris is too busy sobbing into Tirini's handkerchief. The little piece of yellow silk cloth is clearly not up to the task. Captain Julius produces a more functional white cotton handkerchief and hands it over. Lisutaris buries her face in it while Hanama adds her support to the arm Tirini is using to cradle her friend, apparently worried that she might actually topple over with grief. 'Help her to a chair. She needs rest.'

There are plenty of angry glances directed at me. I'm starting to feel angry myself. This is what happens when you recruit women to fight a war. They all start crying and I get the blame. At least there are no more of them likely to appear. Or so I thought, before Ensign Droo enters the room.

'Commander–' she begins, then halts, puzzled. 'What's going on?'

'Captain Thraxas has gone insane and attacked Lisutaris,' cries Hanama.

The young Elf looks at me in alarm. 'Why did you do it? I thought you were getting your temper more under control?'

Having had more than enough of this, I bat Droo out of the way and make for the door. As I leave the room Hanama is informing everyone that it's not the first time I've gone on a violent rampage when maddened by lack of beer. 'I personally had to retrieve him from the penal stockade after he attacked several Simnian officers!'

An emergency canteen has been set up on the ground floor of the Palace. Not for the high ranking officials or officers or politicians but the ordinary citizens, civil servants and soldiers who've been drafted into service to help get the Turai on its feet. They rarely have anything worth eating but I call in anyway, hoping that their food supply might have improved. I find a small queue of people standing in front of two elderly ladies ladling out bowls of unappetising soup. It's not a lot different from the scene you might find out on the streets. Even for Palace workers, Turai is short of food. I decline the soup but take five loaves of bread from the rack, ignoring all protests. Then I march out of the Palace, heading for the west gate where I've arranged to meet Makri. I'm still furious at the scandalous accusation made against me. The sun is beating down. I'm fed up with everything. I sit down by our wagon and brood. Makri doesn't arrive. It doesn't improve my mood. She turns up almost twenty minutes late by which time I'm fuming, and complaining to the horse about the injustices of life.

'So you finally decided to arrive.'

Makri looks at me, not very apologetically. 'I called in at our Commander's office and was delayed by a scene of near hysteria. What the hell did you do?'

'I didn't do anything! I just reported Lisutaris's losses to her and when I handed over the remaining fragments of her gardens she started crying.'

Makri nods her head, and actually smiles. 'I figured it was probably something like that. I managed to dissuade them from declaring you an enemy of the state but you might want to watch your back for a while. Tirini's a powerful sorcerer and we know how good Hanama is at killing people.'

We climb into the wagon and ride out into the streets that will take us south. I'm still unhappy at recent events. 'Twice in one day! First you wailing over some damaged books then Lisutaris in hysterics about her thazis plants. It's a miracle we won the war with women bursting into tears at every opportunity.'

'These women led the army to victory,' declares Makri. 'And I helped.'

'Bah.' I fall silent, having nothing more to say on the topic.

Suddenly sympathetic, Makri reaches out to pat my shoulder. Involuntarily, I shrink back. Makri raises her eyebrows. 'You're going to have to do something about that.'

'Nothing needs doing.'

'Fear of being touched indicates a deep-rooted problem.'

'To you, maybe. Personally I'm fine. Apart from beer.'

We move on in silence. Some of the rubble and debris has been cleared away but there are still work crews everywhere. Refugees and homeless citizens still throng the streets. Already there are beggars at every corner. Beggars were a very common sight in Turai before the war and it will be a lot worse now. Everyone whose own business was destroyed, every employee who no longer has work to go to — how will they earn a living? How will they pay for food, even if the city manages to find any? Will the city be able to provide free provisions while we're getting back on our feet? I realise I've no idea how these things work. I've been involved in plenty of warfare and the sack of more than one city but I don't know what happens after that. Maybe everyone just starves to death.

Makri asks me where we're headed. 'Twelve Seas. I want to talk to Glixius but no one knows where he is. I'm hoping Casax can tell me.'

'Isn't Glixius still with the army?'

'He's missing from their ranks, which is suspicious. Before we talk to Casax we can check on Gurd and Tanrose.'

It's now early evening but the heat is undiminished as we turn into Quintessence Street. At the Avenging Axe, Gurd and Tanrose are still occupying a tent in the backyard. Gurd bought the Avenging Axe a long time ago with money he'd earned as a mercenary but he doesn't have the funds to rebuild it. Many of the other buildings in the street were owned by landlords and rented out to tenants. No one knows if these landlords survived the war and if they did, whether they'll be able to rebuild.

'The government should be giving people assistance,' I tell Gurd.

'Is there any prospect of that happening?'

'No. Not soon, anyway. They're still struggling to buy food.'

'Looks like we took the city back only to starve.'

'Gurd, you can't keep living here in a tent. Not while you're on military duty during the day. And not while Tanrose is expecting a baby. Find a room to rent somewhere. I'll give you the money if you can't afford it.'

Gurd looks at me quizzically. 'Where would you find the money?'

'I won money gambling in Samsarina, in the sword-fighting contest. Lisutaris has been looking after it for me ever since.'

'I know we should go somewhere else,' says Tanrose. 'But we don't want to leave here. It's our home.'

I remember how Tanrose looked just before we entered the city. Despite the trials of life while marching back to Turai, she was healthy, happy that she was pregnant and happy she and Gurd were to be married. Now her healthy aura is fading.

'Is your mother still living in Pashish? Did her tenement survive?'

'Yes,' says Tanrose. 'Not much damage in her street.'

'You should go there for the sake of your health. Gurd, either rent a room or go back to the Sorcerers Auxiliary barracks. You can live there as long as you're still on military duty.'

'But then we'll be apart,' Tanrose looks very unhappy.

I turn to Makri. 'Makri, I expect you know all about pregnancy because you always seem to have read everything about everything. Explain to Tanrose why she can't live in a tent in the middle of a Turanian summer and persuade her to move in with her mother.'

Makri knows I'm right, and she proceeds to do just that. I move along the street, not wishing to hear their pregnancy conversation. Gurd scuffs his way after me, unhappy at everything. 'We don't want to be apart,' he mutters.

'I know, but you can't keep on like this. Until you find a way to get the Avenging Axe rebuilt you'll just have to make do.'

Gurd stares at me for a few moments. 'How did you become the sensible one?'

'I don't know. I think it's lack of beer. I'm having a few day's clarity before I actually lose my mind.'

Chapter Thirteen

We've just climbed back into the wagon when a courier from the Messengers Guild hurries up to me. 'Captain Thraxas? This is for you.' I take the message. The messenger hurries off, keen to continue with his next delivery. I open the envelope.

'The villa was never decommissioned. It still hides its secrets.'

This means nothing to me. I shake the reins and the horse starts pulling our wagon along the street. Makri reads the message. 'What does it mean?'

'I don't know.'

'Who is it from?'

'It doesn't say.' We ride along, heading for the Mermaid to talk to Casax but when we reach Moon and Stars Boulevard I change my mind and turn right, heading back into the city.

'Where are we going?' asks Makri.

'Kushni.'

'Kushni? Why there?'

'I have a hunch.'

'Does that ever work?'

'Plenty of times. Number one chariot at investigating, as you well know.' We head north to Kushni, the disreputable part of town that straddles the river, home to some of Turai's worst criminal elements, an area of gambling dens, brothels, dark narrow streets and continual low-level warfare between the Brotherhood and the Society of Friends.

'Every time I've been in Kushni men assume I'm a prostitute. Then the actual prostitutes get annoyed because they think I'm stealing their business.'

'Try not to kill anyone over it. Not till we've visited the secret villa anyway.'

'Secret villa?'

'You've been there. A villa with rooms lined entirely with red Elvish cloth. Built by a former King so he could carry on his affairs without the Queen's sorcerers being able to discover what he was up to.'

'Of course,' exclaims Makri. 'That was quite a day.' Makri, Lisutaris and Hanama, in collaboration with other disreputable members of the Association of Gentlewoman, had gone there after

89

rescuing Herminis, a Senator's wife who'd been sentenced to death. It all went hopelessly wrong when they found their safe house occupied by a powerful Orcish sorcerer who'd chosen it as a hiding place, not foreseeing that a cabal of Turai's most powerful women might also have the same idea.

Makri laughs. 'What an experience that was.'

'A disaster as I remember it. You'd all have been arrested and executed if I hadn't got you out of the jam you were in.'

Makri brushes this off. 'We'd have managed. But wasn't that villa cleared out afterwards? The authorities removed all the Elvish cloth from the walls so there wasn't a secret room any more.'

'That's what was meant to happen. Perhaps it didn't. There were still two degenerate princes at the Palace who might have wanted to keep a private space for their own use.'

Makri agrees that my hunch might be a good one. 'It could be the villa the message was talking about. Who sent it?'

'I've no idea. I've no idea what we're going to find there either. If we're lucky it will be a huge pile of gold.'

We ride north along the main street before turning off near the river into side streets that narrow into alleys as we approach Kushni. The area shows the same signs of damage as everywhere else but differs in that business is already starting up. Most obviously, prostitutes are back on the streets, easily recognisable from the red ribbons in their hair, the mark of their guild. Many of them would have followed the army back to Turai, never ceasing their trade.

We pass by Vodax's, a seedy gambling den that used to be run by Vodax the Simnian until he was jailed for murdering his wife. The Civil Guards had been bribed to ignore the crime but his son hired me to find evidence. I put Vodax in prison. His son runs the joint now. I'm welcome there any time. We turn north which takes us close to the headquarters of the Assassin's Guild. It's perverse of them to have their guild headquarters in Kushni. I remember I once interviewed Hanama there. She was number three in the guild then, uncooperative and as cold as an Orc's heart. I'm not welcome there. I wonder what her status in the Assassins Guild is now. She might have been promoted. Might even be head of the guild if her superiors died in the war. Working for Lisutaris won't have harmed her status; the assassins aren't averse to having friends in high places.

The villa is on the far side of Kushni. Driving through I recognise more faces than I care to remember, people I've questioned, people I've investigated. Even a few people I've helped. There's some activity around the Three Swans, the tavern run by Barilox, leader of the Brotherhood in Kushni. Workmen are renovating the premises. There's no sign of any beer. If there was there'd be workers from the Draymen's Guild in their distinctive green aprons, rolling barrels off their wagons and into the cellars. Sadly, no draymen are anywhere to be seen. We pull up in Cedar Avenue, a wider road that leads out of Kushni to the city beyond. I've still no idea what we might find inside the villa. It's in good condition, apparently undamaged. The doors and windows are shuttered and there's no sign of habitation. We walk up the short path to the door. It's locked and it's sturdy.

'Well?' says Makri.

I used to be able to use some minor spells. I learned them in Sorcerers College before I was ejected. An opening spell, capable of opening most locked doors. A sleep spell, for incapacitating opponents. Both of these were very handy in my line of work. I knew a minor lighting spell, a spell for increasing stamina, and I retained the power of far-seeing while using a bowl of kuriya. Sorcerers college was many years ago and even these small accomplishments have faded over time. I can't remember when I last used any of them. Possibly not since I left the city. I speak the words of the opening spell. The door rattles but it doesn't open. I try again. Nothing happens.

'We should break it down.'

'I can open it.' I try again. This time I succeed. The door swings open. I turn to Makri. 'No need for violence. Just a little rusty.'

Makri laughs. 'You or the door?' We walk inside. It's gloomy and I know I'm not going to be able to use my lighting spell so soon after my opening spell. We walk along the hallway and come to a very sudden halt as a candle appears at the top of the stairs. In its feeble light I can just make out the figure of a woman holding a saucer with the candle perched on top. Not an elderly woman, but slow-moving nonetheless, limping as she comes down the stairs. She's using a cane which she's not controlling well. Though she doesn't seem threatening my hand's on the pommel of my sword anyway, just in case. When she reaches the foot of the stairs she examines us briefly, then nods to herself.

'In here.' We follow her towards a door. She's a little more mobile on level ground but still slow and it takes her a few moments to open the door. As we enter the room beyond, it lights up more than it should. There doesn't seem to be any source for the extra illumination. Suspecting sorcery, Makri's knife slides into her hand. I can see our host more clearly. Middle aged, hair starting to turn grey, looks underfed, walks with a pronounced limp. Could be any Turanian woman who's been through the war. She's led us into a large parlour with a fine carved wooden table. The whole room is rather fine. That's to be expected; it did host the secret dalliances of our Royal Family. After pulling out a chair, the woman sits down. There's something strange about all this. She beckons to the chairs at the other side of the table. 'Take a seat, Captain Thraxas and Ensign Makri.'

It just became stranger. 'Who are you?' I demand. 'And how do you know our names?'

The air grows a little colder. The woman's features flicker. 'We've met before,' she says. 'Several times.' Her face takes on a different cast as she transforms in an instant into an Orcish woman of indeterminate age. An Orcish woman I have met before, more than once. Deeziz the Unseen, strongest sorcerer in the Orcish Lands, now sitting calmly at a table though I recently saw her turned into a bloody pulp by Lisutaris, Mistress of the Sky. Startled, I draw my sword, as does Makri. 'We just can't get rid of you, can we?' I take a step forward but find my progress slowed. Suddenly I'm walking through mud.

'Captain Thraxas. I'm not at my best but I'm not going to let you stab me. Nor you, Makri, though I remember your skill with weapons.' Deeziz's powers of deception include her voice. She's talking with a common Turanian accent. Coming from an Orc, it's disconcerting. For a moment I feel adrift, unsure of what to do.

'Take a seat and I'll explain why I brought you here.'

I remain standing. 'Did you send the message?'

'Yes. I knew it would lead you here.'

Makri is glaring at Deeziz. 'I was pleased when Lisutaris smeared you and your Prince over the Palace walls. Why aren't you dead?'

'I have strong protection against sorcery. Much stronger than those protection charms you wear. I'd assumed I was safe against anything Lisutaris might use.' She pauses. A note of weariness enters her voice. 'That was unwise. Lisutaris had somehow learned something I wasn't ready for. The moment I found myself thrown back I created an illusion of my death. When I saw that Prince Amrag had really been killed and our forces were on the run, I decided to maintain the illusion. That wasn't easy. Lisutaris's spell wounded me badly.'

I take a seat. 'I take it you're still wounded. Otherwise you wouldn't have scurried off here to hide.'

'*Scurried* isn't the word I'd use. Travelling all the way here while maintaining my human disguise despite being injured wasn't easy.'

'How did you know this safe house existed?'

'I located it as soon as I arrived in Turai. It wasn't difficult to find.' Though she's sounding weary, Deeziz talks quite calmly, aware of her sorcerous prowess. Yet she's obviously damaged too severely to safely leave the city. I wonder if Makri and I could kill her if we attacked simultaneously. I'm also wondering why she led us here. So far it's not making sense. I can't interpret her motives. I've long experience of deducing the thoughts of Turai's criminals but I can't read anything in Deeziz's Orcish features. Her reddish skin is a good deal darker than Makri's and her features are strong, with a straight nose, a well-defined chin and a wide mouth. I'm slightly troubled by the thought that she's not really unattractive. Now I'm hoping she can't read my thoughts.

She looks at Makri, and then at me. 'You still belong to Lisutaris's Security Unit. As Lisutaris's trusted agents, I assumed she'd send you to hunt for the missing gold.'

Makri and I look at each other. We're wondering how Deeziz knows about the gold though we're not that surprised she does. I ask her anyway. 'How do you know about the gold?'

'I discerned its presence beneath the Palace as soon as I arrived in Turai. Using my advanced sorcerous powers.'

'You don't mind bragging about your powers, do you?'

Deeziz doesn't deign to reply to this, her attention suddenly caught by Makri. She leans forward, studying her. 'Now I understand. You were related to Prince Amrag and your blood was in Lisutaris's spell.' She nods, satisfied to have learned why the spell was so powerful. 'Interesting. Not something I'd have expected Lisutaris to be able to do. Unless she found a formula written by a superior practitioner. Julia the Bad for instance.'

I'm becoming fed up with this. 'Did you just bring us here to boast about your powers of learning everything about us? Because we have gold to locate. Right after we've brought sorcerers here to drag you off to prison.'

Deeziz starts to give me another contemptuous look but suddenly winces. Her hand goes to her leg. For a moment she can't control her reaction and it takes a while before she recovers.

'Sore leg?' I'm not sounding sympathetic.

'I have much internal damage. I need you to bring me a selection of healing herbs. You should be able to locate them.'

'Why would we do that?'

'Because I can lead you to the gold.'

'We'll find the gold anyway.'

'No, you won't. Not before your city starves. I can already hear the traders at the harbour making plans to sell their grain to Nioj and Simnia.'

I'm not certain if she means she can hear them literally or is talking figuratively. She's correct anyway.

'Where is the gold?' asks Makri.

'First I need the herbs.'

'And then you'll tell us where it is?'

'Not exactly. But I know enough to point you in the right direction. I learned much of interest when the theft was underway.'

'Why? Were you close?'

'Very close,' says Deeziz. 'I passed by while making my escape.'

I raise my eyebrows. 'You passed by? You mean you thought you might as well take some gold on the way out?'

'I have no need of your gold. I do need your herbs. Bring them to me, and swear not to let anyone know I'm here.'

'Not a chance.'

'You will, if you want to recover the gold. I'll tell you what I know, then I'll slip out of the city unnoticed.' Deeziz makes a brief motion with her hand and a jewel appears above her shoulder. Or rather, an image of a jewel, bright green in colour. 'I'll also return this, which Lisutaris will appreciate.'

I recognise the green jewel immediately. I once spent a long time chasing round Turai looking for it. It's an important sorcerous item that gives Turai's chief sorcerers powers of far-seeing that can't be blocked. Lisutaris hired me to recover it after it went missing and it turned into a very strange case involving Horm the

Dead, many fake jewels and a rash of unicorns and other mythical creatures.

'It might have saved Turai had Lisutaris not been too incompetent to use it before your walls fell.'

'Lisutaris wasn't incompetent. She was ill. You probably had something to do with that.'

Deeziz shrugs her shoulders. 'There was no need. You managed the plague all by yourselves. Don't blame me for Turai's poor sanitary conditions and incompetent governance.'

I'm becoming more annoyed by the moment. Having just defeated the Orcish army there seems no reason to be sitting here being mocked by one of their survivors. Also I'm irritated by the word *governance*. It's the sort of fancy word only Makri would use. Damn these intelligent Orcish women, making fun of me in my own city.

'Why would we trust you?'

'You've no reason not to. With Prince Amrag gone, the Orcish nations will not attack Turai again for many years. Nor will you see me again. I plan to travel to the furthest East, in search of Gobekli.'

'Gobekli?' Makri sits up straight, interested. 'That doesn't exist, does it?'

'I think it may. I intend to look for it.'

'What's Gobekli?'

'A mythical city, far to the East, beyond the lands of the Orcs,' says Makri, who's sounding far more interested than she should. 'Populated by a race who are neither Orcs, Human or Elves. But I'm sure it's just a story.'

'Certain writings in my library suggest it may not be. I have a scroll which purports to have been written by the chief researcher in the Great Gobekli Library four centuries ago.'

'Really?' Makri leans forward eagerly. 'That's fascinating! Could it be genuine?'

'I think–'

I slap my palm against the table and glare at both of them. 'Makri, control yourself. This is no time to be fascinated by libraries. As for you, Deeziz, you're weak and wounded. I'm still thinking we should just drag you up to the Palace.'

'That would go badly for you and it would not help your city. Far easier to bring me the herbs I require.'

There's a long silence. Deeziz turns to Makri again. 'I'll add a few herbs to my list. I can heal the pain in your womb.'

Makri's face lights up. 'It has been troubling me!' She controls her emotions. 'I mean it's fine. I don't need any help.'

Deeziz smiles. She draws a strip of parchment from a pocket inside her dress. 'I'll add them anyway.' The Orcish Sorcerer looks towards me. 'Before I leave, I'll show you how to open the hidden wine cellar in the basement.'

'Hidden wine cellar?'

'Very well stocked. The princes who used this house liked to keep themselves well-supplied. I noticed several bottles of klee with three golden moons on the label. The mark of the Abbot's Special Distillation, I believe.'

I raise my eyebrows. 'The Abbot's Special Distillation? Here, in the basement?' The Abbot's Special Distillation is so rare and fine as to never be seen in Turai outside the Imperial Palace and a few exclusive residences in Thamlin. It's the best klee available anywhere and the only reason I know that is because Lisutaris once gave me several bottles as a reward for saving her life. I can still remember how fine it tasted, and the warm glow that lingered afterwards.

Deeziz nods her head. Oddly, she's smiling. 'There are also several bottles of the Grand Abbot's Dark Ale, preserved in a special underground compartment, cooled and protected by a spell.'

I rise to my feet. 'I need to see this cellar right away.' The Grand Abbot's Dark Ale was the only beer ever served to the Turanian Royal Family. Beer was normally seen as beneath them but an exception was made for a drink so excellent, so skilfully brewed and in such short supply that it was hardly available outside the Palace. It's the finest drink in the known world. With the current beer famine afflicting the city, I must have it.

'Show me the beer.'

Deeziz shakes her head. 'Not until you bring me the herbs.'

'I'll find it myself.'

'You can't. The cellar's hidden by a spell and protected by another spell.'

'Lisutaris will open it for me.'

'I'll destroy it before she gets here.'

'You'd destroy the Grand Abbot's Dark Ale? What sort of monster are you?'

Makri rises to her feet. She winces slightly, and rubs her abdomen. 'We should go.'

'We're not finished here yet.'

'We can discuss it outside. If I have to see you salivating over beer any longer I'll be ill.' Makri walks out the room. I follow her unwillingly, taking a long look behind me, wondering where the cellar might be hidden and if Deeziz is telling the truth about the contents.

Chapter Fourteen

I'm standing on the outskirts of Kushni with a long list of ingredients and a puzzled expression. Makri's similarly puzzled, and actually scratches the tip of her left ear, something I've rarely seen her do.

'What are we supposed to do now?'

I shake my head. 'I don't know whether to help Deeziz or not. Maybe we should just tell Lisutaris and let her decide.'

'Good idea, let's do that.'

We head towards the wagon. I halt. 'Except then Deeziz won't tell us how to find the gold and the city will starve.'

'Will that really happen?'

'Hungry citizens are already drifting towards the Palace. Soon there will be an ugly mob outside, demanding food.'

Makri screws up her face in concentration. 'Maybe Lisutaris could force Deeziz to tell us?'

'Deeziz survived the most powerful spell ever unleashed in Turai and then managed to travel to a safe house. I'm not sure anyone can make her do anything.'

There's another long pause.

'I think we should tell Lisutaris,' says Makri, eventually. 'That's what our Commander would want.'

I shake my head. 'I'm thinking the opposite. We can do more good if we help Deeziz. Besides, I have a feeling she might know if we report her to Lisutaris. She might destroy the beer out of spite.'

Makri rolls her eyes. 'I didn't think it would be long till the beer won the argument.'

'Not just the beer, Makri. There's the Green Jewel too. Very important item for Turai's defence.'

We hover uncertainly on the cracked, filthy pavement. Shady looking characters glance at us at they filter into Kushni although no one approaches us. A large man in a captain's uniform and an Orcish-looking woman with two swords at her hip aren't easy targets for casual criminals. Makri still shows a preference for reporting Deeziz'z presence to the Palace.

'Don't forget about your womb,' I remind her. 'Deeziz says she can heal it.'

'You don't care about my womb!'

'Of course I do. It's been concerning me for some time. We should find these herbs.'

Makri scowls at me. 'I know you're only doing this for the beer.'

'Nonsense. My only interest is the welfare of the city.'

We walk towards the wagon.

'If people find out what we're doing I'll probably be executed as an Orcish spy,' says Makri.

'Don't worry, I'll be executed as well. Where are we going to find healing herbs?'

'Chiaraxi, I suppose. She was travelling along with the baggage train. She'll be back in her shop now, if it still exists.'

Chiaraxi is a herbal healer in Twelve Seas. I've had cause to use her services in the past. Makri knows her quite well, partly through their involvement in the Association of Gentlewomen. Not that I'd class Chiaraxi as a gentlewoman and Makri obviously isn't, but apparently they let anyone in. We climb back into our wagon. I can feel perspiration running down my neck. 'Is Chiaraxi going to have a full stock of supplies so soon after the war?'

Makri isn't certain. 'When I talked to her on the march she only had a few basic herbs. She gathers up a lot of her supplies from the local area though, so she's probably been busy re-stocking. And there's Cospali too, she sells herbs right next to Chiaraxi's.' Makri studies the list. 'I've never heard of some of these things.'

When we reach Twelve Seas there are still no signs of the repair crews visible in wealthier parts of the city. To get to Chiaraxi's we don't have to ride past the ruins of the Avenging Axe, which is a relief. I've no idea what's going to happen there. Will it be rebuilt? Where will I live if it isn't? I don't know how long Lisutaris intends to keep me housed in the Palace. I don't know how long I'll be obliged to remain in the army and I don't know quite how I'll manage when that ends. Probably best not to think too much about the future. It's now near dusk. Chiaraxi's shop is virtually undamaged and there's a light in the window. Inside, Chiaraxi greets us affably. There's dirt on her hands and face and she's unloading herbs, flowers and plant stems from several bags.

'I've been walking round the shore, found a lot of nice plants and seaweed. I met an old friend of yours.'

'Old friend? Who?'

'Dandelion. She's been living in a cave along the shore since the Orcs arrived.'

I'm actually moved to smile at the mention of Dandelion. She worked as a barmaid at the Avenging Axe and was a notably strange young woman, much given to walking around with bare feet and a skirt embroidered with patterns of the zodiac, and talking to dolphins. I wouldn't describe her as an old friend but I'm pleased to learn she survived the war.

'How was she?' asks Makri.

'Quite well. I think she enjoyed her time with the dolphins. She's waiting for some dolphin festival to take place before she comes back to the city. A princess's birthday, I think.'

Neither Makri nor I are surprised to hear that Dandelion will be celebrating a dolphin princess's birthday. I'd be more surprised if she wasn't. Chiaraxi asks how she can help us. Makri takes out our long list and hands it over. The herbalist healer scans it and raises her eyebrows. 'That's quite a list. Some unusual items. What's it all for?'

'We can't say,' I tell her. 'Official business.'

'It looks like you're trying to heal someone with Orcish blood. It's not you is it, Makri? You look healthy enough.'

'No, it's not me, it's…' Makri pauses, and looks hopeless.

'Official business,' I repeat.

Chiaraxi's eyebrows remain raised. I'm thinking she's going to mock the idea of me being an official but instead she does the opposite. 'I was pleased when I heard you were working for our War Leader,' she says. 'Both of you. Shows Twelve Seas in a better light than normal.'

With that she busies herself behind her counter, hunting for herbs. A few things she locates easily, some take longer, and after searching of her shelves she disappears through a curtained door into her storeroom. She's gone for quite a long time and when she re-appears she's frowning. 'I found dried edivas leaves and the carp scales but I'm missing two items on your list. Gobaras leaf is rare around here and I can't remember when I last stocked Panadier root. That's hard to come by at the best of times.'

I scan the list as Chiaraxi lays out her supplies on the counter. 'So you're missing two items. Is there anywhere else we could find them?'

'Copali might have had them. Unfortunately–' She comes to a halt.

'What?' says Makri.

'She was killed when the city fell. Never made it out of Twelve Seas.'

'Her shop's right next door isn't it?'

'Yes. Locked up.'

'We'll search it. We need these herbs.'

The herbalist isn't enthusiastic. 'You'd be breaking in to a dead woman's shop.'

'Can't be helped, Chiaraxi. Important official business. I'll need you to come with us to identify the items.'

Chiaraxi scowls, not liking this but trusting Makri and I enough to go along with it. 'We'd better go through the back. I don't want anyone to see me breaking in. It wouldn't look good.'

'You're right,' says Makri, tactlessly. 'Might look like you were burgling her for supplies.'

'I know.'

We walk through Chiaraxi's storeroom and out into her yard which is separated from Copali's yard by a small wooden fence. Makri leaps over it agilely. Copali clambers over nimbly enough, despite her long skirt. It takes me a while. I'm not great at climbing over things. Makri shakes her head as I stumble gracelessly into Copali's yard and considers making a sarcastic comment about my size but thinks better of it. The yard is empty save for two broken barrels. The back door to Copali's shop is closed and locked. I hesitate.

'Do you want me to break it down?'

'I can manage.' I speak the minor spell to open the door. Nothing happens. I try again. Still nothing happens. Now I'm making a fool of myself. When my spell fails for a third time Makri tells me to step aside so she can kick the door open. She could do that easily enough. So could I, but I don't want to. I speak my simple spell a fourth time. There's a loud click as the lock springs back. I grasp the handle and open the door. We walk through Copali's storeroom to the front of the shop where we're confronted by the sight of two young vagabonds rifling through the contents of the shelves.

I grunt at them. 'I see the local drug addicts have moved in already.'

The older of the two youths who's around eighteen, pale-faced and doesn't look like he ever served in the army, snarls at me. 'Who are you calling a drug addict?'

They both have knives visible in their belts. I draw my own knife and step forward. Makri steps forward with me. Knowing that this is a lot more than they could handle, both youths depart at speed through the front door which is hanging loosely on its hinges. Unlike Chiaraxi they hadn't shown any qualms about entering from the street outside.

'We've only been back in the city a few days and already people are looting the place.'

'This is terrible.' Chiaraxi is upset. 'How could they just break in to steal things?'

'Probably need money for dwa. That's what life is going to be like for a while, Chiaraxi. It'll be some time before things are back to normal.'

'Are the Civil Guards coming back?'

'I doubt our provisional government has the manpower to organise a proper Civil Guard. Not for Twelve Seas anyway.'

Chiaraxi looks downcast. 'I hate this. Everything is wrong. I don't feel safe.'

I know what she means. I don't like it either. I'm not worried about my own safety because if anyone troubles me I'll punch them in the face and if that doesn't put them off I'll run them through, but even so, the chaotic state of the city doesn't feel good. I can see the disorder getting worse, particularly if there's a food shortage. 'I'll talk to Lisutaris and see if she can send some sort of patrol down here. Maybe they can spare some troops from the walls. The Orcs are a long way away by now.'

Chiaraxi is upset but makes an effort to focus. She studies the list we gave her and begins to hunt on the shelves and on the floor where many of Copali's herbs have spilled. There's a sweet smell in the air from the opened pouches of dried herbs.

'Found some Gobaras leaf.' Chiaraxi rises from the floor and hands a bundle of dark brown leaves to Makri. 'I'll try the next room for Panadier root.'

Makri studies the leaves in her hand. 'We've almost got everything. Are you sure this is a good idea?'

'I'm not sure at all.'

'If we help Deeziz to heal herself a lot of things could go wrong.'

102

'They could go right. Lisutaris gets the Green Jewel back, we find the gold and we feed the city.'

'I know...but it doesn't seem like we should be taking this decision.'

'Who should?'

Makri shakes her head. 'I don't know. People in the government, I suppose.'

'They're all idiots. Apart from Lisutaris, and she has her idiotic moments.' A thought strikes me. 'I have a feeling she wouldn't mind leaving the decision to us. So she wouldn't be responsible.'

Chiaraxi returns. There are scraps of leaves and herbs on her knees and elbows from rooting through the stock. 'I found the Panadier root. That's everything on your list.'

'Thanks Chiaraxi, you've really helped us.'

The herbalist looks thoughtful as she hand the roots over. 'It really is an unusual combination. The only time I've ever seen edivas, gobaras and panadier used together was when my old teacher used sell potions to a trader who travelled the Wastelands, catering to the half-Orcish travellers who lived there.' Chiaraxi looks at me inquisitively.

'Official business,' I say. 'The city greatly appreciates your help. I'll fasten the door shut before we go.'

Chapter Fifteen

Late in the evening we find ourselves, for the second time today, hovering uncertainly outside the villa on the outskirts of Kushni. Above us is an oil lamp on a pillar that, like most of the others around here, has not been lit. Few of the city's lamplighters are back at work.

'Should we really be helping Deeziz the Unseen? What if she explodes the city or something?'

'Then she'd blow herself up as well. She didn't seem suicidal.'

'Are you certain this isn't all because she offered you beer?'

'Makri, I'm shocked. Do you really think I'd let a few bottles of beer influence a decision like this?'

'Yes, I've seen you do worse.'

I'm about to give forth with an angry retort when a figure appears though the gloom. A young woman with red ribbons in her hair, signifying her membership of the Whores Guild.

'Looking for company?'

Before I can reply the young whore notices Makri. She glares at her angrily. 'Hey, you're not a member of the Guild. Get off of my patch or we'll throw you off.'

Before Makri can make an angry retort of her own I take hold of her arm and lead her towards the secret house. 'We've got enough problems without starting a fight.'

'She thought I was a prostitute! That's insulting!'

'At least you've got a second source of income if everything goes badly.'

'That's not amusing!' Makri's not really that insulted. She sympathises with the city's prostitutes. She probably knows some of them quite well from her involvement with the Association of Gentlewomen. I wonder if that organisation has re-emerged now the city's back under our control. Maybe they have. Maybe they stole the gold. I knock on the door. It takes Deeziz some time to answer. She's limping badly as she leads us back along the corridor and into the front room. Her condition is getting worse. If I just left without handing over the herbs, she'd probably die soon. When she sits down heavily at the table I take out my bag and look her in the eye.

'You'd better have some good information. If you don't...' I leave the sentence unfinished. I don't know what I'd do if she doesn't. I empty the herbs onto the table. Deeziz mutters a word and the light in the room grows brighter. Her face looks drawn and fatigued. She examines the goods.

'I didn't think you'd find them all so quickly.' With that, she snaps her fingers, bringing two small copper cups from the sideboard floating over to the table. But her next piece of magic fails, as she snaps her fingers again, attempting to fill them with water. After a second failure, she looks rather apologetically at Makri. 'I'll need you to fill these for me.'

'Running out of magic?' I say.

'Obviously.'

The effort of bringing the cups floating over has cost her and her brow is now furrowed in pain. Makri leaves the room to fetch water. I'm left on my own with the most powerful living Orcish sorcerer. Probably the most powerful Orcish Sorcerer in history. I can't think of anything to say so remain silent. Makri arrives back with a bronze pitcher of water and sets it in front of Deeziz. The sorcerer's strength is waning by the second. She's dying in front of our eyes. Though I've been ambivalent about this I'm suddenly gripped by a desire for her not to die. Not right now anyway. Not when she's sitting right next to me. I take hold of the pitcher of water and fill the cups for her. Focusing all her attention on the task, Deeziz places most of the herbs into one of the cups. With the last of her strength she mutters the word of another minor spell, causing the herbs to dissolve as the liquid slowly swirls around. After this she sits back heavily in her chair. Her shoulders slump and her head droops forward. We wait for a moment.

'She doesn't have the strength to drink it,' says Makri. 'Should I help her?'

'I suppose so.'

Makri picks up the cup. She hesitates. 'Are we absolutely sure about this?'

'Yes. But if she kills us I'm going to be really annoyed.'

Makri holds the cup to Deeziz's lips and the ailing sorcerer slowly drains the liquid. It takes some time. Afterwards Deeziz's eyelids droop. He eyes close. She slumps forward.

'That's great. We probably brought the wrong herbs and now we've killed her. I'll have some strong words to say to Chiaraxi.'

105

For a few moments I do really fear that Deeziz has died in front of our eyes. I'm wondering if I should search for a pulse — and wondering if Orc's pulses are in the same places as human's — when she coughs, straightens up and opens her eyes. She coughs again, then wipes her mouth with her sleeve. Colour is returning to her features.

'Are you all right?' Makri speaks Orcish for the first time. It's not something she does often. Me neither, though I'm also a fluent speaker, which is rare in Turai.

'I will now recover,' replies Deeziz. She sits up straighter. I feel a little suspicious at the pace she appears to be recovering. When I speak, I use Orcish too, following on from Makri, for no real reason. 'You seem to be getting better quickly after almost being dead.'

'I have a permanent spell cast over me. The correct herbs will rapidly restore me.' She pauses. 'You both speak common Orcish. That's something I didn't know. How did you learn?'

'I grew up in a Orcish gladiator slave pit.'

'And I've dealt with a lot of dubious characters.'

'Do you also speak Elvish? I've heard you use some of their words.'

Makri nods. 'Common Elvish and the Royal Language.'

Deeziz looks impressed. I interrupt before they embark on some rambling conversation about linguistics which Makri is capable of even in the most unsuitable circumstances. 'We need information. About the gold.'

'Yes, information. Thank you both for bringing me the herbs,' says Deeziz, and sounds quite formal for a moment. She scoops up a few leaves that she hadn't used in her own potion, dropping them into the other goblet.

'This will heal the internal damage caused by Lisutaris's spell.' She hands the goblet to Makri. Makri hesitates.

'I perceive you have Orcish, Elvish and Human ancestry. Very unusual, though I have come across it before. The potion will be quite safe for you. As well as healing your womb it will boost your fertility. In your case that means returning it to normal after the damage you've done to yourself by ingesting dwa along with turix. I'm surprised you've had access to turix, normally sorcerers keep it for themselves.'

Again, I'm impressed by Deeziz's powers of perception. Lisutaris did provide Makri with the sorcerer's potion before the assault on the city to assist her in the strenuous work she was engaged in. Lisutaris shouldn't have done that and I'm not surprised it damaged Makri. Makri shrugs, then drinks the concoction.

Deeziz turns to me. 'I'll now tell you what I know. As I passed though the Palace I was trying to stay ahead of the invading soldiers. With my severe wounds that was difficult. I had to pause and hide, sometimes taking on human form for disguise, sometimes using illusion to keep myself unseen. This became more and more difficult. My powers were low. I was on the verge of being trapped in a corridor when I came across a small door that led into a storage area. I entered the room, used the last of my powers to cast a spell of concealment on the door, then fell unconscious on the floor.'

Deeziz pours herself water from the bronze pitcher and drinks. 'I believe I was unconscious for an entire day. My concealment spell must have held as no one discovered me. However I was still trapped, and injured, with no provisions. Now that the corridors had cleared, I decided to leave as soon as possible.'

I'm quite impressed at Deeziz's resilience though I don't let it show. She was badly wounded by Lisutaris's spell and her position must have seemed hopeless. Keeping going despite that says something about her character.

'When I left the storeroom two men had just emerged from the corridor opposite and were walking swiftly along the tunnel. One was a sorcerer. Not dressed as such, but I knew from the way I could glean nothing from his aura. He had effectively concealed it. Also, he was carrying a magic pocket beneath his tunic.'

'How do you know that?'

'Because it's the sort of thing I know. The other man was shorter, hooded to hide his features. As they'd come from the corridor where I knew the vault was I'd say it's certain they were the thieves.'

Deeziz falls silent. I stare at her. 'What else did you learn?'

'Little else. I was injured after all, more concerned with making my escape than examining strangers.'

'That's all you've got? This doesn't tell us who the thieves were! All you saw was one man in a hood and another who might have been a sorcerer! That doesn't solve anything? Makri, prepare to drag this woman into custody.'

Deeziz appears unmoved. 'I didn't say I could tell you everything. I made it clear I could only lead you towards the culprits. You, as investigator, will have to do the rest. Besides, I do have more information. The shorter man was recently scarred, both on his chest and back.'

'Wasn't he wearing a shirt?'

'He was, but I have the ability to discern any recent wounds, and any remaining scars. I believe he had a tattoo on his shoulder as well, though that was less clear to me.'

I'm still not particularly pleased with her information. 'So all we have to do is examine the entire population of Turai for men with scars and tattoos who might be friends with sorcerers. Shouldn't take more than a few years.'

'It does narrow the field,' says Makri. 'The two men would both fit into your suspicions about the Brotherhood. Maybe the Society of Friends as well. They have sorcerers, and usually gang tattoos.'

I ponder this for a moment. 'That's true, but it's still not much to go on. Deeziz, I regard this information as only marginally useful. I was a fool to let Makri convince me to bring you healing herbs. Nonetheless, it might turn out to be helpful. Kindly keep your other part of the bargain and disappear swiftly from Turai without ever letting anyone know I had anything to do with your recovery.' I rise to my feet.

'You're forgetting something,' says Deeziz.

'What?'

'The Grand Abbot's Klee and Dark Ale.'

'Yes…I suppose I may as well take it with me.'

'I'll take you to the cellar.' Deeziz rises. The effect of the herbs is very marked. Already she's looking a lot healthier though her hair still hangs messily around her face. I follow her along the corridor and down a stairwell towards the cellar. Light appears as we walk, sorcerously produced though Deeziz doesn't utter any spells. It seems to be something she can produce merely by the power of thought. The cellar is much as I was expecting in a house used by royalty. Carpets richer than you'd find in most dwellings, walls painted in the rare and expensive royal purple and even an elvish tapestry on one wall. There are shelves aplenty and several doors leading to pantries, storerooms and wine deposits. To my disappointment, the shelves are empty and the pantries hold nothing of interest. Mustn't have been restocked for a while. Probably because the errant princes spent most of their time in drug induced stupors in the Palace before the war. I wonder again about Princess Dees-Akan. She's presumed dead though there are no eyewitness reports of her death. I still remember the time she hired me to retrieve some compromising letters. That all led to a complex case which nearly ended up destroying the city. She lied to me at the start of the affair which made it more difficult. I don't remember her too badly however; unlike most of my clients she did have good manners.

I watch anxiously as Deeziz hovers over a section of tiling on the floor. She bends down and lifts a section revealing a concealed trapdoor which she opens with a wave of her hand. She then makes a gesture as if summoning something from below. The top of a wooden case appears. I'm trembling with excitement. Unfortunately Deeziz'z powers haven't been restored sufficiently to complete the task. Her hand drops and the case disappears with a clanking noise. As she's about to try again I barge her out the way.

'You'll break the bottles! Let me do it.' I get down on my knees, reach into the underground space and take a firm grasp of the wooden case, lifting it swiftly to the surface. Underneath it there's another case which I also grab and haul into the room. I wrench them open and there, as promised, are four bottles of the Abbot's Klee and nine bottle of the Abbot's Dark Ale.

'Klee and beer, as stated. Sorry I doubted you.'

The sorcerer is looking very displeased, 'How dare you barge me out of the way!'

Makri shakes her head. 'Thraxas can't help himself where beer is concerned. It's like a mental condition.'

'A mental condition?'

'Uncontrollable desire. Rather like the youngest son in the Elvish comedy 'Desire of the Heart' who couldn't stop eating lemon cakes.'

Deeziz nods. 'I have read that comedy. It is an apt comparison.'

'You're read it? Not many people have. Elvish comedy isn't widely known.'

'I have a few examples in my library. There is nothing like it in the Orcish lands, though we have produced many fine epic sagas.'

109

I stand up, clutching one of the wooden cases. 'Makri, is there nothing you can't turn into a discussion about Elvish literature?'

'It's a very comprehensive genre.'

'Help me get these cases into the wagon.'

'Are we suddenly in a rush?'

'I'm always in a rush when you get on to Elvish writing. And I've never heard of Elvish comedy. I don't believe any Elf ever said anything funny.'

I carry the case back up to the ground floor, Makri following on with the other. We place them carefully in the wagon. I'm smiling, and I haven't done that for a while. 'Finally we're making some progress.'

'You're not talking about the gold, are you?'

'In a way. Now I have beer I can start thinking properly. You can't expect Turai's number one chariot at investigating to get things done when you restrict his beer intake. Everyone knows that.' I clamber into the wagon.

'So are we just leaving Deeziz here?' asks Makri.

'What else can we do? Now she's healthy she can sneak out the city and go look for her mythical city in the East.'

Makri climbs in beside me. 'I hope so. If she stays around and causes trouble and Lisutaris finds out we let her go, she's not going to be pleased.'

'I'll be me that's blamed, not you.'

'Why?'

'I'm the senior officer and head of the Security Unit. It's my responsibility.' I start unscrewing the top of one of the bottles of beer. 'First we need to talk to Casax and see if that leads us anywhere. I'm still suspicious about the Brotherhood. Then we'll go back to North Walls and ask the Society of Friends some questions.'

'The only new information we really have is that the thief has scars on their torso and a tattoo.'

'I know. It's not great but it's more than we knew before.' With beer in hand, I'm more optimistic. I drink from the bottle as we ride though Twelve Seas, feeling more cheerful than I have for some time. It's a familiar phenomenon. Remove beer from Thraxas and he just doesn't function properly. Restore it and everything starts to improve. We pull up in front of the Mermaid, haunt of the

Twelve Seas branch of the Brotherhood. I stride in confidently. Some puny thug places himself in front of me.

'Thraxas, Palace Investigator, here to see Casax.'

'He's busy.'

'So what? I'm working for our War Leader so run upstairs and fetch him before I bat you out the way.'

It's not the most tactful of entrances but I do have a full bottle of the Grand Abbot's Dark Ale inside me and it's powerful stuff, particularly for a man who's been denied beer in recent weeks. I'm not in the mood to bandy words with Casax's minor thugs. He turns on his heels and hurries away up the stairs. I notice Makri has her hands on the pommels of her swords but there's no real indication that the other members of the Brotherhood at the tables in the tavern are about to attack us. Possibly the mention of Lisutaris and the Palace has an effect on them. No one wants to get on the wrong side of our War Leader.

Karlox, Casax's giant enforcer, appears at he top of the stairs and motions us up. He's sneering as we reach him but even he doesn't make with his normal abuse. I'm starting to feel like an actual important official. It doesn't last. As I walk into Casax's office the Brotherhood leader is sitting behind his desk and doesn't pretend he's pleased to see me.

'Thraxas, if you think the Palace and Lisutaris would protect you from us you're a bigger fool than I imagined and that's hard to credit because I already regard you as the biggest fool in Turai. Whatever you want, make it quick before I throw you downstairs.' He pauses, and looks at Makri. 'Not you, of course. The job offer as a dancer is still open.'

Makri walks round the desk. Her knife appears in her hand. Moving so quickly that Casax is unable to react, she grabs his tunic and slits it open, then she wrenches it apart, meanwhile placing the tip of her knife at Casax's throat to prevent him from moving.

'Tattoos but no scars.'

I'm startled by this development. I wasn't expecting Makri to take such direct action. It's effective, however. Casax's exposed torso shows no signs of scarring. Casax himself shows every sign of exploding with rage but he's unable to move because of Makri's knife. She takes a step back. Karlox leaps towards her then halts abruptly as he finds the point of Makri's sword at his throat, Makri again having performed this action so quickly that's it's almost impossible to see how she did it.

'Thank you for your co-operation,' I say, and nod in Casax's general direction. We stroll out of the room and down the stairs.

'Nice moves,' I say to Makri, outside the tavern. 'Took me by surprise.'

'Casax annoys me. I don't like the way he keeps offering me work as a dancer. It's insulting.'

'He probably won't be doing it again.'

We mount up and ride off in the wagon. Makri reaches over and puts her hand into the bag at my feet and pulls out a bottle of klee. She opens it, puts it to her mouth and drinks, shuddering as the fiery spirit trickles down her throat. I stare at her.

'What? I'm feeling the strain too. It was a difficult war.'

Chapter Sixteen

At the Palace we head for my office. 'Something just occurred to me. Deeziz's information about scars might be more useful than I thought. Remember Anumaris's list of suspects? Senator Agresius was on it. Friend of Cicerius, party treasurer, probably knew about the vault and in debt to the Society of Friends. He's also a man with a lot of scars on his torso.'

Makri is surprised. 'How do you know that?'

'Because he loves showing off his war wounds. He's one of those senators who lets his toga hang loose while he's making a speech in the Senate so people can see the scars on his chest. Reminds everyone that he's a war hero, wounded honourably in combat. Always plays well with the younger senators who haven't had a chance to fight for the city.'

'Are we going to talk to him?'

'We should.' I frown. 'That's going to be awkward. A man like that won't appreciate being investigated.'

When we reach my office I find Anumaris pacing the room anxiously while Droo lounges in a chair, running her fingers through her spiky blonde hair.

'Captain Thraxas! Our Commander has been asking for you. She's very eager to know if you've made progress.'

Droo sniggers. 'She's been yelling at Anumaris.'

'I wouldn't say she was yelling,' says Anumaris, stiffly. 'Voices were raised.'

Droo grins. 'She was yelling. Not at me. She was pleased with me.'

Droo, while failing to find beer, has been more successful in locating thazis for Lisutaris. The young Elf has a remarkable talent for hunting down illicit substances, managing it so cheerfully and shamelessly that she already seems to have opened up a wide array of contacts. Lisutaris is particularly appreciative of this.

'I need to talk to Lisutaris,' I tell Anumaris. 'Come with me.'

Makri is following us out the room when Droo calls to her. 'A man came to ask you out.'

This brings us to a halt.

'What?'

'Someone called Lieutenant Derigus. He came here twice, looking for you.'

'What did he want?'

'To ask you out.'

'I don't think we can say that,' protests Anumaris. 'He was just asking if you were here.'

'He wanted to ask her to dinner,' continues Droo, cheerfully. 'He's probably salisting for her.'

'Salisting? What does that mean? Never mind.' Makri has now disappeared from my office. I hurry after her, catching up with her in the corridor halfway to Lisutaris' office.

'What does *salisting* mean?'

'A crude Elvish term for lusting. Droo is fond of the term.'

I don't enquire any further. I have other things on my mind. Besides, any romance Makri becomes involved in will inevitably end in disaster and I'll hear more than I want to about it anyway. When we reach Lisutaris's stateroom we're waved in by the guard with only a brief delay, a sign of the importance of our mission. I can remember Lisutaris keeping me waiting for hours while she had her hair done. She's extinguishing a thazis stick as we enter, with an air of mild distaste. 'Inferior brand. Not so bad in the circumstances, I suppose. Ensign Droo certainly has a talent for locating thazis.'

'She's good with beer too, though she's let me down this time.'

'And yet you have been drinking beer, I perceive.'

'It must be tough being a sorcerer, perceiving things all the time. We have a lead on the gold and I need your help. There are several prime suspects. One of them is Senator Agresius.'

'Agresius? Are you trying to make my life difficult? You know how Consul Cicerius will react if you question him.'

'That's why I've come to talk to you first.'

'Is he really a suspect?'

'A strong suspect. Cicerius was in the habit of discussing Palace finances with him. He's rumoured to have heavy debts to the Society of Friends.'

'That's hardly enough reason to suspect him of masterminding a bullion robbery.'

'There's more. I have it on good authority that one of the people involved in the robbery is heavily scarred on his torso.'

Lisutaris digests this for a moment. She's aware of Agresius's habit of showing off his battle scars. 'Do you have a witness for this?'

'Yes. Sort of.'

'Sort of? Who is it?'

'I'm not at liberty to say. I need to protect my sources. I'm sure you understand.'

'No, I don't.'

'Standard investigating practice, Commander.'

'Senator Agresius is a friend and ally of Cicerius. He's one of the most important men in the Traditionals. He's a war hero from the last war and he did his part in this one too.'

'That's why I need your help. If I approach him in the Palace he'll tell me I have no authority to question him.'

'You do have the authority.'

'I know, but he won't cooperate. It would save a lot of time if you'd help. Make it clear he'd better come clean about everything or you'll explode him with a spell. Something like that.'

Lisutaris raises her eyebrows. 'You expect me to question suspects? That's not going to help my reputation.'

'Recovering the gold will be good for your reputation.'

'No one knows the gold is missing yet. If that does become known my reputation evaporates in a wave of food riots.' Lisutaris glances at the marked candle on the table that counts down the hours. 'If I help you with this it will cause trouble with Cicerius. You appreciate that isn't good for Turai?'

'I know, but Agresius is the best suspect I have at the moment.'

Lisutaris sighs. 'I have a meeting with the Turanian Sorcerers Guild in one hour that can't be delayed. I can assist you till then.'

'Good. Agresius is involved in Temple upkeep. If he's working late like everyone else he should still be in his office.'

Lisutaris informs her aide Captain Julius that she'll be gone for a short while but will be back in time for the meeting. As we leave the stateroom I ask her what the meeting is for.

'Still trying to get the Sorcerers Guild back on its feet. The situation is bad. We just learned that Kemlath Orc Slayer died of wounds he received during the assault.'

Kemlath was another powerful figure. A rogue, but powerful.

'It's left us very short of top line sorcerers at a time when the city is under pressure.' Lisutaris looks over at Makri and smiles.

'Fortunately we have still have Makri's strong arm to protect us. Unless she's too distracted by the young officer who's been pursuing her round the Palace.'

'How do you know about that?'

'Palace gossip travels very quickly.'

Makri scowls, not liking to be the subject of Palace gossip. 'Droo probably blabbed it to everyone already.'

Lisutaris laughs. 'Young Lieutenant Derigus did well in the war. And he was very helpful in obtaining some rare thazis plants from the South for me. Not that I admit that ever happened.'

We've now reached the Palace rooms requisitioned by the Office for the Upkeep of Churches and Shrines. It's a prestigious department so it isn't surprising that Senator Agresius has been temporarily assigned to oversee it. The Traditionals have very strong links with the True Church. Inside we find Senator Agresius and three younger men standing around a table examining a map of the city. 'Commander,' he greets Lisutaris. 'Has your office made a decision?'

'If it's about money you need to repair churches, we're still considering it.'

'There's so much damage. We must at least repair the city's main temples quickly.'

'We can't do that at this moment, Senator.'

'The population needs their places of worship, Commander.'

'They also need food, water and roofs over their heads.'

Agresius seems inclined to argue though the others — clerks, builders, architects, I don't really know who works in this department — stand back respectfully.

'Senator Agresius, we need to talk to you in private about a confidential matter.'

'And who are you?' Though I've never talked to Agresius before, I know his type. There are many of them in the Senate. Born wealthy, conservative by nature and not much given to interacting with Turai's lower classes. Cropped grey hair, upright posture, keen on their Senatorial privileges and outwardly extremely respectable, no matter what they might be getting up to in private. I feel a further surge of sympathy for Lodius and his Populares Party: Turai might be a better place with fewer wealthy Senators running things.

'Captain Thraxas, Head of Security for our Commander.'

Agresius narrows his eyes. 'Thraxas? I've heard that name. Are you the Thraxas who was once denounced from the pulpit by Bishop Gzekius?'

'The same. Quite a memorable sermon, so I was told.'

'Commander, this hardly seems like a man who should be making enquiries in this department.'

Lisutaris brushes this aside. 'We need to talk to you, Senator. Somewhere private.'

The Senator shrugs, then leads us to his private office, a decent-sized room with two thick rugs on the floor and no sign of war damage. I begin questioning him immediately. 'I want to know if you were in the Palace the day after we retook the city.'

'Why?'

'Please just answer the Captain's questions,' says Lisutaris.

'Very well. Yes, I was at the Palace. After we defeated the Orcs, orders came through for all officials to report there.'

'What did you do there?'

'Waited for a long time in a reception hall until finally being called by an officer I didn't know who told me that our Commander had ordered all Palace Employees to commence work as soon as possible. At that time I hadn't yet checked to see if my house was still standing, so I went home, found it was, then returned to the Palace to commence work. I've been here ever since.'

'Did you talk to any sorcerers while you were at the Palace?'

Agresius looks questioningly at Lisutaris. 'Am I to be allowed to know what this is about?'

'Just answer Captain Thraxas's questions,' says Lisutaris, firmly. She's making my life a lot easier. If she weren't here Agresius would have thrown me out of his office moments after I arrived.

'I don't remember talking to any Turanian sorcerers but I was greeted by Lemisphir, a Niojan sorcerer who'd accompanied my unit into combat the previous day.'

'You went into battle with a Niojan sorcerer? Were you near the Palace then?'

'Of course. That was our objective.'

'Why was you unit accompanied by a Niojan?'

'I presume he was assigned by our Sorcerers Guild because there weren't enough Turanian sorcerers to go round.'

117

I take a moment to digest this information. 'When you met this Niojan sorcerer the next day in the Palace, did you go anywhere with him? Walk through any corridors?'

'No. We merely greeted each other civilly in the reception hall.'

'Can anyone else confirm that?'

'Commander, this man's impertinence is intolerable! I refuse to answer any more questions without an explanation.'

Lisutaris doesn't offer him any explanation. She does inform me that it's time for her to return to her own office. Knowing that I'm not going to get any more out of Senator Agresius, I leave with her. Makri accompanies us as we walk back through the corridors of the Palace.

'That all sounds suspicious,' says Makri.

'It does. Entered the Palace with a Niojan sorcerer during the fighting then met him there the next day. He's a man with scars too, and serious debts.'

'None of that would explain how he could organise a major crime like robbing the vault,' says Lisutaris.

'We've been thinking about Turai's criminal gangs but what if it was Nioj, for instance, with the full resources of their intelligence services? They'd have access to sorcery, manpower and intelligence. Everything needed for the crime.'

'It would count as an act of war against Turai.'

'Do you think they'd be much concerned about that, with their army right outside and Turai so weak?'

'Possibly not.' Lisutaris is worried by the thought.

'Do you know the sorcerer he was with, Lemisphir?'

'Not really. Niojan sorcerers tend not to socialise.'

'No idea if he might be a master criminal?'

'None. No idea if he might have a magic pocket either. I'm presuming you still think the gold is hidden inside one?'

'That's my best guess. Can't think of anywhere else it could be.'

'I should still be able to locate the sorcerous mark on the gold. It's very troubling that I can't.'

We're almost back at Lisutaris's stateroom when inspiration suddenly strikes her. Unfortunately, as it turns out. 'Thraxas, do you remember that secret house in Kushni? The one the Royal Princes used to use for their assignations? Wasn't that lined with Red Elvish Cloth? What if the gold is hidden there? That would

118

explain why we couldn't trace it by sorcery. No sorcery can penetrate that cloth.'

This is a bad development. Makri has already gone pale. She's a terrible liar. Faced with questions from Lisutaris she's likely to just admit everything. I step in to avoid disaster, thinking rapidly. 'We've already been to that house to check it out. Didn't want to burden you with unnecessary details and I didn't want to mention it because that's where I found beer.'

Lisutaris raises her eyebrows. 'Why was there beer there? Was there anyone in the house?'

'No, there was no one there. I found the beer in a secret cellar in the basement.'

'A secret cellar? Yes, I remember that. Tirini installed it when she was having an affair with one of the princes. I forget which one.'

At this moment Harmon Half Elf appears, hurrying along the corridor. 'Am I late for the sorcerers' meeting?'

'No, just about to start,' Lisutaris informs him. She's still regarding me suspiciously. Makri is looking paler and paler and may faint at any moment from the stress of concealing something from her. A young sorcerer, Capali Comet Rider, appears in the corridor. It's time for their meeting to start. I make good our escape, dragging Makri off in the opposite direction.

'We're doomed,' wails Makri when we're out of earshot.

'No, we're not.'

'Yes, we are. Lisutaris will find out we helped Deeziz and I'll be thrown off the walls as an Orcish spy.'

'Makri, have I ever mentioned that you have something of a pessimistic nature? Deeziz should be long gone by now. There's nothing to connect us to her, unless you panic and start admitting everything to Lisutaris. Even if she did find out, so what? We've been acting solely for the good of Turai.'

Makri isn't much comforted, being sure that she'll be executed for treason.

'Lisutaris isn't going to execute us for treason. We have a lot of history together. Why, last time the Orcs attacked–'

'Don't tell me that story again about you and her being together on the walls when they collapsed. That's not going to protect you forever.'

We carry on towards my office. Makri's worried. I'm annoyed that she interrupted my story about being on the walls with Lisutaris, heroically fighting off the swarming Orcs during the last war and more or less saving the city by ourselves. It's a good story. Not one I tell too often either. By now it's close to midnight. We have a lot of work still to do but decide to end the investigation for today and take it up again early in the morning.

Chapter Seventeen

After an unsatisfactory breakfast of bread, an undercooked yam and a tankard of water, I'm in a poor mood as I approach my office. It doesn't improve when Droo accosts me in the corridor carrying a scruffy-looking piece of paper.

'Thraxas, look at this!

I take the paper. It's covered in small writing, a poorly produced news sheet bearing the title *The Renowned and Truthful Chronicle of All the World's Events*. I'm surprised to see it. The Renowned and Truthful Chronicle was something of an institution in Turai, though not one anyone was proud of. It concentrated mainly on scandal involving senators' daughters, young officers, rich widows, greedy young politicians, and the often-degenerate goings on among Turai's upper classes. That, along with a healthy dose of sensational crime stories was guaranteed to whip up outrage among its readers. It was published regularly before the Orcish invasion though it disappeared from view during the war. I'm surprised to see a new edition appearing so soon after we've retaken the city.

'*Missing Gold — Palace scandal!*'

I'm already scowling. This can't be good.

'*Sources at the Palace indicate that a very large sum of money in the form of gold bullion has disappeared from the Palace vaults. This was earmarked for the purchase of food and is a terrible loss to a city already on the brink of starvation. The whole affair smacks of corruption at the highest levels. Our revered War Leader Lisutaris, Mistress of the Sky, is of course beyond suspicion but the sad truth is she's surrounded by a coterie of very dubious characters including assassins, degenerate sorcerers, half-Orcish ruffians and several shady figures from the lower depths of Turanian society. Our readers will be amazed to learn that among these figures is Thraxas, about whom the Chronicle has had reason to warn the city before. As the food intended for our starving population disappears to the Simnian, Samsarinan and Niojan encampments, many curious glances will be cast towards the Mistress of the Sky, wondering why her most trusted companions all seem to be characters of the very lowest repute...*'

I stop reading. 'Droo. where did you get this?'

'From the angry crowd at the Palace gates. Someone was handing them out.'

Makri appears at our side, also carrying a sheet of paper. 'They called me a half-Orcish ruffian!'

I shake my head. 'This is bad. The population isn't going to like it.'

'Indeed they are not!' comes a loud and angry voice. Lisutaris strides into view. She's brandishing her own copy of the Renowned and Truthful Chronicle and she's not looking enamoured by its contents. 'Who's been speaking to these people?'

'No one here, Commander. Probably someone from Lodius's camp, looking to cause trouble.'

'How did Lodius learn of the gold? Never mind, I'll find that out later.'

'There should be laws against publishing these lies.'

Lisutaris glares at me. 'I don't know, it does describe me as *revered and beyond suspicion*, unfortunately surrounded by dubious characters. They might be on to something. Find the gold before people start rioting.'

'Enquiries are proceeding well.'

'Last night you told me the only lead you had was some vague story about a man with scars on his torso. Is that still all you have?'

'Yes, Commander.'

'Someone made off with millions in gold right under our noses and my Head of Security is now roaming the city asking men to remove their tunics. Let's hope that news doesn't make it into the Chronicle or we'll be laughed out of the city.'

'Hey, there's more about Thraxas on the next page!' Droo says brightly. 'Were you really denounced by the Archbishop? And then by a Bishop as well after you robbed his church? And another time you and an Orc woman started a big sword-fight in another church?' Droo laughs gleefully. 'You must really hate the church.'

'Now they're calling me an Orc!' exclaims Makri.

'Hey, what's this?' Droo suddenly sounds aggrieved. 'They're saying Lisutaris's messenger is a small Elf who's always drunk and goes around stealing wine. That's outrageous. Why's everyone looking at me?'

Anumaris appears in the corridor. Lisutaris speaks sharply to her. 'Anumaris, assist Captain Thraxas on his mission to examine

Turai's male population for scars. Get it done quickly. If anyone resists blast them with a spell.'

'Yes, Commander.'

'Try not to do anything disreputable. You at least seem to have avoided being denounced by the Chronicle.'

'I don't know about that.' Droo pipes up again. 'She could be the '*Incompetent young sorcerer who only got promoted due to her father being a Senator.*"

'That's not true!' Anumaris looks furious. 'It's not true, is it Commander?'

Lisutaris regards her sourly. 'Ask me again once you've finished investigating. Captain Thraxas, I am at this moment attempting to reassemble the Turanian Sorcerers Guild, rebuild the city's walls, rebuild the city's infrastructure, strengthen and reorganise our army, and negotiate for food we have no money to pay for. Meanwhile you're hanging around the Palace drinking beer. Find the gold, and quickly.'

Lisutaris turns on her heel and storms off down the corridor. There's a moment's silence.

'Do you have beer?' enquires Droo.

I decline to answer. Instead I ask Anumaris if she has her list of suspects on her. She has. 'Then it's time to investigate. Follow me to our wagon.'

'I did not get promoted because my father's a Senator.' Anumaris is still aggrieved. 'I worked hard at Sorcerers College.'

'What does your father do?' asks Droo.

'He's the Senator responsible for liaising with the Sorcerers Guild. But that has nothing to do with it.'

'Why do they always concentrate on Orcs?' complains Makri, as we leave the building. 'You have one drop of Orcish blood and suddenly you're an Orc.'

'At least you weren't connected to robberies, unexplained murders and cowardice in battle,' says Droo.

'Who was?'

'Thraxas. They put a lot of information into that paragraph. Needed very small writing to fit it all in.'

Our wagon, complete with a fresh horse, is waiting for us at the stables. We climb in. I'm fairly grim-faced as I turn to Anumaris. 'Who's nearest on our list of suspects?'

'Probably the soldiers — Lubatox, Carox and Durun.'

'The ones who carried the gold into the vault?'

'Yes. It still seems strange that Captain Ularax trusted them to do that. Senior Trooper Lubatox is in charge of a unit at the East Wall.'

'Fine, we'll start with him.' I shake the reins, enough to start the horse moving. The horses provided to transport government employees around the city are well trained animals, in good condition and probably better fed than the employees. As we leave through one of the main Palace gates we find ourselves riding through a crowd of surly onlookers. It's not exactly an angry mob but you can feel the tension in the air. By now everyone will be aware of the report in the Renowned and Truthful Chronicle.

As is now customary we make slow progress through the city. I'm already sick of picking my way past repair crews and teams of builders. We're just north of the parkland where we entered the city and some of the government buildings close to the Palace have been completely destroyed. We even come across the remains of a dragon, a few jagged bones still mixed with the rubble of the building it crashed on to. I stare at it morosely as we pass. I hope I never see another live dragon. At the main guard tower on the east wall I ask for Senior Trooper Lubatox. We're directed south to the next watchtower where he's in command of the unit.

Lubatox is a few years older then me. From his accent I'd say he grew up in Twelve Seas and from his manner, both confident and guarded, I'd guess he's been a solider for a long time. As a Senior Trooper he hasn't advanced very far up the ranks but that's difficult for a poor man from Twelve Seas to do. Officer's positions are almost always awarded to the sons of wealthy families, who are regularly placed in charge of soldiers far more experienced than them. It's a weakness in our military structure which should be attended to but probably won't be.

'Captain Thraxas. How can I help?'

'I'm making enquiries about a problem at the Palace and I need you to answer a few questions.'

The Senior Trooper doesn't object, knowing I'm here as Lisutaris's Head of Security. He leads us to his own small billet inside the guard tower, while casting a few curious glances at Makri, knowing her by reputation and interested to see her up close.

'So,' he says, cordially enough once we're in his room. 'Am I in trouble for something?'

'You led your unit back to Turai and took part in the assault on the walls. You were commended several times.'

He nods his head modestly.

'Before the war you were assigned for several years to guard duty at the Palace, under Captain Ularax, then in charge of Palace Security.'

'I was.'

I get straight to the point. 'Did you help carry gold into the secret vault?'

Lubatox's manner changes immediately. He doesn't answer.

'Tell me about the gold.'

He hesitates. 'I can't talk about that.'

'I'm afraid you have to. Captain Ularax was killed in the war so I can't ask him. I need to know why you were assigned to carrying the gold when it was a state secret that it even existed. You have a good military record but it's not something a Senior Trooper and two privates should have been doing.'

'What is this about? Am I being accused of something?'

'Answer my question. I'm here on behalf on Lisutaris and our War Leader doesn't send me to ask questions for no reason.'

He remains silent for a few moments, unsure of what to say. He doesn't want to talk but Lisutaris's name carries a lot of weight.

'Captain Ularax sometimes wasn't as careful as he should have been about transporting the gold. We had to help him out when…'

'When he was drunk? Intoxicated on Dwa?'

'Drunk, mainly.' Senior Trooper Lubatox looks unhappy at the memory. 'He was still a good officer. He was killed fighting the Orcs. I don't want to spoil his record.'

I nod my head. 'It won't. It can stay in the past. That explains why you were carrying the gold. I know that Private Carox and Private Durun helped you. Was there anyone else?'

'No. Just us. We knew it was meant to be secret, we never involved anyone else.'

I believe him. I like Senior Trooper Lubatox. I'm sorry about what I'm going to have to say to him next. 'I'm making enquiries about a man with scarring on his torso. Do you have scars?'

'One small scar from an arrow.'

125

'I need to see.' As I say it, it sounds ridiculous. I knew it was going to. Lubatox is immediately insulted.

'You want me to take my tunic off?'

'Yes.'

'I don't believe our Commander would make a demand like that.'

'She did. I'm following her orders. I need to see your chest and back to check for scars.'

'I refuse. You can't make me. I have legal rights.'

'Not really. Most of them were suspended for the duration of the war and that order hasn't been rescinded yet. Don't make this difficult. I have a sorcerer with me who can paralyse you if need be.' I indicate Anumaris, who tries not to look embarrassed about the whole thing. Even Makri has taken a step back. Demanding that honest Turanian citizens take their tunics off is proving to be just as uncomfortable as I thought it would be.

'I'll report this to General Osbus.'

General Osbus is an important man. He's not as important as Lisutaris. 'Anumaris, place a spell on Senior Trooper Lubatox.'

The young sorcerer steps forward. Lubatox is alarmed. No one likes having sorcery worked on them. He abruptly unties his tunic and throws it furiously on the floor then looks at us defiantly. 'Satisfied?' He has one small scar on his ribs, quite recent, and nothing on his back. He doesn't qualify as heavily scarred.

'Thank you for your cooperation.' I lead Makri and Anumaris from the room.

'General Osbus won't let his men be treated like this,' Lubatox calls after us.

Outside we head for our wagon. 'We can strike him off the list.'

'General Osbus will be down on you like a bad spell for this,' says Anumaris.

'We're following our Commander's orders. Not my fault if people get upset.'

We climb in the wagon and ride off. Once again the sun is beating down and it's as hot as Orcish Hell with not even a breath of wind. 'This is going to be a very poor day,' I mutter, as we head towards the next name on Anumaris's list.

Chapter Eighteen

It's early evening by the time we arrive back at the Palace. We ride into the grounds in silence. When I pull up in front of the stables, Makri finally speaks. 'That was one of the worst days I've ever had investigating.'

Anumaris shakes her head. 'I feel degraded. Everyone is so insulted when you ask them to take their tunics off. I don't want to do that again.'

'There are more names on the list.'

'Is there really no other way? It's insulting. They get so angry about it.'

'I'm fed up with being called an Orc bitch,' says Makri, sounding more depressed than angry.

It's true that most of the people we questioned today didn't take kindly to the proceedings. 'At least no one actually turned violent.'

We clamber out of the wagon. Anumaris sighs. 'Private Carox was absolutely furious. Long history of loyal service to the city. Fought in the last war and this one. I felt sorry for him.'

I hold up my hand to bring this to a halt. 'Yes, people were insulted. They always are when you investigate them. That's just the nature of investigating. Most cases I work on I'm as welcome as an Orc at an Elvish wedding. You just have to ignore it.'

'Poor choice of expression.' Makri sounds unhappy.

'Possibly. But you're only one quarter Orc and you'd probably be quite welcome at some Elvish weddings. I mean, you speak the language and you know all their poetry.'

'I'm a quarter Elf too. Why do people never focus on that? Every time someone gets annoyed it's Orc bitch or Orc whore. It gets me down.'

Inside the Palace I tell Anumaris she's off duty for the evening. 'I'll talk to Cicerius's assistant Hansius to check if there's anything else he can tell us about government officials. Makri, come with me.' We travel down the long corridor towards my office. It's empty. Quite bare too, apart from a wooden table and a few chairs. There's a small chest in which I could put case notes if I had any, which I don't. There is one new addition that Makri spots immediately.

'You have a safe?'

'Government issue. It has a combination number and a protection spell, courtesy of Anumaris. Wouldn't keep out an expert safe-cracker but it's enough to make it Droo-proof, anyway.'

'Why does it need to be Droo-proof?'

I speak the word to open the safe. 'Investigator Thraxas.' There's a click. I turn the dial, entering the numerical code and there's another click. I open the safe. 'That's why.' Inside the safe are my precious bottles of klee and ale. Four bottles of the Abbot's Special Distillation, one half full, and eight remaining bottles of the Grand Abbot's Dark Ale.

'How did you persuade Lisutaris to give you a safe?'

'Didn't come from Lisutaris. Came from her supplies manager after I reasonably pointed out that I need a secure place to keep vital evidence.' I take out the opened bottle of klee and pour some into two cheap metal goblets. I hand one to Makri then drink the other. She tells me she's going to visit Derigus, the young lieutenant who's been asking to see her. Were Droo here there would be a lot of comments about Makri going on a date. I don't make any comment myself though for some reason it makes me feel slightly sour. After she leaves I drink another goblet of klee and wonder if I should investigate anything or just doze off in my office chair. It's a decent Palace chair, better than the one I had in my office in Twelve Seas. The decision is taken out of my hands by the arrival of Hansius.

'The Consul and our War Leader need to see you right away.'

I haul myself out of my comfortable chair. 'What about?'

'They're in a meeting with Senator Lodius.' He looks at me meaningfully. I fail to catch his meaning.

'Why do they need me?'

'After the report in that news sheet Senator Lodius is demanding to know if the story about the gold is true and if it is, what are we doing about it?' Hansius is worried. I've encountered him fairly often in the past few years. He's competent, and honest as far as I know. Dedicated to helping the wheels of government run smoothly. Not really friendly towards me but not hostile either. 'It's important for Turai that the Ruling Council doesn't split apart.'

'I know.'

'Lodius has come close to accusing Cicerius of neglecting the poor to make sure the aristocracy survives. It would be helpful if you could reassure us that the gold will be recovered.'

'I know that too, but I'm not close to recovering it. Do you want me to lie?'

'I don't know. The situation is confusing. Do you know Senator Lodius?'

'I've come across him. I once prevented him evicting a large group of tenants down in Twelve Seas.'

Hansius's face falls. 'That can't have endeared you to him.'

'It didn't. But not long after that I cleared him of a murder charge. So you could say he owes me.'

'It would have been better for the city if he'd been hanged for murder.'

'He was innocent.'

'It would still have been better.'

That's more hostile than I'd have expected from Hansius, perhaps a reflection of the pressure the Council is under. Now the King is dead it will be an interesting time for politics in the city, unless we become a vassal state to Nioj or Simnia, something that could happen if we can't feed or defend ourselves. I'm sober and worried as I enter the state room where Cicerius, Lisutaris and Lodius are sitting round a table. This state room is undamaged, an opulent collection of elegant furniture with Elvish tapestries on the walls and expensive Samsarinan carpets on the floor, quite incongruous to anyone who's seen the state of the city outside the Palace walls. Hansius departs leaving me alone with Lisutaris, Cicerius and Lodius. Lisutaris speaks first. 'Captain Thraxas, I've been waiting for your report. I hope it's not going to be simply that enquiries are ongoing.'

As I don't really have any more to say than that, it puts me in a difficult spot. 'Enquiries *are* still ongoing, Commander, but I've made progress. Good progress, with information I can't divulge at the moment.' This doesn't go down well.

'Not satisfactory. Turai needs money quickly.' Lodius doesn't sound quite as hostile as I'd have expected; perhaps he is actually grateful I cleared him of that murder charge.

'Foreign merchants are already positioned at the harbour, waiting to buy all available supplies,' adds Lisutaris. 'Is there any chance of you finding the gold in the next thirty-six hours?'

'There's a chance. It's not certain.'

'That's not good enough!' Cicerius slaps his palm on the table, something I don't remember seeing him do before. He's tired and stressed. Cicerius is getting old and he was never a robust man. He collects himself. 'Do you need any assistance? Can we provide you with anything?'

'I don't think so, Consul. We're questioning everyone we need to question, and we've gathered evidence. It's not hopeless.'

Cicerius eyes me, not sure how upset he should be with me. Lodius asks why they've been receiving complaints from General Osbus.

'We upset some of his men during our investigation. Couldn't be helped.'

'According to the General you've been forcing law-abiding soldiers to remove their tunics. Why?'

'Part of the investigation. I can't tell you the exact reasons.'

Lodius leans forward. 'Normal civil rights may have been suspended for the duration of the war, Captain Thraxas, but that doesn't mean you can go around abusing Turanian citizens.'

There doesn't seem anything to say to this so I remain silent. Senator Lodius turns to his fellow Council members. 'I don't regard Captain Thraxas as the worst investigator in the city but there are others. With time being short, we should be using them.'

'I've already considered that,' says Cicerius, immediately. 'Paulius Grachus ran a very respectable agency on the outskirts of Thamlin that the Palace occasionally had reason to use. Unfortunately Grachus was killed in the invasion and I haven't been able to trace any of his employees.' From the regretful way he says this, Cicerius obviously doesn't regard me as respectable. It's no surprise. At least Lodius doesn't think I'm the worst investigator in the city.

'What about the Civil Guards? Some of them are back in Turai.'

'Not as many as we need for maintaining order. Praetor Samilius was wounded in the assault and his deputy is struggling to cope.'

Praetor Samilius is head of Turai's Civil Guard. I've had a few hostile encounters with him in the past. He's not particularly well suited to his post though he isn't the worst government appointee either.

'I'll ask his deputy if he can spare any men to investigate.'

I don't object to this. I wouldn't expect any of Turai's Civil Guards to come up with anything but there's always a chance they might. I can feel time pressing. 'Commander, I'd like to talk to you in private about a sorcerous matter.'

From the way Lisutaris agrees immediately and rises to her feet she's not much enjoying being in the meeting. Outside the office she shakes her head. 'I'm not cut out for government meetings.'

'It's your own fault for being a good War Leader.'

'When this is all over I'm going to rebuild my greenhouses and sit on my balcony smoking thazis till I pass out in a coma.'

'You'd smoked yourself into a coma the first time we met.'

Lisutaris smiles. 'When Horm the Dead attacked the city. That was quite an affair. I've been wondering what happened to Horm. Strange that he didn't seem to be with Prince Amrag's army. He was one of the strongest Orc sorcerers.'

'One of their strongest leaders too.'

'Deeziz wasn't impressed with his behaviour when we all met in Twelve Seas at the card game. Denounced him as disloyal to the Prince.'

Uncomfortable at the mention of Deeziz I move the conversation along. 'I'm suspicious of a sorcerer called Mabzus. He works with the Society of Friends in North Walls.'

Lisutaris frowns. 'Mabzus? There's no registered sorcerer of that name in Turai.'

'I met him and that's what he called himself.'

'Any sorcerer who enters Turai has to register with the Sorcerers Guild. Was he powerful?'

'Not sure, though I did get that impression.'

'What does he have to do with your investigation?'

'Maybe nothing, but it's possible he was with some Society of Friends men near the Palace at the time of the theft. I'd like to know exactly what Mabzus has been up to since we retook the city but it's difficult to exert much pressure on him when he's surrounded by his Society companions. I'll try again anyway.'

'I'll come with you.'

'You're offering to help me investigate?' I'm surprised by Lisutaris's enthusiasm. 'Didn't you say that would be bad for your status?'

'I've changed my mind. I need to get out of this damned Palace for a while.'

'All right. You'll scare them. Do you want to get changed first?'

Lisutaris looks at me, surprised. 'Changed? What do you mean?'

'Put on the leather tunic you wore when we stormed the city. We're visiting a den of thieves in North Walls, you never know who might pull a knife.'

The Head of the Sorcerers Guild scoffs at this. 'I just led the army back to Turai. I'm sure I'll be quite safe in a local tavern.'

'I expect you will be. But I'm your Head of Security, I have to be careful, especially with your bodyguard not around.'

'Where is Makri?'

'Visiting Lieutenant Derigus.'

In the stables we debate which wagon to take. Lisutaris has access to many vehicles. 'I don't want one of these fancy state carriages,' I tell her. 'Just draw attention to ourselves. But I don't want to carry you in my small open carriage either.' In the end we settle on a small phaeton with a covered seat for Lisutaris. I've no actual reason to worry about her safety but I do anyway. 'We'll be going past Thamlin. What's Tirini Snake Smiter doing?'

'Learning construction magic to rebuild her house, shouting at workmen for getting things wrong and sending desperate missives to nearby cities looking for beauticians and fashion designers seeking employment.' Lisutaris smiles at the thought of her friend. 'She's already a master of every known hairstyle spell but she needs the human touch to round things off. She has very high standards.'

'Sounds like she has plenty of time on her hands. We'll pick her up on the way to North Walls.'

Lisutaris regards me curiously. 'Still worried about me? We've faced plenty of danger together, Thraxas.'

'I know, but Makri would literally kill me if let anything happen to you.'

We pass out of the Palace grounds. There are larger crowds outside and a sense of mounting anger. The returning population is hungry, and worried about the future. It won't take much to make them riot. They're not that well behaved at the best of times. We make better time through the city though we're held up by a construction crew repairing a branch of the aqueduct that takes water to Thamlin. Lisutaris sticks her head out of the covering. 'We're making progress with reconstruction.'

'In Thamlin. Not in Twelve Seas.'

'We'll get to it as soon as we can, Thraxas.' Lisutaris waves to an officer with the construction crew. Surprised to see her, he salutes very smartly. We move on.

'So Makri is visiting Lieutenant Derigus?'

'That's what she said.'

'During the march back to Turai a surprising number of my junior officers felt a sudden need to confer with her about sword-fighting techniques.'

'She is an excellent swordswoman.'

'I know. She's also a considerable beauty, even if my junior officers didn't want to come right out and admit that, with her Orcish blood.' Lisutaris leans forward so she's almost level with me. 'Does it bother you she's visiting the young lieutenant?'

'No. Why would it?'

'I always assumed you had strong feelings for Makri, no matter how unsuitable a match that would have been. You were never out of each other's company. But then you got together with Sareepa. Quite a suitable match, as it turned out. Then Sareepa was killed.'

By now I'm sitting rigidly upright. I don't like any part of this conversation and curse under my breath at the clearance crew currently blocking the road as they haul away the remnants of a collapsed wall blocking access to Tirini Snake Smiter's villa.

'Makri suggests you're traumatised by Sareepa's death but don't want to acknowledge it.'

'Makri is talking nonsense.'

'That's exactly what you'd say if you didn't want to acknowledge it.'

'I'm not the only one who lost someone in the war.'

Our War Leader might have more to say on the subject. Fortunately we round the corner and catch sight of Tirini in her desolate front garden, pointing at her house and shouting at it. As we approach she's scowling.

'Tirini, why are you shouting at your house?'

'I'm trying to repair the front balcony, without success. Have you ever tried construction sorcery?'

'No. They didn't teach it at college.'

'I know! It turns out that was a mistake. If I can't make these repairs myself I'll have to wait on workmen to arrive and God knows how long that will take. They insist on repairing aqueducts and sewers first, it's very inconsiderate to the residents here.'

Tirini is dressed in an indoor version of her usual finery, a robe and long jacket of yellow silk, a necklace of pale blue queenstone, and pink shoes with some sort of wedged heel design that I'm unable to put a name to. She barely acknowledges me as she asks Lisutaris why she's here.

'We're going to North Walls to question criminals. Captain Thraxas is concerned for my safety and suggests you accompany us.'

'Why not?' cries Tirini, crossly. 'I've already been reduced to the role of common workman. May as well fraternise with criminals in a cheap tavern. She glares at me. 'I presume we are going to a cheap tavern?'

'One of the cheapest.'

Tirini climbs into the wagon with difficulty, her shoes and robe not really being suitable. I don't bother to ask her if she'd like to change outfits before accompanying us, knowing she'd refuse. While the other sorcerers in the assault squadron all wore protective clothing, Tirini scorned the idea, declaring that she hadn't fought her way back to the city just to let people see her in army boots and an unflattering tunic. We set off. Tirini and Lisutaris settle down in the back of the phaeton. I'm lost in some gloomy thoughts and don't listen to most of their conversation though a few sentences do penetrate. 'You simply can't imagine life in Thamlin at the moment, Lisu! Nothing is available! Not a hairstylist, not a beautician, not a seamstress — absolutely nothing. Even dear Emilian's parlour is closed, sacked and looted during the occupation, though what the Orcs wanted with his make-up supplies is beyond me. Honestly, had I not had my own supply buried in a vault beneath my cellar, I would simply despair.'

'You had make-up buried in your cellar?'

'Of course. And a few outfits, just in case. Turai has always been in danger of invasion, you know that. It was as well to be prepared. Do you like these shoes? I've had them in reserve for some years now, keeping them safe for just such an emergency.'

No one listening to Tirini's frivolous conversation would guess at the amount of sorcerous power she possesses. It took me a long time appreciate it. And bravery too, I suppose. Throughout the war she was never absent from Lisutaris's side when asked to be there. No one would guess her origins either. If Lisutaris differs from other Turanian sorcerers in being from a higher social strata than most, Tirini Snake Smiter is the opposite. She comes from a very humble background, something she keeps well hidden and I only learned accidentally in the course of an investigation.

We pick our way through the streets to the north of the city. 'Here we are. Benevolence Lane.' Construction work is continuing at the Hero of Turai, Darisax's tavern.

'As awful as I imagined,' mutters Tirini as we leave the wagon.

'Let me do the talking. You can look powerful and menacing.'

Tirini raises her eyebrows. '*Menacing* is not a look I aspire to.'

Lisutaris takes her arm. 'Just pretend someone's trodden on your shoes.'

We enter the tavern. It's dark, gloomy and no less hot than the street outside. There are puzzled looks as we step through the door. Not so much at me as at the two richly dressed women at my side. Not everyone served in the army and some don't recognise Lisutaris as our War Leader. The tavern is much the same as on my last visit. Fifteen or so Society of Friends men, one or two women, none of them that cheerful. Even for our criminals, the good times haven't yet returned. From outside comes the monotonous banging and hammering as the roof is repaired. Darisax and Mabzus are sitting at a table at the far end of the tavern. We head straight towards them. The Society of Friends men are uncertain whether to obstruct us or not. They might not recognise Lisutaris but the rainbow motif is clearly visible on her cloak and it rarely pays to get in the way of a sorcerer. Darisax clearly does recognise Lisutaris and rises to his feet uncomfortably. 'Commander Lisutaris…'

'We need to talk to you in private. Right away.'

Darisax glances at Mabzus. He might be hoping Mabzus is powerful enough to oppose Lisutaris. That would be amusing. Mabzus is too wise to make any such attempt. There's a brief, awkward silence before the Society of Friends boss shrugs his shoulders and leads us into his private room at the back of the tavern. Inside it's dark. Darisax fumbles to light a lamp before Lisutaris snaps her fingers, illuminating the room. Darisax has a chair and a large desk and not much else. I'm disappointed.

'Not got round to redecorating?'

'The Orcs took everything worth taking. Business hasn't really started up yet.'

'I expect it will soon.'

Lisutaris regards Mabzus. 'I'm told you're a sorcerer. Why haven't you registered your presence in Turai with the Sorcerers Guild?'

'I didn't think they were back in operation yet. As soon as the Guild office opens again I'll report to them.' Mabzus addresses Lisutaris respectfully. He doesn't want to offend her.

'Make sure you do. Now, Captain Thraxas has some questions for you both and I'd appreciate swift and honest answers.'

Darisax scowls at me. Despite his lack of stature he's still quite an imposing figure, having a lot of bulk. He looks strong. Not that that's any good when faced with a sorcerer as powerful as Lisutaris.

'You said you didn't go near the Palace. That was a lie.'

'Was it?'

'Yes. The brooch we found belongs to you. A Palace sorcerer found your aura all over it.' This is a lie but it could have happened. 'Also, you were spotted. There's a guard who recognised you from your days along the coast. He saw you entering the grounds the day after we took the city. Or re-entering perhaps.'

'None of that's true, fat man. No sorcerer at the Palace would recognise my aura. I've never had any contact with them. The brooch you found could have come from anywhere. And the day after the invasion was chaos. There were troops all over the city. You're trying to make me believe some random soldier recognised me at the Palace gates? You're making it all up.'

I'm only making some of it up and I hoped it would go better than it has. Darisax apparently isn't a man to panic in a crisis, even when faced with the array of authority confronting him here.

'I've got a reliable witness and that's enough to take you into custody for further questioning.'

'Not until I've talked to my lawyer it isn't. You don't get to come here and bully people, investigator, no matter who you've got with you. I have legal rights.'

'Standard legal rights have been suspended for the duration of the war.' I'm fed up saying this. It goes against the grain to be informing Turanian citizens that their civil rights are currently suspended. I'm meant to be on their side. Before I can ask any more questions, Tirini interrupts us.

'I'm bored. Is this how you spend your time? Asking pointless questions to people who don't want to talk to you?'

I ignore the interruption. 'Do either of you have scars on your torsos?'

'What the hell does that have to do with you?' Darisax reacts angrily.

'Just answer my question. Both of you — any scars?'

'This interview is over. I don't need to talk to you.'

'Answer Captain Thraxas's question,' says Lisutaris.

'We have no scars and it's none of your business anyway.'

'I need to see your torsos.' I tell them. Mabzus is looking uncomfortable, less willing than his boss to confront authority.

'No.' Darisax folds his arms across his chest.

Tirini sighs. 'This is even more tedious than I anticipated. I really must get back to repairing my villa.' With that, she mutters a few indecipherable words and raises her arm. Darisax and Mabzus's tunics vanish from their torsos before re-appearing instantly on the table behind them. Both neatly folded, I notice. It's an impressive display of Tirini's clothes magic. I doubt anyone else could have done it. The Society of Friends boss and his sorcerer open their mouths to protest but don't get the chance to speak as Tirini motions with her hand, causing them to levitate a few inches and rotate in the air.

'No discernible scarring,' says Tirini. 'Can we go now?'

'I have more questions.'

'Is there no end to this? I can't spend all day here. Answer Thraxas's questions or I'll change the air in your lungs to fire.'

I glance at Lisutaris. This is all very illegal. You can't threaten Turanian citizens with torture. However, Lisutaris is a much higher authority than me and she's not doing anything to prevent it.

'Why were you at the Palace?'

Darisax keeps his mouth shut. Even the threat of his body being set on fire won't make him talk. I sort of admire him for that. I can see why he became a Society of Friends boss.

'Mabzus, you're far from home. If you die here no one's going to miss you and no one's going to ask questions about it. So tell me everything you know.'

Mabzus is smart enough to be worried about the sorcery he's facing. 'Fine. We were after the gold in the Palace.'

That's more than I was expecting. I hide my surprise. 'Go on.'

'The day after we entered the city a messenger brought us a key. The note that came with it said it was the key to a vault in the

Palace and the vault wasn't guarded. If we got there quickly we could empty it out. All it needed was the key and a particular spell. There was someone at the Palace we could pay to learn the spell. We had to move quickly so we went down there in a wagon before dawn.'

'Who were you to meet at the Palace?'

'I don't know. All we knew was we were to meet him at the East Door at five in the morning. We didn't get that far. When we entered the grounds we were attacked.'

'Attacked? Who by?'

'We don't know. A sorcerer. Too powerful for me. We were frozen out and ended up unconscious on the grass. We woke up a few hours later. The key was gone. It was daylight and people were looking at us so we left. That's all I know.'

I turn to Darisax. 'Anything to add?'

'I've nothing to say.'

I question Mabzus some more but he doesn't seem to know any more details. He doesn't know who sent them the key and he doesn't know the identity of the person they were to meet at the Palace. I think he's telling the truth. He'd rather upset Darisax than Lisutaris and Tirini. I tell my companions it's time to go.

'We still don't know where the gold is,' protests Lisutaris.

'We're not learning anything else here.'

Tirini is still complaining as we leave the tavern. 'This has been the most tiresome day! Why anyone would want to investigate for a living is quite beyond me. Though I must say it is rather less dangerous than Captain Thraxas made it out to be.'

'Yes, it's an easy life,' I grunt back in reply. 'Commander, I'm going to need sorcerous power for the next step.'

'For what?'

'For examining locations. Mabzus gave us a lot of information. I need to check out the East Gate of the Palace and the grounds between there and the East Door. Then we need to check out the wagon Mabzus travelled in. He said they left that in the Palace grounds, someone must know what happened to it. We might learn a lot from sorcerous examination.'

'You mean looking back in time? That hasn't been easy recently. The three moons are very poorly aligned. I already tried to look back to the theft of the gold with no success.' Lisutaris shakes her head. 'So blank was the past I wondered if some powerful sorcerer had interfered with any examination.'

'That would make sense, Commander. Mabzus did say their attempt to get the gold was ended by a powerful sorcerer.'

Lisutaris doesn't like it that there might be a powerful sorcerer on the loose in the city without her knowing. Neither do I, and I'm hoping the powerful sorcerer in question wasn't Deeziz. According to her own story she was far too badly injured to be attacking anyone at the Palace. I still believe her but it's a concern anyway.

'Even if the past is hidden there are other things to learn. Auras, for instance. Or any fragment of material left behind that matches up to a fragment now carried by another person in the city. You can learn a lot from very little. I'll have to wait till daylight but as early as possible we should examine the area where Mabzus says he was attacked.'

'It might be helpful,' agrees Lisutaris. 'But I can't help you. I'm meeting the commanders and ambassadors from Nioj, Samsarina and Simnia at dawn and I can't fail to turn up in case they decide to parcel out Turai for themselves.'

'Is that a possibility?'

'Yes. We've been hinting to Nioj that it's time for them to leave but they're not taking the hint. We're so weak, it's a worry.'

'Anumaris can help me.'

Lisutaris shakes her head. 'Anumaris isn't experienced enough to garner every piece of information from a crime scene. Few people are. Tirini, would you—'

'Most definitely not.'

'Tirini, Turai needs you to help.'

'My balcony needs to be repaired and I haven't even started on sorting out my winter coats. Do you realise what the Orcs did to my wardrobe? I'm sorry, Lisu, I was willing to protect you from danger but I draw the line at scrabbling around in the dirt helping Captain Thraxas investigate a crime scene.'

Lisutaris looks Tirini in the eye. 'We need your help.'

Tirini folds her arms in front of her. 'Are you actually pulling rank on me, Lisutaris, Mistress of the Sky?'

'No. I'm appealing to your better nature as your oldest friend, companion, confidante and fellow Turanian sorcerer.'

Tirini Snake Smiter scowls. 'Fine! I'll do it. You have successfully morally blackmailed me. But my reputation may

139

never recover. If Rosewater Satinius hears I've been investigating like a common Civil Guard I'll never hear the end of it. She'll have it spread round her dining club before the moons rise.'

Lisutaris laughs. 'We all have to make sacrifices, Tirini. We need to find that gold. Meet Captain Thraxas at the east gate at dawn.'

Chapter Nineteen

Early next morning my Security Unit gathers in my office. Anumaris and Droo are here though there's no sign of Makri.

'I expect she's still with Derigus,' suggests Droo, quite enthusiastically. 'Probably spent the night with him.'

'She did not.' Anumaris corrects her. 'I know because I heard her stumbling into her room early this morning.'

'Stumbling?'

'Must have been drunk,' says Droo, again quite enthusiastically.

'How would she manage that?'

'Maybe there's still some Elvish wine in the Palace.'

We head outside. As the sun appears over the horizon it's already warm though not yet intolerably hot. To my surprise, Tirini Snake Smiter is waiting for us. I was half-expecting her not to turn up, despite encouragement from Lisutaris. She's sitting on an undamaged bench that's shaded from the sunlight by one of the few surviving trees.

'Tell me when you need help that doesn't involve scrabbling round in the dirt.'

We haven't been scrabbling around in the dirt for long before Makri appears.

'Hi Makri,' shouts Droo. 'Did you have a nice time with Derigus? I heard you stumbled in drunk.'

'I did have a little Elvish wine,' admits Makri.

'I thought the Council drank it all?'

'He'd managed to keep a bottle in reserve. Last one, he said.'

'We have work to do,' I inform everyone. 'So stop talking about Elvish wine and get busy.'

'What are we doing here?' asks Makri.

'Next stage of the investigation, examining a related crime scene. All torsos have been examined with no results except a flurry of complaints about my behaviour. However we have learned that someone tipped the Society of Friends off as to the secret vault. A Society boss and sorcerer went to retrieve it but were interrupted in the Palace grounds by an even more powerful sorcerer who knocked them out, stole the key and presumably made off with the gold.'

141

Makri looks alarmed at the mention of a powerful sorcerer, thinking no doubt of Deeziz.

'We're now examining the patch of ground where it happened. If we find anything that seems out of place, Tirini will help us with aura examination and any other sorcery she can think of.'

'I could do that,' says Anumaris.

'As well as Tirini Snake Smiter?'

'No,' she admits. 'Not as well. Who is this powerful sorcerer we're looking for?'

'We don't know. I've been wondering about Glixius Dragon Killer again. He hasn't been a major suspect since we eliminated Casax for not having scars but Casax might have sent another Brotherhood man with Glixius to pick up the gold, someone we don't know about. Though I wouldn't really expect Casax to trust anyone else when there was so much gold involved.' I realise I'm not sounding very convincing about anything.

'We have about twenty-four hours to find the gold or we can't buy food for the city.' Anumaris grimaces. 'It seems hopeless.'

The sun is climbing in the sky. It'll be hot as Orcish Hell soon enough. It doesn't take long before the sweat is pouring off me as I crawl around looking for clues. Even the nimble Droo and the athletic Makri feel the strain. We're attempting to do a fingertip search of the Palace grounds between the east gate and the east door and it's a long stretch of ground. Tirini Snake Smiter stays out of the sun and offers no help in searching, though the first time we take her an item we've found she does produce an impressive response. Droo hands her a small knife that was hidden under a bush. We stand around Tirini eagerly while she remains seated. She mutters a spell I've never heard before. The knife is momentarily enveloped in a purple cloud. Tirini studies it for about twenty seconds.

'Simnian knife, forged six years ago, carried here by a soldier, never been used to stab anyone, never been inside the Palace, never been close to strong sorcery. Probably dropped by accident.'

The purple cloud dissipates along with our hopes. The knife isn't connected to the crime. It's an impressive display of discovery sorcery but it hasn't helped us.

'Can I keep the knife?' asks Droo.

'Yes. Now everyone back to work.'

Minutes later I'm again on my hands and knees, sweat running into my eyes, mentally cursing the poor alignment of the moons that's rendering sorcerous inquiries into the past increasingly difficult. Even the best practitioners aren't certain when things will improve. I rise wearily to my feet just as Anumaris exclaims that she's found something close to the Palace door.

'A silver ten-guran piece, trodden into the dirt.' She hurries over to Tirini. Tirini, by now dozing off, wakes and looks at the coin with a bored expression. 'This really is the most tedious of days. I will regard Lisutaris as greatly in my debt when it's finally over.' Tirini intones her spell again and the coin becomes indistinct as a small purple cloud envelops it. She stares at it till the cloud fades away. 'Multiple owners. Last handled by a Samsarinan officer. Dropped accidentally. Trodden on by several people as troops swept through the grounds. No hint of sorcery and never handled by a Turanian citizen till Anumaris picked it up.'

Again it's an impressive piece of sorcery and again it gets us nowhere. Droo flops down on the glass. 'I'm roasting to death. Is Turai always this hot?'

'No. Sometimes it's freezing and sometimes it rains so hard the streets are underwater. It's a terrible location for a city. Whoever built it here was an idiot.' I look around at the parched grounds. 'This doesn't seem to be getting us anywhere.'

Anumaris is filthy from assiduously searching the soil and withered grass. 'There are general spells for locating all items that don't belong in an area.'

'Can you do that?'

Anumaris shakes her head. 'No. I haven't advanced that far. Perhaps Tirini…'

All heads turn towards the elegantly clad and not-at-all-exhausted Tirini Shake Smiter.

'Do you have some sort of general searching spell that might help?'

'A spell like that contains very many variables, comparing the locations of many items at many different times. It takes a lot of power.'

'But can you do it?'

Tirini purses her lips. 'Expending so much power does not come without a cost. It takes time to recharge oneself. I have urgent home repairs to perform and many clothes to rescue.'

'It would be very helpful,' says Anumaris, respectfully but firmly. 'I'm sure our Commander would approve.'

'My dearest Lisutaris would never interfere with my garment sorcery.' She glances at the sky and scowls. 'I would like to get out of this damnable sun. She rises to her feet. 'Everyone stand behind me where I can't see you. And keep quiet.'

We do as instructed. Tirini stands very still, examining the scene in front of her. Finally she raises both her hands to shoulder level and intones a spell, much longer than those she's previously used. As she speaks, tiny beams of purple light flicker around her fingers. For what seems like a long period, nothing happens and then, magically, twenty or so purple beams of light shoot up from the grounds in front of us. Tirini sits down heavily. 'Gather them in before the light fades.'

I glance at her for a moment. Her eyes have gone completely purple and are slowly returning to normal, She looks drained though she retains her composure. Having no time to waste I set off with Makri, Anumaris and Droo to gather in whatever hidden items Tirini's spell has uncovered, each of which will be something recently brought to the area. I appreciate Tirini's work and don't resent her sitting back in the shade to rest.

Chapter Twenty

Not long afterwards we're walking back into the Palace on our way to my office. We have twenty-two items to examine. Though none of them are obviously clues they're all worth investigating. Lisutaris is waiting in my office.

'Captain Thraxas, I hope you have good news because I haven't.'

'Bad meeting?'

'Terrible. The Niojan ambassador is a vile excuse for a human being and if he does bring us to war I'll make sure to kill him before his legions trample over us. What are you carrying?'

'Pieces of thread, scraps of paper, one blade, a fork, a sandal and various other small items located between the east gate and the east door by Tirini's general finding spell.'

Lisutaris raises her eyebrows, impressed. 'Really? Tirini, you're a marvel, that's not an easy spell to control.'

'I have quite exhausted myself! One's exertions were something to behold. But anything for the city, of course.'

'I'll be sure to inform the Council of your excellent work. You should go home and rest now.'

Anumaris, Droo, Makri and I are filthy from crawling around the gardens though it doesn't seem to register with Lisutaris that we've been busy too. 'We were hoping Tirini could help us examine the items.'

'We can't work poor Tirini to death. Others must share the burden. I'll take care of the examination.' Lisutaris summons a guard from the end of the corridor. 'Sergeant, escort Tirini Snake Smiter to the stables and have her driven home in a landus. Ensure her journey is comfortable, she's been under a great deal of strain.'

The sergeant salutes smartly then escorts the sorcerer along the corridor. Lisutaris follows me into my office and tells us to lay out the items on a table for examination. She takes a small stick of thazis from inside her cloak and lights it with a snap of her fingers. 'Nothing here stands out as obviously significant. Perhaps something will surprise us.' The Head of the Sorcerers Guild picks up the sandal. Without her making any apparent effort or even uttering a word, a faint purple cloud envelops the item. 'Orcish sandal. Owner now dead. No connection to the gold.' She picks up the fork. 'Standard Simnian army issue, dropped by a soldier during the fighting. It has been in the Palace...' She pauses. 'However no connection to the gold or any crime.' Lisutaris moves on to examining several pieces of thread and scraps of cloth. Her examination seems to take almost no effort. When she's about half way through the items she pauses and frowns. 'Nothing at all so far. If this is another dead end, we're in trouble. We need money by tomorrow.'

'Does the Council have a plan for us not having it?'

'Not really. The city will go hungry, people will riot and we'll have to beg for food from our allies. That will probably be the first step in losing our independence.'

'Maybe you should just requisition the grain. Take it from the ships.'

'That would probably lead to war.'

'Better to go down fighting than begging.'

'It could come to that. Cicerius and Lodius detest each other but neither of them are willing to give up Turai's independence.'

'Could you defend the city? You're the most powerful sorcerer in the West.'

'I might hold them off for a short while but Nioj, Simnia and Samsarina have their own Sorcerers Guilds. Turai's guild is now so weak there's hardly anyone to support me.'

Anumaris rises to her feet. 'I'll be there to support you, Commander.'

'I appreciate it, Anumaris. So would Tirini and Dearineth and Harmon. And so would Thraxas and Makri all the other Turanian soldiers who helped retake the city. But there's not enough of us to fight three nations and I'd rather not get you all killed.' She shakes her head. 'Let's carry on.'

Lisutaris quickly checks several scraps of paper, finding them to be meaningless, before pausing over a fragment of red ribbon. 'Belonged to a prostitute,' she says. 'Not been inside the Palace, but did dally with Senator Klezius between the bushes and the Palace wall.' She shakes her head. 'If Senator Klezius really needed to cheat on his wife only a day after re-entering the city, you'd have thought he could have found somewhere better.' She smiles. 'Strong ally of the Traditionals. Cicerius would be horrified. I probably won't tell him, it would ruin his mood.'

'Ruin his mood? Isn't it bad enough already?'

146

'Not as bad as you'd imagine. He just authorised a medal for his son Cerius following a report on his bravery from his commanding officer.'

'Ah. That would please him.' The Acting Consul's son had been sheltering in semi-disgrace following a sordid scandal a few years ago involving Turai's degenerate Princes, Turai's criminal underclass and Horm the Dead, Half-Orcish sorcerer. They were all implicated in importing drugs into the city and Cerius would have ended up in jail without my investigation. He won't be the only man who's managed to resurrect his reputation in the war. Lisutaris carries on, finding nothing interesting in the next few items. I'm now fidgeting with worry. If nothing comes of this investigation we're nowhere with not much time left to do anything. Makri looks on impassively. Droo has fallen asleep in a chair. Lisutaris picks up the hilt of a broken knife. 'This is curious. Makri, is this Orcish?'

Makri shakes her head. 'I'm not sure. I've never seen that design before.'

'Nor have I.' Lisutaris concentrates. The handle is enveloped by a darker purple cloud. 'This has a very odd aura. It's been inside the Palace. It was used in anger recently. Could just be a war relic but I can sense something Orcish about it. Something Orcish and sorcerous.'

We watch in silence as Lisutaris extends more power. Something is troubling her. The purple cloud enveloping the knife handle grows darker till it's almost black. Lisutaris stares into it, concentrating fully. A tinge of purple appears in her eyes. After some moments she shakes her head and lays down the item. Her eyes clear. 'I can't interpret this and I don't like it. This knife hilt has Orcish connections and I'd say it's been used by an Orcish sorcerer recently except I can't trace it to anyone. I should be able to connect it to its owner but I can't.'

'Maybe the owner is dead?'

'I don't think so. It feels more like the owner is hiding.'

'An Orcish sorcerer hiding in the city? That's impossible.'

'I know.' Lisutaris scowls. 'I'd detect them right away. This is troubling.'

I glance at Makri. The colour has drained from her cheeks and I can tell she's close to confessing everything about Deeziz the Unseen. Anumaris wonders if the Orcish sorcerer might be too far away for Lisutaris to detect. 'He'd have fled when we took the city back. He might be far over the Wastelands by now.'

Lisutaris purses her lips. 'I should have been able to detect some trace of him leaving the city.' The sorcerer turns to me. 'Thraxas, I don't know what this means and I don't like it. Could some Orcish presence still be in the city?'

'Highly unlikely, Commander. They wouldn't be able to hide from you. Besides, why would they be here?'

'I don't know. To steal the gold, perhaps?' She frowns deeply. 'None of this makes sense. I'll need to examine–' She's interrupted by the arrival of Captain Julius. 'Trouble, Commander. A crowd is gathering outside the Gates and I'm not sure we have the manpower to protect the Palace.'

'A crowd?'

'More an angry mob, honestly. The Chronicle printed another story about the missing gold. It suggests widespread corruption inside the Palace. Blames almost everyone, yourself excepted.'

'This is intolerable!' cries Lisutaris. 'Who publishes this nonsense? Don't they realise the harm they're doing to Turai?'

'It gets worse, Commander. They published a schedule for the sale of grain informing everyone that provisional contracts are already in place for the transfer of incoming supplies to Nioj and Simnia. They claim Turai is bankrupt and we're all going to starve.'

'Well at least that part's accurate,' I say. 'Can't fault their reporting.'

'There's more bad news, Commander.'

'Of course. What is it?'

'Senator Lodius is demanding an immediate inquiry into Palace corruption and is threatening to withdraw from the Council. Cicerius accused him of planning a civil war. There was a terrible argument before Lodius stormed off to talk to his supporters. Many of whom are outside the Palace gate at this moment, as it happens.'

Lisutaris eyes her young assistant bleakly. 'Is there anything else?'

'The Niojan ambassador hinted that Nioj might be willing to pay for food for Turai in return for perpetual free access to our harbour and the position of Harbour Sorcerer being awarded to a Niojan. There were a few other conditions…'

Lisutaris slams the broken knife hilt down on my desk. 'The city is falling apart. Thraxas, I don't know what this hilt means and I don't have time to pursue it. See what you can do. Anumaris, come with me.' With that our War Leader strides from the room followed by Anumaris and Julius. Makri and I are silent for while. Droo continues to slumber in her chair.

'To sum up,' says Makri eventually, using a phrase she picked up from her professors at the Community College. 'Only days after we recaptured Turai, the city is about to fall either to starvation, civil war or foreign conquest. Meanwhile we're on a fool's errand hunting for gold on the advice of the most powerful Orcish sorcerer, an implacable enemy of Turai, currently concealed in a safe house in Kushni, who we somehow agreed to cooperate with despite me warning your that it was a really bad idea, a warning that is now coming true. Lisutaris will find out soon enough that this knife belonged to Deeziz and we've been helping her. My own prospects are either execution for treason or death protecting Lisutaris from the maddened citizens.'

'You know Makri, you've become much more eloquent recently. It speaks highly of the Community College.'

'Why did we ever believe Deeziz? She's obviously been mocking us, sending us on a wild-dragon chase for people with scars. Meanwhile she's been wandering around the Palace stabbing people. She's probably half way to Kose or Gzak by now with a magic pocket full of gold, looking forward to telling her Orcish friends how she tricked us.'

'Calm down Makri, no need to get carried away. We saw how badly injured she was. She couldn't have been wandering around stabbing people. I don't think this knife belonged to her.'

'Then whose was it? Another undetectable Orcish sorcerer? How many of them are?' Makri sits down heavily. 'It's the end. We're defeated. I'm never going to the University. The only question is whether I'll be exposed as a traitor in time for them to throw me off the walls before the city falls.'

'Makri, for the sake of St Quatinius, stop this nonsense.'

'It's not nonsense. We've been tricked, we're doomed and I don't believe in your western saints anyway.'

'The situation is not as bad as you're making out. This knife hilt has opened up a lot of new possibilities for investigation.'

'What possibilities?'

'I don't know. I need to think.'

'Think? You need to think? There's an angry mob outside the Palace gates. Foreign ambassadors are running rings round Cicerius, and Lodius is about to start a civil war. Meanwhile the city is full of Orcish sorcerers stealing our gold. I'd say time for thinking is limited.'

I feel myself becoming angry. 'Things look bad but I've been in tough spots before. I'm not giving up so easily.'

'You know what I hate the most?' Makri rises to her feet. 'The scarred torso business. How could we fall for that? We wasted our time checking for scars on a bunch of petty criminals for no reason. It was preposterous. We should never have believed Deeziz, she was obviously making fools of us.' Makri glares at me. 'I blame you. I'm going to denounce you from the scaffold.'

'What scaffold?'

'The scaffold they hang me from before they throw me from the walls.'

'Your execution is sounding worse all the time.'

'I'm expecting it to be grisly. I'm going to my room. Let me know if you think of something useful. I'll be reading Elvish literature and despairing that I'll never got to study it at the University.'

Makri departs. I take a bottle of beer from my safe, drink it while sitting in my chair then I fall asleep.

Chapter Twenty-One

When I awaken it's late in the evening. It's dark, though not too dark to recognise the Orcish sorcerer sitting in the chair previously occupied by Ensign Droo. I leap to my feet.

'Deeziz! What are you doing here? What did you do with Droo?' A terrible suspicion grips me. 'Have you been imitating Droo? Were you her all along?' By now I'm fumbling for my sword.

Deeziz looks puzzled. 'Droo? You mean the young Elf? Why would I imitate her?'

'Because you like going round disguised as other people.'

'Not Elves. I find them distasteful. And arrogant. Have you noticed how arrogant Elves are? As if they have the only worthwhile civilisation in the world. They really over-estimate their worth. And their poetry is greatly over-rated.'

'I've often thought that myself. Even if — wait, stop talking about Elvish poetry! What are you doing here?'

'I came to see how your investigation was proceeding.'

I'm now eyeing her very suspiciously and my hand is on my sword pommel. 'How did you get here?'

'I rode up in a wagon, disguised as a soldier. Quite an easy aspect to take on, I find no one studies soldiers too closely in war time, there are so many of them.'

'Why haven't you left Turai? You should be back in Orcland by now.'

'Orcland? There's no such place.'

'I mean whichever Orcish nation you come from. On your favourite mountaintop. That was the agreement.'

'An agreement I intend to keep. I still appreciate that you brought me the necessary herbs for healing. The process is slower than I anticipated. I'm not yet back to full strength. I need to wait a day or two before traversing the Wastelands.'

I don't know what Deeziz is doing here and I don't like being alone with such a powerful enemy sorcerer, no matter how well-intentioned she claims to be. Not liking the darkness I light the oil lamp. Deeziz is certainly looking a lot healthier. She's brushed her long dark hair, she's calm rather than in pain, and she's wrapped herself in quite an expensive-looking blue cloak. She's wearing a pair of women's boots, practical but quite fancy, the sort of thing a rich Turanian woman might wear outdoors.

'How is your investigation proceeding?'

'Badly. No sign of the gold and we're almost out of time. There have been suggestions I wasted a lot of time on a fool's errand to find a man with a scarred torso.'

She raises her eyebrows. 'That was not a fool's errand. Why would it be?'

'Because while you were pretending to be injured you were really creeping around the city stabbing people.'

'That makes no sense.'

'Possibly not. But how else would you explain this?' I pick up the broken knife hilt and brandish it.

'Part of a knife?'

'Part of a knife that's been inside the palace, has recently stabbed someone and is connected to powerful Orcish sorcery which now can't be traced. No one but you could have hidden its origins from Lisutaris.'

The Orcish sorcerer frowns. 'Let me see it.'

'And have you destroy evidence? I don't think so.'

Deeziz regards me curiously. 'I've observed you before, investigating, quite efficiently. Slowly, admittedly, but you did seem to follow a logical pattern. Now you seem to be acting irrationally. Why is that?'

Not willing to admit I'm acting irrationally, I decline to answer. Deeziz stares at me. She has dark, penetrating eyes. I don't like it. It reminds me of Lisutaris on a bad day. 'Is it simply stress from the predicament Turai is in? I have observed angry crowds.'

'That isn't helping.'

She leans forward. 'It's not just the effects of the war. You've seen too much war for it to seriously disrupt your mind.' She studies my face. 'I perceive you lost someone dear to you.'

Her words strike me like a blow. For a second I get the urge to shout at her and deny it. The feeling disappears almost instantly, apparently taking my own strength with it. I slump into my chair and say nothing. Deeziz nods her head sympathetically. 'Do you want to tell me about it?'

Which is how I end up telling my problems to an enemy Orcish sorcerer after having been completely unable to speak about it with Makri, Lisutaris or even Gurd.

152

'On the march back to the city I started seeing Sareepa, a Matteshan sorcerer. Walking out, you might call it. I wasn't expecting it to happen. It was the first relationship I've had for a long time. I didn't expect that we'd become so close, but we did. I didn't realise how much I'd miss her either. She was killed at the walls. It's left me numb inside. I can't really describe how bad I feel.' My head is resting on my hands and I feel as close to shedding tears as I have for a very long time.

'I'm sorry to hear it. If you were to hold me responsible I would understand. You may be interested — or pleased — to hear that I lost everyone I was close to in the war.'

'You did?'

'Yes. Three people. A leader I respected. My oldest friend whom I'd known since childhood. And my lover of many years. All dead. Sitting in the house in Kushni, I realised how alone I now was in the world.'

'Didn't you used to spend all your time alone on a mountaintop?'

'I exaggerated that. Really I had visitors.' Deeziz sighs. 'The war was foolish and unnecessary. I told Prince Amrag that, though when he led the Orcish nations I did assist him to the fullest extent of my powers.' She's silent for a few moments. 'Sareepa Lighting Strikes the Mountain. I never encountered her. She had a very good reputation.'

'Head of her Guild. Mostly responsible for the dragon shield. I don't know what she saw in me.'

'I sometimes thought the same about my lover. These things are often inexplicable. Was Sareepa happier from her time with you?'

'I think so.'

'Then the reason for the attraction doesn't matter. You would have been a great comfort to her in difficult times.'

We fall silent. I feel a little better for having finally told someone how sad I feel about the death of Sareepa. Deeziz takes the knife hilt from my desk to examine it. I don't make any effort to stop her. My eyes turn towards the safe in the corner. Probably I should be drinking beer by now. I cross over to my small safe, enter the correct combination and mutter Anumaris's opening spell, not caring that Deeziz can hear me. If she wanted to rob my safe a simple spell wouldn't stop her. I take out a bottle of the Grand Abbot's Dark Ale. I take two metal tankards from a shelf, neither of them quite clean, and fill them both before placing one in front of Deeziz. She's studying the knife hilt intently. She must be using a different form of sorcery than Tirini and Lisutaris as no purple cloud appears, though the temperature in the room does quickly drop a degree or two.

'This item has been used in anger recently. It has also been enveloped in sorcery. Sorcery from the East.'

'You mean Orcish?'

'Yes. Whoever was responsible has cloaked themselves in powerful spells of hiding.' Deeziz looks puzzled. 'Spells I would not have expected anyone to master, except for me.'

'That's why you're a suspect.'

'I should not be.'

'You are. Do you know any other Orcish sorcerers who could be responsible?'

'There are several powerful practitioners. Gezineka from Kose. Misadras of Grykur. I'm sure I'd know if they remained in Turai. So would Lisutaris.'

'Maybe one of them found another safe house.'

'Why would they stay?'

'Who knows? Maybe you're all in a plot together to retake the city.'

Deeziz sips from her tankard. She's about to speak when heavy footsteps sound in the corridor outside. Someone thuds against the door. In an instant the Orcish sorcerer transforms her appearance into that of a Turanian foot soldier, taking the shape so quickly and so completely that it's startling to see. I don't have time to think about it as my door opens and Makri stumbles into the room.

'Thraxas!' she cries, before pitching forward onto the floor where she lays face down. 'I have important news.'

I swiftly grasp the situation. 'Are you drunk?'

'Yes.'

'How?'

'I borrowed a bottle of your klee.'

'Borrowed? You mean you stole it from my safe?'

'Borrowed.'

'My precious supply of the Abbot's Special Distillation? You know how hard that is to—'

Makri raises herself on her hands and knees. 'Shut up, I have important news. Derigus has scars on his chest and his back. Recent scars from the war. And a tattoo.'

154

After my unexpected encounter with Deeziz and the shocking news of Makri stealing a bottle of klee, I'd practically forgotten I was working on a case. 'Derigus? Lieutenant Derigus in the emergency aqueduct repair unit?'

Makri sinks back down to the ground. It's a pathetic sight, though one I've encountered before. She's not a great drinker. I help her to her feet and onto a chair. 'Tell me what happened.'

'I took a bottle of klee and went to visit him. We drank a lot of klee and talked about a few things then when he was taking his tunic off I noticed his scars. Quite prominent.'

'Why was he taking his tunic off?'

Makri regards me sourly. 'Don't ask stupid questions. As soon as I saw the scars I knew he was the person we've been looking for. He was probably just trying to get information from me! I'm disgusted at his behaviour!'

'What happened then?'

'I was looking for some tactful way to leave when events took over.'

'What events?'

'I vomited over the rug. I'd drunk too much klee. After that he didn't mind me leaving.'

'Did he guess you were suspicious?'

'One moment.' Makri stumbles over to the side of the room to a fireplace that sits empty and unused. She leans over and is sick again, quite heavily. I sigh, then help her back to her chair. 'You really shouldn't gulp down high quality klee. It takes a man of my experience to do that. I'll get you a lesada leaf.' Lesada leaves, from the Elvish Isles, are the greatest known cure for hangovers and intoxication. They're fast-acting, efficient and undoubtedly the Elves' greatest contribution to the happiness of mankind. I've been carrying a good bundle of them around with me and carefully secreted a small packet in my safe. While I'm retrieving one Makri raises her head.

'Why is there a soldier hiding in the shadows?'

Deeziz transforms. 'It's me.'

'Thraxas, it's Deeziz. Do I need to stab her?'

'No, we're still on the same side.'

'So you say. Not everyone is convinced.'

I pour water from my pitcher into a wooden goblet, a little cleaner than the one I used for beer, and crumble the dried leaf into

155

it, swirling it around to mix it properly, then hand it to Makri. She makes a face as she drinks it down. It's not the first time I've had to do this for her. She really doesn't have a high tolerance for alcohol. The leaf will help her to recover swiftly. Deeziz meanwhile has emerged from the shadows and looks at me with satisfaction.

'A man with a scarred torso, as I told you.' She turns to Makri. 'Has he been your lover for long?'

'I wouldn't say we ever reached that stage' says Makri, still sounding sour. 'The vomiting really brought it to an end.' She shakes her head sadly. 'I didn't even like him that much. I was just drunk.' Makri notices the two goblets of beer on the table. 'I see you were getting along cosily.'

'I wouldn't describe it as cosy.'

'You shared your precious beer with her.'

'Standard Turanian hospitality.'

Makri scoffs at this. 'Turanian hospitality? You'd kill a grandmother if she tried taking your damned special ale.' Colour is returning to her cheeks as the leaf takes effect. 'Quite strange, finding you're now late-night drinking buddies with Turai's arch-enemy.'

'At least I wasn't helping some traitorous young lieutenant take his tunic off! The man's been playing you for a fool.'

'I'm aware of that.'

We glare at each other.

'I have noticed you argue a lot,' Deeziz interjects. 'When I was spying, I mean. I would have thought this was a time for action, rather than arguing. Do you want my assistance?'

'Thraxas, why is Deeziz being helpful?'

I can't answer that. Nonetheless, Deeziz reaches out so her hand touches Makri's sleeve, concentrating for a few moments before announcing that the man Makri has been in recent contact with, Derigus, is undoubtedly connected to the Orcish sorcery she detected. 'I sense the presence of gold as well.'

I drink from my goblet. 'I need to talk to Derigus right away. Makri, was he as drunk as you?'

'I don't think so. Not that I was really drunk. Just tiredness, I expect.'

'Have you recovered how? Then let's go.'

'Do you want me to accompany you?' asks Deeziz.

'Why not? You might be able to help.'

156

Makri looks doubtful. 'I'm still not convinced we can trust her.'

'Time is too short to worry about it. Either we solve this tonight or there will be food riots tomorrow.'

Deeziz transforms back into a male Turanian soldier as we leave my office and head for the east wing of the Palace where Lieutenant Derigus has his private quarters.

Chapter Twenty-Two

We're striding along the Palace corridors which are quiet though there are guards keeping watch at strategic points.

'How did you get into my safe to take the klee?'

'I watched you when you put in the combination.'

'What about the spell?'

'I got help.'

'You mean Anumaris Thunderbolt?'

'I can't comment on that.'

The Palace has now been cleansed of all signs of Orcish intrusion. The opulence on show only makes me think of Gurd and Tanrose, homeless in Twelve Seas. I still don't know where I'm going to live once I'm finally discharged from the army. A cheap room somewhere in Twelve Seas, I suppose. I look rather bleakly at the newly burnished silver chandelier hanging at the next intersection. It's been expertly renewed in the space of a few days. Its candles light up the corridors in a brilliant warm glow, and it's not even an important part of the Palace. 'Lodius is right,' I mutter to myself. 'There need to be changes.'

'Derigus's room is just round this corner,' Makri says, and sounds bitter about it.

'Don't stab him, we need information.'

'I know.'

Derigus's private room is just one door in a long corridor of rooms used by soldiers who've been drafted in to help run things for the Council. Without bothering to knock I turn the handle. The door opens and I stride inside, followed by Makri and Deeziz. There are only two small rooms and they're both empty. I'm surprised. 'It's two in the morning. Why wouldn't Derigus be here? Makri, was he going anywhere?'

'He didn't plan to.'

'Are you sure? Did you give him any sort of hint he was a suspect?'

'I didn't even know he was a suspect.'

'He might have picked up something when he was talking to you. If he was trying to gather information he probably asked you some leading questions about the investigation, without you realising.'

'I'd have known if he was doing that.'

'You drunk enough strong klee to vomit over the man's carpet. I'd say he might have tricked you easily enough.'

Again Makri looks unhappy but doesn't contradict me. I turn to Deeziz. 'Derigus might be involved in moving the gold right now. Can you do some magic and find where he is.'

'Do some magic?' Deeziz the Unseen is offended. 'My sorcerous art does not consist of parlour tricks. It is the result of many years of study.'

'Fine. Can you put your years of study to good use and find Derigus?'

Deeziz, still in her soldier's disguise, glances round the room. There's not much here. She glances at the papers on the table, puts her hand on the chair where Derigus would have sat, then disappears into the bedroom next door. I look at the papers but they only consist of his unit's plans for renovating Turai's broken aqueducts. Deeziz emerges from the other room carrying a pair of soldiers boots.

'These boots have been in Kushni. Not in the house I occupy, but not far away.'

'Another house in Kushni? With more red elvish cloth?'

'I don't think so. I can't sense the absence of space that would normally produce. However I feel that this Derigus may be there now.'

'The gold can't be sitting in a house in Kushni,' says Makri. 'Deeziz would have sensed it by now. So would Lisutaris.'

'True, but it's the only lead we have. We'll take a wagon.'

'I have to get weapons from my room.'

'Fine, meet us in my office.'

Makri hurries off to pick up her weapons while I hurry back to my office. We pass several night guards on the way but I'm a Captain on official business so they don't trouble us. They're not suspicious of Deeziz either. She's taken on the form of a young male soldier so completely that there's nothing to be suspicious of. Her powers of transformation are far superior to any I've ever encountered before. My goblet of ale is still half full. I drain it swiftly while putting on my jerkin and checking my knife and sword are both securely in their scabbards. My office door opens. I turn to greet Makri only to find it's Anumaris and Droo, one on either side of Lisutaris who appears to be barely conscious, her

159

head lolling from side to side as they practically drag her into the room. When they sit her down on a chair she slumps forward so her face is resting on the table.'

'Thraxas,' cries Anumaris. 'You're not going to believe this–'

'Lisutaris has smoked so much thazis she's put herself into a coma. I've seen it before.'

'You have?'

'Several times. Happens when the stress become too much for her. It's a character flaw but hey, we all have character flaws. People have occasionally said I drink too much.'

'You're taking this far too lightly,' says Anumaris, crossly.

'She'll come out of it without any harm done.'

'There would have been harm done if Droo and I hadn't met her by chance in the corridor when she was stumbling towards her room. We had to bring her here in case anyone in the smart section of the Palace saw her. Think of the scandal! This is our Commander!'

'It will be fine. Just let her rest here. I'm leaving as soon as Makri gets here, we have investigating to do.'

'What's happening?'

'A good lead in Kushni.'

'Did you know there was a riot in Twelve Seas this afternoon?'

'No, but I'm not surprised. If Turai doesn't find some money soon it will get a lot worse. I'd ask you to come with us but you'd better stay here and look after Lisutaris. Just lock the door and make sure no one enters.'

'Can I come?' asks Droo, who's always keen to be involved.

'Yes.'

'Can I drink that half goblet of beer?'

'Go ahead,' says the soldier who's been silent till now. Anumaris looks at her.

'Who is this?'

'Margax,' I tell her, lying instantly and convincingly. 'Old friend of mine from the army. Bumped into him in the canteen this evening and invited him round for beer. We've been reminiscing. Here's Makri, we have to be going.'

Makri however isn't so easy to shift. When she sees Lisutaris she demands to know what's going on and when she learns that Lisutaris is currently in a thazis-induced stupor she's very reluctant to leave her. 'I'm her bodyguard.'

160

'I think you should go with Thraxas,' says Anumaris. 'He needs your help when he's investigating, it never goes so well when you're not there.'

'That's true,' agrees Makri.

'I'll send a message to Hanama, she's billeted not far away. We'll be quite capable of looking after Lisutaris until she recovers. We're safe here anyway.'

Makri is reluctant. I tell her she has to decide quickly. 'Lisutaris would want you to come with me. We need to find the gold and she isn't in any danger.' Makri accompanies us from my office, still reluctant, though seeing sense in my words. We hurry through the Palace and head for the stables where a sleepy-looking attendant helps me attach two horses to the pinions of a fast carriage. We've only just set off through the grounds towards the gate when Droo turns to Deeziz. 'There's something funny about your aura. Are you an Orc?'

'Droo, stop rambling. Of course he's not an Orc. It's my old friend…' I realise I've forgotten the name I made up. Droo doesn't notice but it doesn't prevent her from carrying on.

'There just seems something funny about him. I'm an Elf. We can tell things like that.' We're saved from further investigation by our young Elvish companion by the noise at the Palace gates. Even though it's now the middle of the night there's a large crowd there and they're making a lot of noise. There's no immediate sign of violence but they're faced by an unhappy unit of soldiers, fewer soldiers than would normally be used in the circumstances, there being quite a shortage at the moment. People are shouting as we make our way past.

'Who stole our gold?'

"We need food!'

'The Palace is corrupt!'

'You can't argue with any of that,' mutters Makri, as we head South towards Translucence Street. It won't take us long to reach Kushni though we're not sure where we're going when we get there. Translucence Street runs from one side of the area to the other and it's home to some of Kushni's most dubious establishments — brothels, gambling dens and small theatrical establishments where the chorus line tends to be notably under-dressed. I've spent quite a lot of time there. Mostly in a professional capacity.

161

Droo pipes up again. 'There's definitely something odd about —
what's his name again?'

'Marax.'

'I'm sure that wasn't it. Why don't you know your friend's name?'
Droo pauses. 'Thraxas, are you sure this is really your friend?'

There's a very muted sound as Deeziz abruptly drops her
disguise.

'Is you friend meant to be an Orcish woman?'

'It's all right, Droo. She's helping us.'

Droo pokes her face close to Deeziz. 'I'm sure I've seen you
before somewhere.'

As we approach the outskirts of Kushni we start to hear a dull
roar, the sound of many voices. It grows as we approach the centre
and by the time we're almost at Translucence Street it's swollen
into a roar. Wisps of smoke are visible in the oil lamps that hang
outside Kushni's establishments.

'It sounds like a riot.'

'Strange. People in Kushni are usually too busy gambling and
whoring to start rioting.'

I nudge the horses forward. The sound becomes unmistakable. If
you've lived in Turai for any length of time, you know what a riot
sounds like. I look around us, selecting a yard next to a closed
tavern, destroyed in the war. I ride the wagon in there and quickly
unhitch the horses, looping the reign around the horse rail. 'We'd
better go on foot from here. Deeziz, do something so you don't
look like an Orcish sorcerer.'

'Deeziz!' cries Droo. 'I knew I'd seen her before. Wait, aren't you
dead?'

'I can no longer disguise myself,' admits the sorcerer. 'I'm not
back to full power.'

'We have to do something.'

'How about putting on that ragged cloak that's lying on the
ground?'

'With appropriate bloodstains.' Deeziz shrugs, picks up the cloak
and wraps it around her, drawing up the hood to disguise her
features.

'Follow me,' I say. 'Stay close, don't get involved in the riot and
look out for anywhere that looks like it might be a hiding place for
a sorcerer and a pile of gold.' We walk into Translucence Street.
Not far away a rioting crowd are throwing rocks and setting refuse

162

containers on fire. We advance cautiously. It's going to be tough to make our way through the mob. Tough for Deeziz to sense anything unusual with so much hostile activity going on.

'Why are people rioting?' wonders Droo, but none of us has an answer. It could be dissatisfaction about the missing gold and the lack of food, though again I'd have expected riots about that to happen in other parts of the city, not Kushni.

'Thraxas!' I'm assailed by a voice in my ear as I'm hailed by a rather large woman in a tight red dress that wouldn't normally be considered suitable for outdoor evening wear.

'Hello, Murzi.'

'Haven't see you here for a while. Picked a bad time if you're looking for entertainment.'

'I can see that.'

Murzi steps forward. The last time I saw her she had red ribbons in her hair, but she doesn't have them now. She notices me looking. 'I've moved up in the world. I have my own establishment.' She takes a step forward to study Makri, and raises her eyebrows. 'This your woman? No wonder we haven't seen you around so much. Pretty thing. Not quite human, I see. You always did have exotic tastes.'

'Murzi, maybe you can help me–'

'Shouldn't have brought that young Elf here. Elvish ambassadors don't like it, always leads to trouble.'

'Have you noticed anything strange recently?'

'Strange?' Murzi laughs. 'Everything's strange. We just got back into the city, no one has any food, people are trying to gamble without money and there's a riot going on. What more do you want?'

'Are we going to hear more about Thraxas's exotic tastes?' asks Droo, enthusiastically.

I ignore her. 'I mean strange in some other way. Like someone who doesn't belong here. Or someone using magic. You've been here a long time, Murzi, you know what doesn't belong.'

Murzi considers my words. Stones crash into the wall above us and we huddle in the doorway for cover. Murzi glances at the captain's rank on my shoulder. 'Are you working for the Palace again?'

'Yes. Official business.'

'Not a phrase I ever like to hear.'

'I'll tell them to look kindly on your endeavours.'

The rioting grows louder. The mob is slowly advancing towards us.

'Can you help me or not?'

'Maybe, for old time's sake. Two of my girls have been making visits to a house in Celestial Row. Quiet place, off the main track. No trouble, but an odd character, they said. Sorcerer they'd never seen before. Good customer too, paid them in gold.'

'That might be just what I want to hear. Can you identify the house?'

'Yellow door at the end of the row. Now the Palace really does owe me a favour.'

'Yes, they do. I won't forget it.' I turn to my companions. 'We can get to Celestial Row through the backstreets.' I lead them away.

'When that woman said for old time's sake, what did she mean?' asks Droo. 'What happened in old times?'

'Just concentrate on the present, Droo.'

'Probably something to do with his exotic tastes,' she whispers to Makri, loudly enough for everyone to hear. There's a small alley not far ahead. Unfortunately there are quite a few angry people between us and the entrance. I notice the riot seems unfocused and I'm still not certain what it's about. I can't see any definite target. It reminds me of something but I can't remember what. I use my bulk to force my way through the crowd, Makri assists, using her strength. Deeziz doesn't help. I'm hoping she's preserving her power because I have a feeling we're going to need it. We make our way into the alley then hurry along. It's dark, without a streetlamp, but I know the backstreets of Kushni well and lead us through several interconnected alleys to a narrow passage that emerges into Celestial Row. Not the poorest dwellings in Kushni but not wealthy either. I'm looking for a yellow door but I can't make out any colours in the darkness.

'Yellow door,' says Makri, pointing to the end of the small row. We advance rapidly, coming to a halt in front of a nondescript two story dwelling. 'Deeziz, can you sense anything?'

'Yes, a great deal, though it's not easy to interpret. If you wait—'

'No time to wait. Everyone, get ready for anything.' I march up the steps to the yellow door and hammer on it with my fist. It swings open immediately revealing Glixius Dragon Killer.

'Glixius! You're under arrest for–'

Glixius waves his hand and an energy bolt knocks me backwards. I end up flat on my back. The door slams shut. Makri appears at my side. 'Are you hurt?'

'My protection charm took most of the force.'

'It took some of the force.' Deeziz corrects me. 'I dissipated the rest. Who was that sorcerer?'

'Glixius Dragon Killer. Associate of the Brotherhood.' I clamber to my feet.

'Didn't you eliminate him from the inquiry?'

'Apparently I was wrong.'

The door opens again. This time it's Lieutenant Derigus which adds to my confusion. A known associate of the Society of Friends shouldn't be working with a Brotherhood man. It's unheard of.

'Makri,' he says. 'You should leave. I don't want you to get hurt.'

Makri draws her weapons. She has a murderous look in her eyes. 'I'm not in any danger.'

'You're in a lot of danger. Glixius will kill you all. We're heading for the harbour. Step aside and let us pass, it will be best for everyone.'

'How can you be working with Glixius? He's a Brotherhood man and you're with the Society of Friends. You hate each other.'

'We decided it was worth teaming up, given the stakes.'

I'm dissatisfied with this. 'That never happens in Turai. Do our traditions mean nothing to you?'

'Not when a pile of gold bullion is involved.'

I step forward. Derigus shakes his head. 'I wouldn't come any closer if I were you. We're leaving now and you'd better not get in our way.'

The door closes. 'How powerful is Glixius?' asks Droo.

'Quite powerful. Not as powerful as Deeziz.' I turn to the Orcish Sorcerer, still mostly concealed in her tattered cloak.

'He was at the card table, was he not?' she says, referring back to the night Turai fell. 'I didn't care for him. Yes, I am more powerful. Though my agreement to help you find the gold did not extend to fighting other sorcerers.'

'Our agreement was fairly open-ended. It could extend to fighting other sorcerers.'

'I wouldn't even be here had my health recovered more rapidly.'

'But you are here and we need your help.'

'You wouldn't want to just let Thraxas and Makri die, would you?' says Droo, brightly. 'Not after they brought you herbs and medicine and everything. That would be treacherous.'

Deeziz pulls back her hood. 'I've done my part. Destroying Glixius is not my responsibility.'

'Could you destroy him?' asks Droo.

'Of course.'

'Maybe you couldn't. You said you weren't really recovered yet. Maybe you should just sneak away before he opens the door.'

'I do not sneak away from awkward situations.'

'You're always sneaking,' I say. 'That's why you're called Deeziz the Unseen.'

Deeziz looks offended. 'Sorcerous concealment is not sneaking.'

'It's basically the same. Now, are you going to help us because when that yellow door opens Makri is going to mount a suicidal attack on whoever steps out because she's really annoyed that Derigus pretended he was attracted to her when really all he wanted was information. I'll be obliged to attack with her because I never abandon a companion in battle so if Glixius kills us it will be your fault and you'll feel bad about it afterwards.'

'Why will I feel bad?'

'Your conscience will torment you.'

'Orcs don't have consciences,' says Droo, not very helpfully.

'Yes, we do!'

'I was taught you don't.'

'Elvish education concerning Orcs is very incomplete!' says Makri, also offended.

'At school I had to read the epic poem Lord Dalikia Sails East and the Orcs don't have consciences in that. Whole point of the epic, as far as I remember.'

'Not one of the Elves' finest works,' sniffs Makri. Despite her hatred of Orcs, Makri's own Orcish blood does on occasion make her defend their culture against inaccurate assumptions.

'Where did this so-called Lord sail to?' demands Deeziz. 'It makes a difference which Orcs he encountered.'

'They were all bad.'

'Then in that case–'

Fortunately for my sanity, the yellow door swings open. Glixius glowers at us. He's a large, square-jawed man and he's never really forgiven me for once punching him in the face when he'd run out of spells.

'Deeziz?' he calls. 'Is that really you? You were supposed to be dead.' He laughs, and takes a step forward. 'So you survived. You're a lot weaker than the last time we met. I am considerably stronger.' With that he raises both hands, barks out a few words in a sorcerous language, unleashing a powerful spell. It's aimed at Deeziz but it's strong enough to throw us all backwards. I land heavily. As I'm scrambling to my feet I see that Deeziz was knocked over too which probably shouldn't happen to the most powerful Orcish sorcerer. If she's still seriously weakened we're in trouble. As Deeziz rises her cloak falls to the ground, revealing a short black cape that covers her shoulders. On it are black symbols and letters, barely discernible marks of her status among the Orcs. She stands quite steadily, raises one hand and utters one word. The result is gratifying. Glixius is blown backwards, shattering the yellow door as he crashes through it.

'Nice spell,' I mutter, and draw my sword in preparation for running up the steps. I don't get the chance. Seconds after vanishing Glixius re-appears, apparently unharmed. 'Oh dear, Deeziz, is that the best you can do? Being dead must have had a very bad effect on you.' With that he barks out another spell. This one is better directed. It doesn't touch me, Makri or Droo but slams into Deeziz. She's thrown along the road, enveloped in a ball of orange light that momentarily threatens to consume her before she manages to cast it off. She stands there for a moment, shaken.

'Damn you!' she cries, the only time I've heard her utter an oath. She rasps out a short sentence, a collection of ugly words from some secret Orcish sorcerer's language. The words alone are enough to make anyone shiver. The spell itself makes no visible sign but Glixius is raised into the air, almost to the level of the second floor of the house, then slammed down onto the ground. This time he's shaken. Unfortunately he isn't defeated. He climbs to his feet. 'It will take more than a little fall to trouble Glixius Dragon Killer!'

I'm still unsure if his resilience is due to Deeziz's weakened state or because he actually has got stronger. Glixius did assist the Sorcerers Guild in the defence of Turai. He marched all the way back to the city with the army, fighting dragons on the way. Maybe he learned some new skills. He's about to utter another spell when

167

we're interrupted by a shout from Makri. 'There's a dragon overhead.'

For a second I'm consumed by a feeling of unreality. There simply can't be a dragon overhead. When I look up, there is. Quite small, by dragon standards. Not the sort of huge war dragon I've grown used to in recent times, but a younger, nimbler beast, gliding downwards quite gracefully. It halts thirty feet or so above us and hovers, flapping its wings. A black clad figure vaults from the beast. It should be a painful descent but before he hits the ground the figure halts in the air, then lands softly.

'There you are, Glixius. I hoped the riot would draw you out of hiding.'

'Horm!'

I shake my head. Horm the Dead. This is a really bad development.

Chapter Twenty-Three

Horm the Dead is half-Orcish. His features are unusually pale, said to be the result of him dying and coming back to life in some grim sorcerous ritual to increase his power. His eyes are black, deep set. His thick black hair hangs round his shoulders. There are dark eagle feathers woven into his plaits along with black and gold beads. For a fairly insane sorcerer he does take care of his appearance. While the overall effect is both dramatic and frightening, he's not exactly ugly and with his noticeable cheekbones he might even be called handsome by some impressionable young people. Every time I've encountered him he's been dressed in black.

'Glixius Dragon Killer. Deeziz the Unseen, Thraxas, the cheap investigator. Makri the most beautiful. Quite the reunion.'

'You forgot about me.' Droo sounds piqued to be left out. 'Ensign Sendroo-ir-Vallis.'

Horm raises his eyebrows. 'You would be best not to come to my attention, Elf. It can be bad for your health.' He turns towards the shattered yellow door. 'So, Glixius, you decided to betray me. I thought you had more sense. Investigator — I discovered the presence of the gold in the Palace, I obtained the key and provided these men with the means to raid the vault. And how have they repaid me? By attempting to hide from me and keep the gold from themselves. Perfidious behaviour, would you agree?'

'Turai's criminals aren't known for their good behaviour.'

Horm smiles. 'In my kingdom of Yal, they have some honour.'

'You'd have been better off staying in Yal,' says Deeziz. 'As ordered by Prince Amrag.'

'Yes, the Prince. Now unfortunately dead, to the overwhelming sorrow of all the Orcish nations.' From the way he's smiling, Horm isn't grieving too much. 'Personally, I have not quite forgiven him for banishing me.'

'You deserved it. You were never a loyal follower. I remember the card game.'

There's a moment's silence. Horm, Makri, Deeziz, Glixius and myself were all in the Avenging Axe on the fateful night the city fell. I remember Deeziz telling Horm that Prince Amrag was not going to be pleased with his disloyal behaviour. That was only moments before she brought down the north wall, letting the Orcish armies flood into the city.

Horm turns his attention to Makri. 'Makri, you are still the most beautiful and the most strong. I regret you refused to leave Turai with me. It pains me to see you still grubbing around in the company of a cheap investigator when you could be sharing my throne.'

Makri looks angry but doesn't reply. I ask Horm if he's responsible for the riot in Kushni.

'I am. Only a minor spell. Just something to make Glixius show his face. And now Glixius, it's time for you to pay for your treachery.'

'Treachery?' Glixius laughs. 'You know you planned to make off with all the gold yourself. Your pathetic Kingdom of Yal is bankrupt after Prince Amrag took against you. Your own citizens will throw you out if you can't feed them.'

This angers Horm. Giving no warning he suddenly fires a spell at Glixius. Glixius is not caught unprepared. He shields himself effectively with a curtain of purple light while simultaneously firing back a spell of his own. Horm takes a powerful hit, so powerful that I'd guess Glixius has been preparing some sorcery for just this occasion. Horm falls, rises, and fires another spell. Deeziz joins in against him and suddenly the small street erupts in a vortex of whirling wind, flashing lights, shouted spells, fire and lightning as the three sorcerers battle it out between them. I grab Makri and Droo and withdraw to the side of the road where we take cover behind a small wooden fence.

'We should help Deeziz.' Makri has a sword in each hand and isn't comfortable hiding from the action.

'We can't walk into the middle of that storm of magic, we'll die.'

'We have protection charms.'

'We'll still die, that's a lot of high level sorcery.'

'How about if I sneak in the back door and kill Derigus? I could do that.'

'That wouldn't really help.'

'But I want to kill Derigus.'

'We can deal with Derigus later. Right now we just have to hope Deeziz can defeat Horm.'

'Are they ganging up on her?'

'It's hard to tell.' Several deafening explosions make the ground shudder and there's now so much smoke it's impossible to see what's going on. I'm wondering if we should flee. Make our escape while the sorcerers are all occupied. That wouldn't be glorious but it might be sensible. Though I don't want to abandon Deeziz. She's our ally, for better or for worse.

Makri looks round, away from the fighting. 'What's that?' I can't see or hear anything but Makri has sharp Elvish eyesight and hearing. 'Someone's coming.'

A burst of light from a spell illuminates the gloom for a second, just long enough to let us see a carriage approaching. Three figures leap out and run towards us. We're enveloped in utter darkness for several moments as another spell blankets the area. When that clears I find Lisutaris, Anumaris and Hanama standing beside us.

'What is going on here?' demands Lisutaris.

'We found the gold,' I tell her, giving her the positive news first. 'Deeziz, Horm the Dead and Glixius are currently fighting each other over it.'

Lisutaris's eyes open wide in shock. 'Deeziz? I killed her.'

'No, she escaped.'

'Damn her! I'll put an end to her this time.' Lisutaris scans the scene, trying to pick out Deeziz among the chaos. She slowly raises on arm. I rapidly grab hold of her sleeve.

'You can't attack Deeziz, Commander. She's on our side.'

'Don't be absurd, Thraxas. She's Turai's deadly enemy.'

'Most of the time, yes. But for the past few days…'

Lisutaris glares at me. 'For the past few days what?'

'We helped her recover and then she helped us find the gold,' says Makri. 'It was mostly Thraxas's idea.'

I've rarely seen anyone look so appalled as Lisutaris does at this moment. The shock of learning of Deeziz's survival added to the revelation that we actually assisted her seems to numb her for a moment and she struggles to speak.

'Commander, you can deal with Thraxas's traitorous behaviour later,' says Hanama. 'The sorcerous combat is threatening to ignite the houses.'

Lisutaris turns her head to examine the scene. It's still chaotic and tongues of flame are visible on the house with the yellow door.

'I'll deal with it.' Lisutaris takes a step forward. Once more I interrupt her.

171

'You can't harm Deeziz, Commander. I guaranteed her safety and we owe her for leading us to the gold.'

'Damn you all!' From Lisutaris' expression she's tempted to end the discussion by blasting us out of existence. Fortunately she controls herself. 'You will all suffer the consequences of this,' she growls.

'See, I knew this would happen,' mutters Makri.

'I wasn't involved in any of it,' adds Droo. 'Complete surprise to me that Thraxas recruited an enemy.'

'Anumaris,' says Lisutaris. 'Get ready to fight.'

'Yes, Commander.'

Lisutaris strides forward. This time I don't interrupt her. She raises an arm and shouts one word. A freezing calm descends on the alley. The fires are extinguished. The sorcery surrounding Deeziz, Horm and Glixius fades away, leaving all three of them looking round confused, wondering what happened. They're all somewhat the worse for wear, particularly Glixius who's down on one knee, exhausted. Horm the Dead is quickest to grasp the situation.

'Lisutaris, Mistress of the Sky. Again unable to keep your nose out of my affairs.'

Lisutaris surveys the scene. 'I followed the aura of an Orcish invader here. Surprisingly not you, Horm. Another Orc. Deeziz. You survived.'

'I did,' replies Deeziz, solemnly. 'Your spell did kill Prince Amrag.'

'Since when you appear to have joined the ranks of my Security Unit at the invitation of Captain Thraxas. Not something I would have approved of. Anumaris, were you aware of this?'

'No, Commander.'

Lisutaris takes a moment to glance backwards and glare at us again. 'I am very displeased. I'll have a lot to say after I deal with Horm.' She turns and walks towards the Orcish sorcerer.

'This is so unfair,' says Droo. 'Now I'm getting the blame too.'

'Life is often unfair, Droo.'

As Lisutaris strides towards Horm he smiles. 'You're going to deal with me, Mistress of the Sky? Grand words.'

'I've done it before.'

'Perhaps. Though never conclusively, I might add. I can't help noticing you're not in the best condition. You have a lot of troubles on your mind. Very distracting for a sorcerer. And then there's your drug use.'

Lisutaris halts, disquieted by the Sorcerer's words.

'What's that substance Turanian sorcerers dose themselves with in action? Turix? How much of that did you ingest before taking the city?' Horm laughs. 'It's really a way of taking dwa without admitting it. At least I'm honest about my tastes. That's not all, is it? I perceive you've only recently emerged from a thazis-induced stupor. It permeates your aura. Do your fellow members of your Ruling Council know about your habits, Lisutaris, Mistress of the Sky?' Horm looks towards Glixius. 'Glixius, if you'd like to avoid me killing you as you deserve, prevent Deeziz from bothering me as I deal with Lisutaris. Afterwords we may come to some agreement.'

'We need to help,' says Makri, and takes a step forward seconds before we're once again thrown backwards as the alley erupts in a violent scene of clashing spells and malevolent sorcery. We find ourselves lying behind the fence, now flattened. Droo's spiky yellow hair is black with soot. Acrid smoke fills my nostrils.

'The dragon's attacking Lisutaris!' Anumaris leaps to her feet. 'I'll deal with it.' She rushes forward.

'We need to help too,' says Makri though it's not obvious what we can do. Lisutaris and Horm are completely concealed inside a whirling ball of sorcerous light. It's impossible to tell what's happening and it would be impossible to enter. Glixius and Deeziz are engaged with each other though it's much less intense. Both are tired and weakened.

'If we get behind Glixius we can deal with him. Then Deeziz can help Lisutaris.'

We set off, sneaking through the tiny, barren gardens in front of the houses at the edge of the row. I'm hoping no one notices. It's possible they won't, with the amount of flashing lights, explosions and occasional moments of utter darkness that envelop us. Our protection charms wouldn't save us from direct attack by these powerful spells but they do protect us from any residual effects. We soon find ourselves crouching beside another ruined fence, only yards away from Glixius who's still engaged in trading spells with Deeziz. He's having the worst of it, mainly focusing on defending himself inside a sorcerous barrier. He doesn't notice as we sneak up to the side of the steps. Makri leaps towards him, far nimbler than me. Unfortunately she bounces off his sorcerous barrier which she probably should have anticipated. It does get his attention. He turns towards us, quite wearily, There's blood dripping down his cheek. His defensive shield flickers for a second. That's long enough for Deeziz. She pierces the barrier with a bolt of lighting that pins him to the wall. He slides to the ground, either dead or not far off.

We pick ourselves up, something we've been doing a lot in the last half hour. I ache everywhere. Lisutaris is still engaged with Horm the Dead. Anumaris is struggling with the dragon and not doing too well. Deeziz walks forward. She's limping. She casts another spell, her voice not as strong as it was. Horm is unable to repel the joint attack from Lisutaris and Deeziz. There's an unexpected moment of calm as his sorcery fails for a moment but he's still upright and doesn't look like he's about to give in. Abruptly he cries out and pitches forward on to the ground. I'm confused. 'What just happened?'

'Someone threw a knife in his back.'

Hanama emerges through the drifting smoke.

'She really is the best assassin in Turai.'

It seems like the action is over until yet another strange event occurs. The small dragon disengages from Anumaris, flies to Horm the Dead, picks him up then ascends rapidly into the sky, carrying him like a sea-hawk with a fish in its claws. No one on the ground has the energy to prevent it happening.

'That's a really well trained dragon,' observes Makri.

Lisutaris's cloak is ripped and her hair is matted over her forehead. She sits down heavily on the steps. Deeziz is standing on her own. Lisutaris calls to her. 'Come and rest on the steps with me, while the rest of my Security Unit locates the gold.' Lisutaris gives me a meaningful look. 'Which they'd better do quickly, after all this.'

Chapter Twenty-Four

Two days later I'm in conversation with Lisutaris. 'You'd have to agree, Commander, examining the whole history of this affair, from the moment Prince Amrag marched on Turai, I've played a vital role in protecting the city. Defended the walls against the Orcs, defeated Horm the Dead in a card game thereby saving Makri and frustrating Horm's plans, rescued you and Makri when the city fell, helped you become War Leader in Samsarina, took charge of your Security Unit as we marched back to Turai, exposed Deeziz the Unseen when she was infiltrating our army, had an important role in bringing the walls down for our attack, and then found Turai's gold thereby preventing the destruction of the city in food riots and consequent capture of our beloved nation by Nioj and Simnia. Quite an impressive record. Not saying you have to erect a statue of me in the Palace grounds, but a medal wouldn't be out of place. Maybe a pension too. We really ought to revive the ancient custom of awarding free dinners for life to the nation's heroes.'

'I've managed to persuade the Council not to put you on trial for treason,' says Lisutaris.

'I really don't think that should have been an option.'

Lisutaris shakes her head. 'You saved the life of the Orcish sorcerer responsible for taking the city. Then you recruited her.'

'It worked out in the end.'

'Yes, it did.' Lisutaris has calmed down in the days since her violent encounter with Horm the Dead. The retrieval of the Palace gold enabled the Council to secure food for the city. The threat of rioting, revolution and foreign takeover has receded. Lisutaris might even have kept the full story secret from the Ruling Council had Lieutenant Derigus not made a confession designed to show himself as an innocent dupe of others, which he certainly wasn't. As he'd actually witnessed Deeziz the Unseen at the scene of the final battle, her presence during the affair couldn't be hidden. The subsequent conversation I had with the Council was interesting, you could say.

'What's going to happen to Derigus?'

'Trial for theft and treason. As an adopted member of the Senatorial class he'll probably be allowed to go into exile.'

'He deserves worse.'

'Did he actually kill anyone?'

'It's possible he stabbed Lemusius to get hold of the key but I don't know that for sure. It could have been Glixius. Glixius started the whole thing off after learning about the gold during the march to Turai.'

'I really had no idea so many people knew about the gold.'

'Secrets are very hard to keep in Turai. You should remember that now you're a politician.'

The sorcerer shakes her head. 'I'll be leaving politics as soon as possible.'

'It probably shouldn't have been such a surprise that Glixius went for assistance to someone connected to the Society of Friends but it threw me off the scent. I never expected a Society of Friends member to cooperate with a Brotherhood man. It goes against all our traditions.'

We're walking through the Palace. I don't know where we're going. Lisutaris has again restored her appearance and in our opulent surroundings she's looking almost regal. Guards stand up straight and salute smartly as she passes.

'How did Horm become involved?'

'Glixius again. He and Derigus realised they couldn't get through the spell protecting the vault so they ditched their partners and approached someone who could. I don't know how Glixius contacted Horm. Maybe criminal sorcerers have their own secret network. What's going to happen to Glixius?'

'He's in the custody of the Sorcerers Guild till he recovers. He took a lot of damage. After that, I'm not sure. Expulsion from the Guild and the city, probably.'

'You still haven't told me why you couldn't trace the gold after they stole it.'

'It's slightly embarrassing,' admits Lisutaris. 'The sorcerous mark should have been traceable even if hidden inside a magic pocket. Glixius put the gold inside his own magic pocket, placed that inside another given to him by Horm, and then put that inside a third, also given to him by Horm. It hadn't occurred to me or anyone else that someone might do that. Magic pockets are rare items, no one is supposed to have three of them.'

'Was Horm still alive when his dragon carried him off?'

'I don't know. Probably. He's difficult to kill.' Lisutaris halts. 'As is Deeziz. Why didn't you just kill her when you met her? She was in a weakened state.'

'She offered to help us find the gold.'

'Makri told me you prevented her from stabbing her even before that. After finding Turai's deadly enemy alive, executing her might have seemed like the natural thing to do. You've killed people in wartime, Thraxas.'

'I know.'

'You didn't want to do it, did you?'

'Not really. It's different in battle. I don't like to execute someone in cold blood.'

'She was close to death when you found her. You could just have let her die.'

I can't think what to say. We walk on. We seem to be heading out of the Palace though we're walking through a part I'm not familiar with, corridors once only accessible to the Royal Family and now only open to senior members of our temporary government.

'Would if have been different if she wasn't a woman?'

'Maybe. Where is she now?'

'That's a state secret.'

Lisutaris is surely joking. 'No, really, where is she?'

'Her whereabouts is a state secret,' replies Lisutaris, firmly.

We leave the Palace by a door I've never used before, the Grand Southern Gate, a huge bronze edifice so perfectly balanced on its hinges it's said a person can push it open or closed with one finger. Outside is the grand marble staircase lined with statues that leads to the Imperial Gardens, also grand. Restoration work has been extensive and while they can't make the flowers and trees grow back in the space of a few days, they have removed all traces of the occupation. There's even a fountain in operation, a statue of Saint Quatinius surrounded by dolphins in memory of some episode involving our patron saint. I can't quite remember the details. Something involving dolphins anyway. Lisutaris's carriage is waiting for us on the paved track to the main Palace gate.

'If Glixius and Derigus hadn't been so greedy they might have got away with it,' says Lisutaris. 'It was a mistake to try and double cross Horm. They planned to sneak out the city and head West where he couldn't follow but it was a huge risk. Horm the Dead is not to be taken lightly.'

I agree with Lisutaris. Horm is not to be taken lightly. 'I still don't know if he was ever in the vault. He's so powerful it would explain how they stole the gold so quickly. But he's so good at hiding any traces of himself it's impossible to tell. He might just have given Glixius a spell for doing all the heavy lifting.' I screw up my face. 'I don't often come up against anyone as powerful as Horm. If I do, it makes investigation difficult.'

Lisutaris nods, quite sympathetically. 'Fortunately there are very few sorcerers like Horm the Dead.'

A soldier in a very smart uniform is waiting at the carriage. He salutes Lisutaris and opens the door. We climb in while another soldier steps up to the driver's seat. Inside the enclosed carriage Makri is waiting. She smiles at me. 'I see they let you off. I told them it wasn't your fault. Deeziz offered you beer. Everyone knows you wouldn't be able to resist that.'

'Thanks, Makri. I'm sure that was a tremendous help.'

The carriage sets off. 'I take it no one blamed Makri for anything?'

'You were the senior officer present, Thraxas. Everything was your responsibility. Besides, Cicerius seems more sympathetic towards Makri these days. I wouldn't exactly say he's taken a shine to her but he admires her determination to attend the University and does intend to make it happen.'

We head south. Outside it's still as hot as Orcish hell but the carriage is cooler, whether by design or some small piece of sorcery from Lisutaris, I can't tell.

'When I emerged from my slumber I sensed immediately that you were with an Orc with sorcerous power.'

'By slumber you mean thazis-induced stupor.'

'I wouldn't really call it that.'

'You should. You have a problem with smoking too much thazis and you should deal with it.'

'I'll deal with it when you stop drinking so much.'

'Then I guess we're both doomed to carry on.'

Lisutaris almost smiles. Her mood is improving. 'I did notice you'd been sharing beer with your Orcish visitor. You wouldn't normally be keen to share your precious Grand Abbot's Ale.'

'That's what I said!' adds Makri.

'Everyone is making too much of me sharing beer with Deeziz. It was simply standard Turanian hospitality.'

'Maybe you just have a thing for powerful female sorcerers.'
'I could understand that,' says Lisutaris. 'We do fascinate men.'
'Where are we going?' I ask, to change the subject.
'Twelve Seas. We have business to conduct before we arrive.' Lisutaris draws a small embroidered purse from inside her robe. I recognise it as her own personal magic pocket. She opens it then reaches inside so that her whole forearm disappears into the tiny purse. There's no limit to the space available inside. While in Samsarina, Lisutaris, Makri and I all entered the purse and walked into the lands beyond. She pulls out a handful of gold coins. 'When Makri won the sword-fighting contest you successfully gambled your way to a very healthy profit. We ended up with 10,500 gurans each. I admit I was impressed.'

'Do you still have it? I thought it would have gone by now.'
'Most of mine has gone in war expenses but I retained your and Makri's full share.'
'Take some of mine,' says Makri, immediately. 'I'll share your expenses.'
'Thank you Makri, but I don't need it.'
'You're as poor as everyone else in Turai right now.'
'True, but my fortune will recover. I still own all my lands and my family share of Turai's silver mines. Meanwhile I'm being paid by the state for my role in the Council. You and Thraxas will both need your share for what I have in mind.'
'What I have in mind is beer and gambling. I can manage that on my own.'
Lisutaris smiles but says nothing. She replaces the gold in her magic pocket and we carry on into Twelve Seas. I notice changes immediately. Government work crews have finally arrived to clear up the mess and the carriage has to pick its way between teams repairing the local aqueduct and others fixing the sewers. Still other are hauling away rubble and there's even building work going on at the local public baths. Quintessence Street, home to the Avenging Axe, is no longer a scene of misery and desolation. There's life, activity and a sense of optimism in the air.
'Now Turai has money I've allocated a budget for repairs in Twelve Seas. The harbour requires extensive work but I haven't forgotten Quintessence Street and the Avenging Axe.'
'Is the city going to pay to rebuild it?'

179

'No, we can't afford to repair every private citizen's house and business. But we will make a contribution and arrange for loans to help with the rest. I've already sent Captain Julius to talk to Gurd.'

I'm glad Lisutaris hasn't forgotten that Gurd is a solid citizen and a stout defender of Turai. When we arrive at the Avenging Axe we find preliminary work already underway. Gurd is assisting with clearing away rubble and debris from the site, helping the work crew load it into a parked carriage prior to it being hauled away. He's working enthusiastically as we approach; age has greyed the old barbarian's hair but hasn't diminished his strength. He greets us with a smile. Seeing Gurd smile makes me appreciate for the first time that the war is actually over.

'Commander! Thraxas, Makri! We're rebuilding!'

For a moment I'm worried he's actually going to embrace me. Fortunately he doesn't go that far. War does strange things to people's manners but so far it hasn't completely broken the dignity of warriors like Gurd and myself; we don't go around embracing each other in public.

'Great news, Gurd. How long will it take?'

'Five weeks, if it all follows the plan Captain Julius brought from the Palace architect's office.'

I gaze at the patch of ground, imagining a new Avenging Axe rising to replace the old one. 'Once the Avenging Axe is rebuilt the city will start to feel like home again. I'm looking forward to moving back in.'

Gurd looks puzzled. 'Moving back in? You're not moving in, so I heard.'

'What do you mean?'

'I don't think moving back into the Avenging Axe is best for you,' says Lisutaris.

'What? You're trying to evict me? After all I've done for this city? I won't stand for it!'

Lisutaris shakes her head in frustration. 'Follow me.' She walks off. I storm after her.

'What's happening? Where are we going?'

She stops at the property next to the Avenging Axe which was also razed to the ground during the war. 'This house belonged to Larizox, an elderly fisherman, retired. Sadly he was killed during the invasion. He died without issue and had no relatives.

Consequently his property now reverts to the state. We're selling it to you and Makri.'

'What?' I'm having trouble gasping any of this.

'It's time you owned your own home, Thraxas. You can't live in a room in a tavern forever.'

'Why not?'

'Because you're a functioning adult, that's why not. It's time to accept your responsibilities as a Turanian citizen and homeowner. Our architects have developed plans for some very practical buildings to replace many of those lost during the war. This house will be rebuilt as two separate units within the same walls. Makri will have the upstairs dwelling where she can study in peace while she attends the University. You can have the downstairs dwelling to live in and to use as your office for investigating. It's an excellent arrangement.'

I fold my arms in front of me. 'It might sound excellent to you but what about my opinion? I didn't agree to buy a house! I'm quite happy in the Avenging Axe.'

'Thraxas,' says Makri. 'Do you realise Tanrose will be having her baby soon? She's going to need more space upstairs and if you're living there you'll probably run into her breast-feeding the baby in the hallway.'

My blood runs cold at the thought.

'And they'll probably have more children. It will be crying babies and breast-feeding for years.'

'Stop saying breast-feeing.'

Makri gazes at the levelled space in front of us. 'I'll be so happy to own my own home! I never thought that would happen. I'll still be nearby to help you investigate but there will be several locked doors between us so you won't disturb my studies.'

'That never happens. Usually it's you disturbing me with fundraising for the Association of Gentlewomen or some such nonsense.' I turn to Lisutaris. 'I'm still not sure this is a good idea. And you shouldn't be ordering people around like this, you don't have the authority.'

'I do actually. I'm still War Leader until the position is officially put to rest by an agreement between the nations. I outrank everyone though I try not to throw my weight around. So I can order you to live here. Not that I would if you were vehemently opposed to it, but really, Thraxas, why would you object? What

181

else are you going to do with your money? Fritter it all away it on drinking and gambling?'

'That was my plan.'

'You'll still have some left for that.'

'It's a great deal, Thraxas,' cries Makri. 'Stop being foolish about it. You should be thanking Lisutaris for taking the trouble to look after your future.'

I glare at them both, not quite ready to be thanking anyone yet.

'I do owe you thanks, Thraxas,' says Lisutaris. 'For all your help during the war. I appreciate it. Now I should go, I have a lot to do.' She turns to leave, then pauses. 'When the tavern is ready to open, Gurd should hold a small ceremony. I'll have a campaign medal for you, Thraxas. And medals for Makri and Gurd. I'll award them to you at the ceremony.' With that she turns and walks grandly back to her carriage, wishing Gurd a friendly goodbye as she passes. At that moment Dandelion, one-time barmaid at the Avenging Axe, appears in her standard attire of bare feet and a long dress embroidered with signs of the zodiac. She's smiling. 'Hello Gurd!' she calls. 'And hello important sorcerer whose name I've forgotten. I've been living with the dolphins in their secret cave. I've been having a nice time. They told me the city was being rebuilt so I've come to see if I can be a barmaid again. I'd like some wages to buy nice things for the dolphins.'

'Welcome back,' says Gurd, who's learned to make the best of it where Dandelion is concerned. She was actually a good barmaid.

I notice that Lisutaris, Mistress of the Sky, Head of the Turanian Sorcerers Guild, Head of the International Sorcerers Guild, War Leader, Commander, and leading member of the Ruling Council of Turai, is laughing as she rides off, another sign that the war is finally over.

The End

182

Martin Millar was born in Scotland and now lives in London. He is the author of such novels as Supercute Futures, Lonely Werewolf Girl and The Good fairies of New York. He wrote the Thraxas series under the name of Martin Scott. Thraxas won the World Fantasy Award in 2000. As Martin Millar and as Martin Scott, he has been widely translated.

Printed in Great Britain
by Amazon

87549198R00109